Buttercup Baby

Buttercup Baby

N. ALIKYAN

Published by Innocent Sinner Publishing LLC

Find me:

https://nellyalikyan.com

Copyediting: Michelle [https://damorodesign.com]

Cover Design : Murphy Rae [https://www.murphyrae.com]

ISBN: 978-1-956847-04-8

First Edition: June 2022

10 9 8 7 6 5 4 3 2 1

To the stories I create in my head to help myself fall asleep.
This was all you.

Also by Nelly Alikyan

Catchers Series
With the Flames Catching Midnight
With the Rains Catching Dawn

Whittle Magic Series
Alluring Darkness
Beholding Darkness
Claiming Darkness
Desiring Darkness

Soundtrack

.

My Brother's Best Friend by Hannah Trager
(OPEN/CLOSE CREDITS)

Kiss the Girl by Brent Morgan *(C2, S2)*

Blue Collar Boys by Luke Combs *(C4, S2)*

Can't Help Falling In Love by Elvis Presley
(C10)

Hooked by Dylan Scott *(C12, S1)*

Colouring This Life by Vybz Kartel *(C15)*

Perfect by Topic & Ally Brooke *(C19, S2)*

I Guess I'm In Love by Clinton Kane *(C21, S3)*

Like My Father by Jax *(C22, S2)*

Breathless by Shayne Ward *(C25, S2)*

I Got You by Erin Kinsey *(C27, S3)*

Hey Stupid, I Love You by JP Saxe *(C28, S1)*

CHAPTER 1

Tommy

DARIUS FLIPS the burgers steaming on the grill while his little *friend* tells everyone how they'd been thrown out of the movie theater even though they had been innocently watching the film.

A load of crap.

Not a single person is going to believe that story, especially with the way the two of them glance at each other as they tell it. They look like they're about to go at it right there in front of everyone.

But who cares because this is Darius Aabeck we're talking about, and everyone knows he's a class A whorebag.

He's my best friend, but the man has seen more ass than Santa has children. He likes to joke that he's just making up for my modest five, but the man is no angel, and that devilish smirk he throws at girls has nothing to do with me. He's just a pig.

But I still love him. My brother.

He took me into his world when I was nine years old, and we've been brothers ever since. Joined at the hip, twins, soulmates.

"Yeah, what a load of crap, asshole." I push Darius as he flips another burger and bring the beer to my lips.

He just winks with that smirk that gets him past just about anything. "I don't know what you mean."

"I *mean* you're a whore." He knows I don't pull for any of his shit.

"Am not." He squares his shoulders, but that glimmer in his eyes says he knows damn well that he is.

"Are too."

I freeze.

Because that wasn't my response or that of anyone at this BBQ. That was the voice of little Emory Aabeck, Darius's baby sister, who was meant to be three thousand miles away in London.

Darius is standing rigid beside me, and we both look at each other before slowly turning around. I drop my beer at the sight of Emory Aabeck standing confidently in front of us with the widest grin across her face.

And fuck, I'm stopped short.

When Emory left for London four years ago after she'd graduated high school and Darius and I college, she'd been a kid sister.

But fuck.

She definitely doesn't look like a kid sister anymore.

She is still the same beautiful woman I last saw four years ago, but this time, I'm frozen. Breathless.

Darius breaks from his astonishment first and barrels toward her to lift her into his arms for a tight squeeze as he laughs giddily. And she holds on just as tight. Tighter even.

Emory's back, and something tells me I'm never going to see her as a kid sister ever again.

After an eternity, she pulls from her brother and looks at me. Her smile is wide across her face, and her perfect brown eyes are warm as they stare into mine.

That dark hair that I played with a billion times through the years blows behind her like that of a goddess, and all I can think is, 'She's so stunning.'

Now my cock is up and wide awake.

Not the right time and most definitely not the right girl.

She's in front of me when she says, "I think I've got enough breath in me for one more bear hug."

And that's when the grin cracks the very structure of my face and threatens to swallow me whole.

Her legs wrap around my waist, and I hold on tight as my face falls to the crook of her neck and I breathe her in. She'd never smelled so good, so perfect.

It's been years since I've been around her, seen her, mostly only talking to her on the phone on the off chance I was around Darius when they were speaking. It's been four years, and I didn't realize until this very moment with her in my arms how much I missed her.

I don't want to let go. I don't want to release the scent that's flooding my every sense. But I have to. If for no other reason than because my cock is stirring again, and I can't have her feeling that specific reaction. The girl looked to me like an older brother, the same way she saw Darius, and the last thing she needs is my dick pressing into her.

Darius throws his arm around her shoulders. "Now, you wanna tell me what the hell you're doing here?"

"I've come home. I thought I'd surprise my two favorite men."

Her smile is too much. Too beautiful. Too hypnotizing. Too…much.

"I can see you've come home, smartass. Why?" Darius walks her over to the grill where Luke has taken over as grillmaster.

"Because I graduated," she states matter-of-factly.

"I thought we were all coming over for a graduation ceremony," I say because I definitely remember her telling everyone the ceremony would be held later than expected and to hold off on buying tickets. "I've been looking forward to checking out London."

She pinches my cheek. "I'll take you."

The phrase is taken completely out of context in my head as erotic images take over, and I have to crush them before they can solidify.

"Be serious, princess," Darius says.

"Graduation is this weekend."

"No ceremony?" Darius asks.

She shrugs. "You know I don't like that stuff. I didn't want to be a part of it."

"Your parents are gonna be upset," I state because they definitely will.

She shrugs again, and it's obvious she doesn't like that she'll be upsetting them, but she pushes the thought aside. "Tough."

"And who is this?" Laura, Darius's current fuck buddy, interrupts the conversation with a grimace.

They're not together and nobody would be stupid enough to think they have feelings for one another, but I think Laura still doesn't want Darius whoring around on her if she doesn't know about it. To keep things safe if nothing else.

And though Darius is a whore, he's a one-woman whore.

For the most part.

I throw my arm over the one Darius has around Emory's shoulders. "This is Emory."

"My baby sister," Darius adds, a smirk telling her he knows why she's asking.

Smiles blossom at the statement, and everyone turns to her, ready for introductions. I stand back as Darius pulls her into his side and moves for one end of the yard to begin them.

There's a good load of friends here, so it'll be a while before Darius gets her through the entire crowd.

I stand by Luke and Drew as they start another argument about some game from a month ago because those two are always ready to argue sports; it doesn't matter how old the game is.

But that doesn't matter to me because Emory's back.

She's back, and her smile is wide and her presence exhilarating.

It's remarkable how in only a few short minutes my life is thrown off it's hinges. Last I heard, she was thinking about taking that job in London after graduating.

And as she stands before me, I'm unable to wrench my stare from her direction, and all I can think is that I'm so happy she didn't take that job.

My nose kind of hates my eyes because they get to continue taking her in while her scent is all the way across the yard.

Her scent. So intoxicating. I can only imagine how intoxicating her *scent* is.

My cock is stirring again, growing harder with each passing second, and I need to stop this. What the fuck is going on with me? I cannot be thinking about Emory *fucking* Aabeck in that way. Darius would kill me.

But then she glances back at me while Darius is introducing her to another small group of friends, and my heart somersaults. Her eyes spark as she stares at me, and I know there's nothing I can do about the stiffening between my legs. I'm a lost boy, and she's my Neverland.

Darius got some brother time in with her after introductions were over, but he'd left her alone about half an hour ago and ran off to the bathroom. The fact that I saw Laura head into the house only a couple of minutes before was no shocker.

Emory's sitting alone at the wooden table we have set out in the yard, but she looks content. She's never been the type to shy away from being alone or looking like a loner. It's why she was always comfortable with the idea of being in another country on her own. She is very comfortable in her own company.

As I watch her, I realize she hasn't eaten the entire time she's been here—going on two hours now—and I can guess that she didn't stop to eat before getting to the house either. She has to be starved.

I grab ingredients for a cheeseburger and make it up the way she likes—mustard, ketchup, pickles, tomatoes, and lettuce with a side of cucumbers. She used to eat those suckers like they were fries.

I grab a water from the cooler and walk up behind her, leaning into her as I place the plate and bottle on the table. "You have to eat."

She relaxes when she realizes the strange intrusion by her ear is me, and the part of me that came alive two hours ago when she got here is excited to see that.

I straddle the bench, and she turns a wide smile my way. I feel like I've won the greatest award of all time to be on the receiving end of that smile.

She just stares at me like she's taking every part of me in. "I've missed you, Buttercup."

My jaw ticks at the nickname, but I also feel the lightness in my eyes as I watch her. She'd given me the stupid nickname the second time we met because I'd fallen off a tree and hurt myself and she'd stayed by my side as Darius went off to find their parents. At five years old, she comforted me by saying, '*It'll be all right, Buttercup*' like her mother always told her when she was hurt.

And somehow, the nickname has stuck.

"Eat," I grit though I can't hide that I'm not mad at the use of the name. I know she can see how much I've missed hearing it.

She mimics my grumbles but takes the burger in her hands and takes a large bite. As her lips close around the burger, all my mind sees is her lips wrapping around my cock —no teeth, of course—but the image is there and clear as day.

Darius takes a seat across from us, and the fucker has a huge I-just-fucked smile on his face.

And I've just been imaging his sister sucking me dry, so maybe I shouldn't be judging. And maybe—okay, definitely —it's a good thing he's here.

He steals a cucumber from Emory's plate and laughs as she calls him a slut through a full mouth, but he doesn't give her time to swallow as he asks, "And do Mom and Dad know you're back?"

"Nope," she says as she swallows the last bite and chugs down some water. "And you won't tell them either. I wanna surprise them."

He smiles. Darius loves surprises. "How?"

I'm curious too, but I can't focus on anything except the fact that she's just finished that burger in a few bites. She must've been hungrier that I'd thought. "Pause." I move quickly, making her another burger and putting it before her as I straddle the bench again, my knee brushing her hip as I sit a little bit closer. "Eat, then, how are we surprising them?"

She smiles warmly at me. "Thank you, Buttercup."

"Eat, baby."

I don't know what possessed me to say that, but her eyes widening a fraction tells me she's very aware of the slip.

And thankfully, Darius is oblivious. "He's right, baby sister, eat. Then we can talk about how we're giving Mom and Dad a mini heart attack."

She's three bites in when she finally puts it down to tell us the plan. She looks between Darius and me before settling on whatever she was thinking about.

She looks to her brother. "Call and tell them you guys wanna go over for dinner. Tell them Tommy's bringing a girl home."

Another flash passes me. This one an image of taking Emory out and introducing her as mine.

Then fucking her against the wall of whatever dark hall we find.

I pinch myself to stop that train of thought as Darius asks, "Why Tommy?" His tone is more curious than offended.

"I highly doubt they're going to believe you're bringing home a girl, whorebag." She takes another bite. "Plus, I need you to show up earlier than us so you can make sure they're both around. No last-minute calls or hopping to the store."

He rolls his eyes, but that grin says he doesn't give a damn what everyone thinks of him. Pretty much because he knows they're all facts.

This is how we work. We never lie, just omit facts.

We won't tell them I want to introduce a girl because that would be a lie. But if we tell them I want to bring a girl over, it could literally be anyone. Even Nana Isla.

Darius is dialing when Emory brings the last bite of her burger to my lips. "It's too much. Finish it for me."

"It's one more bite, Em."

Her lips fall into that pout that she perfected over the years to get me to do whatever she wants. I've forgotten how effective it was after all this time.

I sigh and swipe the last bits from her fingers, my tongue taking the opportunity to taste a bit of her skin. Her pupils dilate a little as she watches me, and I try to manipulate my mind into believing I didn't just see that.

It doesn't work.

But as I turn to listen to Darius talking to his mom, I realize how at ease I am. Truly at ease, something I haven't felt in so long because the opposite has become the new normal. But having Emory back, I feel it again. That contented peace of life with the two of them. I have my family back together, and I don't want to let go ever again.

My eyes flicker to Emory, and I stare as she watches Darius avoid telling their mother *who* I will be bringing. She's back and beautiful and perfect, and I cannot fathom a point where I allow her out of my life again.

And not for the dirty reasons my cock is singing up to me either, but because of this. The three of us. I wouldn't give this up for the world, and I know if she says she wants to leave again, I'll drag Darius and go with her.

Her gaze flickers to meet mine, and that smile relaxes as she meets my stare. She takes the hand I have placed on the table and brings it to her lips for a light kiss. "You miss me, Buttercup?"

"Too much." I don't hesitate.

Darius breaks our stare when he hangs up the phone and takes our conjoined hands. Then it's the three of us holding hands and laughing together like old times.

CHAPTER 2
Emory

I **LEFT** my bags by the gate when I'd surprised the guys. The boys brought them in after everyone left while I helped clean the backyard.

Then Tommy was sweet enough to offer his bed, stating there was no way I was spending any time in Darius's infected sheets.

Darius laughed at the comment and walked right for those infected sheets, not giving a single fuck.

And that's how I ended up in Tommy's bed while he lay out on the couch. And exactly why it took me forever to fall asleep.

I wanted to tell him to join me in the bed. Since we slept together a million times growing up, there was no need for him to take the couch. But I also knew that if he joined me in this bed, my body would be so aware of him that I'd never fall asleep.

And it's already hard enough getting my body to calm down as it is. Because damn, do these sheets smell like him. That tingling of masculinity that radiates off his skin and that engulfed me when Tommy hugged me, then sat beside me all night.

It's insane—how affected I am by all of it. Any of it.

I hadn't expected this.

I thought I'd come back and find the two brothers I'd left behind. Sure, I've always found Tommy attractive and maybe even had a slight crush when we were kids, but there truly has been nothing there.

Even as I was dropped off at the house and stared at the backs of the two men I adored more than anyone else in the world, I felt nothing.

But then he turned to face me, and my heart literally stopped for a few seconds. I had to force myself to turn to Darius because all I wanted was to keep staring at Tommy.

Then he hugged me so tightly, I genuinely felt myself mold into him as I got lost in that scent so uniquely Tommy. The very same one I was drowning in all night as I tried to sleep.

I wanted to stay there, wrapped in his arms and suffocating in his scent, all night. And a part of me—a large part—wanted nothing more than to kiss the skin below his ear, if only to get a glimpse of his taste.

But I let the desire go because I'm Darius's little sister and duh, that makes me his little sister too. Somehow, I forced myself away while Darius introduced me to everyone, but the feel of his eyes on me sent shivers down my spine that should not be happening with Thomas Rutherford.

And the way his tongue brushed my fingers when he took that last bite...Fucking fuck fuck fuck.

Add a special fuck because he noticed how it had affected me and turned away quickly. Yup, just his little sister.

It is a fact I will have to live with. Especially because this reaction must be a random side effect of so long away from him, and I'm sure it will go away soon. It has to. This is my

Buttercup; he's ridiculously attractive, and I haven't seen him in a long while. That is it.

But I can't fight the fact that my panties are soaked through, and I am half tempted to completely take them off because the thought that Tommy has probably jacked off right in this spot is too much.

It's torture.

I have no idea what the fuck is going on with my head because he has never been more than Darius's best friend and brother. I have never felt a desire like this for him.

I've never felt a desire like this for anyone. Ever.

It's too much.

But I've finally tired myself out enough to fall asleep. Surprisingly, jet lag didn't affect me since I tried to switch my sleeping schedule around my last week in London so I wouldn't be as affected when I returned home.

When I wake up grumpy and sexually frustrated, things only get worse.

Because I walk out to the kitchen to find both my brother and his best friend up and chipper, still in their pajama bottoms.

And shirtless. Because of course they are. Of course *he* is.

That's exactly what I need—the sight of the light speckle of hair trickling across his chiseled chest and leading the path down to the motherland. I just changed panties, and now these are soaked too.

"You guys working today?" I try to distract myself, glad neither of them caught me ogling Tommy.

Darius tskes. "No work on Sundays, little sister."

I smile because that's exactly what I thought. "Great! That means we can hang out all day."

"Ooo," he breaths out as he puts his cup into the sink with a bit of mirth in his eyes, "wish you'd told me you were coming. I'd have cleared my schedule."

I cross my arms as a scoff huffs out of my nose. "Too busy to spend time with your baby sister whom you haven't seen in four years?"

I can tell Tommy's trying not to laugh as he leans over the island and watches us.

Darius, on the other hand, doesn't try to hide the wide grin. "A baby sister who is moving in with us. I'll see you plenty."

The little shit is being serious; he is gonna leave—surely to see that chick he was banging last night—instead of spending the day with me.

I narrow my gaze on Tommy. "Is your schedule full too?"

My tone is demanding, but inside I'm dreading the answer. I really don't want to hear him say he's fucking some girl. He's never been the type to whore around, but that doesn't mean there isn't anyone in his life at the moment.

There's a light trickle of dark hair around that heart stopping smile. "Absolutely not, baby. I'm all yours."

There's that word again. *Baby.*

And calling himself all mine. I need to stop thinking about it because he obviously means it differently than how I'm interpreting it.

I turn back to Darius. "You sure you don't wanna come?"

He quirks a brow at me. "How is this gonna convince me to come?"

"Your best friend is taking your baby sister on a date." Lame since Tommy took me out a million times growing up. And this wouldn't be a date date. "You sure you want to allow that?"

Darius's grin is as wide as the Cheshire cat's as he smacks Tommy on the back. "Good luck."

"Really?" It's more annoyed than angry as the word leaves my lips.

He's already walking back to his room. "Have fun on your date!"

I scoff. *Asshole.*

Tommy's still silently enjoying the show when I turn back to him. "So where are we going on this little date?"

His tongue darts out to clean his bottom lip, and it grabs all my attention. Way, way too distracting. I needed Darius's buffer today.

His eyes shine as he says, "You ask me out, and I have to plan the date?"

I clear my head because it's too full of Tommy's tongue before I can speak, but my voice is still weak as it leaves me. "Yes."

I like that he called it a date even though it's not a real one. *Technically.*

It's definitely going to be a date, but not the romantic kind. Just the kind of date that we always went on when we were younger, the kind that Darius would take me on. Hanging out.

Tommy laughs as he finishes his coffee and puts the cup in the sink. That laugh is so rich and dark, I'm gonna have to change my panties again.

This is getting ridiculous.

He stops beside me before walking out of the kitchen and leans into my ear. "Dress casually. We'll leave in half an hour."

My heart flips.

Not only because we're going on this date, but also because of the proximity of his words. My entire body shivers as his breath hits my ear and sends shivers tingling all throughout my body.

This needs to stop. It'll be torture living in this house with them if this...attraction doesn't go away.

I look up into his waiting eyes and nod.

. . .

The way he smiles at me when I walk out of the room in white Vans, dark denim shorts, and a basic black tank has my heart fluttering. He has no right to look at me like that—that perfect heart stopping, panty-melting smile.

And those shining, wicked eyes that say he approves of what he sees.

No.

No, he doesn't. I'm reading too much into everything, and it needs to stop!

As I look him over, I cannot help but approve of everything I see. Very much so.

He's in a plain white shirt and denim over boots. Casual, exactly as he's said. But damn, did he deliver on his end. He looks go *fucking* good, drool actually wants to slip out of my mouth.

He takes me to his car and opens the passenger door, bowing at me to get in. "Madam."

I laugh and push him away as I fall into the scent of him that's filling every inch of the inside of this car.

Then we're driving.

And driving.

We don't actually talk on the ride, too filled with our horrible voices as we sing every country song that plays on the radio.

But it's a perfect start to the day.

We're about an hour into the drive before we begin to slow and pull off the dirt road to park. It doesn't look like there's anything around, and I turn a quirked brow at him.

He just smirks and gets out of the car.

I follow him as he leads me into the bushes. "Planning on killing me, Buttercup?"

"You got me, baby girl."

My breath stops. Completely and utterly, I am frozen. *Baby* was one thing, but *baby girl* is…

Not allowed.

He needs to stop that; my poor heart can't take much more.

Maybe this not-a-real-date wasn't such a great idea.

When we're out of the overgrown bushes, I see a lake, beautifully encompassed by flowers and a family of ducks.

Yeah, seeing this, I know this was a bad idea. This is straight out of a movie.

I watch him as he unlocks a tiny cottage I hadn't noticed at first.

"Bring girls here so often they gave you a key?" I ask even though I really don't want to know the answer.

He laughs while he's in there. And doesn't deny.

Then he comes out with a canoe, and I realize what is going to happen on this date. A real-life fucking movie!

He winks at my gasp as he sets it on the wooded plank by the water. "It's Octavio's. He brings Lynette here all the time. He brought me the keys while you were getting ready."

Octavio is Darius and Tommy's closest friend and partner at work.

"And how many women have you brought here?" I ask again because as much as I don't want to know, hearing the answer will solidify that this is nothing more than him taking the girl he sees as a little sister somewhere pretty.

He smiles like he knows why I'm asking though he can't possibly. That would mean he sees this as anything but platonic. "This is *my* first time here. I've definitely never brought anyone. I've just heard so much from Lynette that I figured you'd love it too."

I force my breath not to hitch.

Okay, so no other women, but he's also never been here, so it still doesn't mean anything.

This is already shaping out to be a pretty awesome date. Motherfucker is going to set my expectations so high, I'll be ruined for anyone else—something both he and Darius have always tried to do, so I never settled.

He's back in the tiny cottage and out two minutes later with some waters and the paddles. "Just don't tell your brother. Octavio doesn't want him asking to bring every other chick around here."

I laugh because Darius is a pig, but I don't see him bringing *every* other chick around.

Tommy pushes the canoe into the water and holds it close with his foot before reaching out a hand to me. "Let's go."

I don't hesitate taking his hand and slowly stepping into the tiny boat. I'm seated when he follows and sits across from me.

"Do you know how to row this thing?" I ask because I don't think I've ever heard of either him or Darius canoeing.

"How hard could it be?" He's cocky, and that has my body reacting almost immediately.

I inhale slowly. *Relax, body. This is Tommy. Only Tommy.*

And he's right. When you're as gorgeously powerful as he is, how hard could it be?

He rows us around the lake as we talk about my time in London. He lets me row almost an hour in, showing me his little technique, while I let his arms take a break.

And damn, does it take all my strength.

But at least now I'm not distracted by the flexing of his biceps.

He laughs at my attempts, but I'm still getting us around. It's just not as fluid or graceful, and definitely not as fast, as his motions had been.

We finally pause in the middle of the lake, and we both laugh as I rub my arms. This was hard fucking work.

We take swigs of our waters, then he's moving again.

Apparently, the benches of this canoe can be pushed back to create enough space in the middle to lie down. Tommy kicks his bench back, then both of his hands settle by my hips and his face stops only inches from mine. I have to hold my breath so I don't get too much of his scent assaulting me, and the way he winks tells me he knows what I'm doing.

But that's impossible. I'm only his best friend's little sister.

He pushes me back, and voilà, there's an open space in the middle of the canoe.

He lays a couple of blankets out—how he keeps himself stable with the rocking of the canoe is amazing—then lies down, a larger blanket under his head to keep it propped up, and opens his arms wide for me to snuggle in.

We haven't done this in four years, and it is one of the things I missed most about being away. Cuddling with Tommy. And that's the only reason I don't hesitate.

I snuggle into his side, my head resting on his chest as my fingers begin playing with the cotton of his shirt, and I'm smacked with his scent. Everywhere. But I don't care as he pulls me in tighter.

"Fuck, Emmie." His breath hits my temple, and I freeze, scared he's gonna pull away. "I can't believe I went four years without holding you. How the fuck did I go from holding you almost every day to not at all, baby?"

My heart is still racing, but at least I can calm down now that I know he has no intentions of pushing me away. "It's the thing I got most homesick about. Cuddling with you. I complained to Darius all the time that I needed him to ship you to me so I could have my teddy bear back."

His laugh rumbles through his chest as his arms bring me in so close, I'm damn near lying on top of him. "He never told me."

I shrug. "He probably thought I was joking."

That laugh again. "Thought? You weren't joking?"

I rest my chin on his chest so I can look into his eyes. "Never." His responding grin is distracting. "I never slept the same. I was so used to getting at least a bit of you every day that not having you was *weird*. I kind of got antsy the first few months I was out there, but then I think my body got used to it."

One of his hands is at my waist, drawing small circles as it holds me close, and the other reaches out to play with my hair. "I'm sorry, baby. If I'd known, I'd have flown out on the next flight."

My lips tug up. "Liar."

He winks, and I drop back to lying on his chest so my heart can ease up a bit. Looking at him is sending that sucker on a sprint.

There's a bit of silence—the comfortable, we could be like this all day kind—before he breaks it. "Good start to the date?"

I scoff, watching my fingers draw on his chest. I'm spelling out my name. "Start? This is the best date period. And it's not even real!"

His chest moves beneath me as he chuckles. "Oh, it's real, baby girl."

He needs.

To stop.

Calling me that!

We spend most of the next hour and a half talking about nothing in particular and playing the cloud game where we come up with what the clouds up above look like. I love when he laughs at my inane concepts for each figure, and that's half the reason I keep coming up with them. But only half!

I honestly think we can lie out there for hours still, continuing this little game and the conversations of nothing in particular if it weren't for our stomachs. Already it's been almost five hours since breakfast, and even that had been a quick bagel and a few pieces of fruit. Not to mention the workout we had rowing earlier.

He laughs as our stomachs make a chorus, squeezing me in tight to him before releasing me and sitting us up. "Time for food."

I feel my bottom lip jut out, and I know my eyes are screaming puppy dog as I look at him.

"Don't give me that pout, baby. It works way too well, and I need to get some food in you."

I deepen the pout. "But I don't wanna go." *I don't want to stop holding you in this perfect movie.*

He flicks my nose lightly though I catch his gaze on my lips. His eyes shoot back up quickly though, like he's reprimanding himself. "I know, baby. I'll bring you back."

All I can think while he's helping me to the bench and pulling the two seats to the middle again is why he would be reprimanding himself. Maybe that was also a figment of my imagination.

I fold the blankets as he rows us back to land. Everything is put away and locked up, and we're in the car in a matter of ten minutes. Then it's back into town.

We do exactly as we had before—sing horribly to country songs the entire way, but it's only about twenty minutes before we stop, shit-eating grins on both our faces.

He pulls into a deli outside of town and forces me to stay in the car as he goes in to grab our food—it's a surprise, he says.

When he returns with a bag and two waters, he pushes his seat back so he has space to turn to me and hands me a sub from the bag. "Best subs. Ever."

I'm already unwrapping. "That's a bold statement, Buttercup."

He winks, but I'm already staring at the beauty that is the

melted cheese and meatball marinara sub. My stomach grumbles in anticipation, and the smell excites me.

I bite into it, and fuck, this is the best sub. Ever.

I look up to find him staring at me. "I told you."

He brings his sub to his lips, but this sub is so good, I'm not even paying attention to his mouth.

Yup. Best date ever.

And it wasn't even a real date.

When we finish, he doesn't adjust his seat to drive back into town. Instead, he reclines it back so he can lie there and turns to stare at me expectantly.

I recline mine too and lie on my side to watch him. "Still planning on killing me?"

His brows furrow. "Thinking about it."

I wait a bit, but he doesn't do anything but stare at me. I quirk a brow at him in question.

His smile is soft. "I like listening to you speak. We don't have to be home for that."

I swear if my heart keeps going like this, it's gonna stop. "What do you want to hear me talk about?" We've already talked so much.

"Tell me where in the world you want to travel to most."

The answer should be more difficult to come up with since I've already been to so many places, but I don't even have to think about it. "Africa. Maybe Zimbabwe or Botswana. I really want to go on one of those safaris."

He lies there on his side and listens to me talk about it. About all the research I've done and how excited the thought of seeing the animals in their natural habitat makes me. And I don't even realize when hours pass by and I've talked about safaris, traveling across Africa in general, then moving on to the Middle East. The man wasn't kidding when he said he enjoyed listening to me.

When the sun is beginning to set in the late summer day,

Tommy goes back into the deli for another round of food for when we're back home, then we're on the road again.

We listen to the music this time rather than destroying it with our voices, and we're about ten minutes away from town when I see a sign for a drive-in movie hidden behind some bushes.

I sit right up. "Tommy! Tommy, a drive-in. We have to go!"

He smiles over at me and doesn't hesitate turning off the road and into the little drive-in.

He pays for our tickets while the old man looks between the two of us with raised brows, then nods for us to continue, only two minutes before the movie starts.

Tommy switches to the station that will provide the audio, and I'm cuddled into his arm, not caring what the movie is about because anything would be perfect for this date.

Except maybe what starts.

Two minutes into the start of the movie, I realize why the man had been looking at us like that at the same moment Tommy barks out in laughter.

I'm gasping and turning away, thankful for the darkness that hides the blush deep on my skin. Because this isn't a normal movie drive-in. It's a dirty movie drive-in.

The moans and groans of two people starting to get it on blasts threw the speakers in the car when I throw my head between my legs to hide, screaming at Tommy who is still barking with laughter. "This isn't funny, Tommy! Let's go."

I turn to see the tears beginning to spring to his eyes and can't fight the laugh that bubbles out of me at seeing him like that.

I push away from him as far as I can go because there's no way I can remain near him with *those* sounds. It's too much.

When the high-pitched moans of the woman in the movie

pierce through the speakers, I finally sit back up and see the man going down on her on the huge drive-in screen.

I'm shaking my head and trying not to look, my hand covering the side of my face as my entire body turns to Tommy. "I cannot believe this."

He's still laughing. "Oh, me neither, but this has officially become the best date to exist."

I smack him on the arm. "Tommy! Let's go!"

"C'mon, baby girl." There's a seductive undertone to him. "Let's stick around a bit, see what happens."

My panties are soaked through so much, I'm scared I'll soak through the shorts as I stare into his eyes and mutter breathlessly. "Stop calling me that."

His gaze dips to my lips, and even though it's dark, I see his dark browns dilating. I know that much I'm not making up in my head.

The way he looks at me kinda tells me he sees the same thing mirrored in my browns.

He's grinning again as he starts the engine. "Fine, we can go." We're out of there, and the station statics out as Tommy shuts it off and turns to me. "But I'm not gonna stop calling you that, baby girl."

I don't say anything more until we're about a block from the house, and I remember what he's said. "This wasn't a real date."

The more I say it, the realer it'll become because I cannot let myself fantasize about Thomas Rutherford, Darius's brother and for all intents and purposes, his soulmate. Because soulmates aren't always romantic.

Tommy turns off the car in front of the house and is opening my door as I grab the bags of food.

He slams the door shut behind me, our bodies almost touching as he hovers over me. "It was real."

CHAPTER 3

Tommy

WORK WAS TOUGH TODAY. Mostly because it was all labor and way too hot out for anyone to be putting in that much work. But it needed to get done and we had the best men in town to do it.

And while this is Darius's and my business, so we could just sit back and let the others do the manual labor, that's not our style. We came into this field because of how much we enjoyed the physical part of it.

Although it was a tough day, I'm thankful for all the hard work. It keeps my mind off a certain date that Darius asked about with a laugh. And a certain woman whom I definitely should not think about, especially with the direction my thoughts seemed to head in every time she popped into my mind.

But no matter how much I try, she's always there. Always hovering at the edge of my thoughts, waiting to make it back to the forefront.

Moral of the story, it's been physically and mentally a challenging day.

When we're back home, it's right to the showers for us.

That's normally the drill, but on days like today when we're extra sweaty and dirty, it's a requirement.

And luckily for us, both our rooms came with ensuites.

I chuck off my boots and socks when I get to my room and head straight for the bathroom, ready to pull my shirt off.

Then I pause.

Because my bathroom isn't empty.

In hindsight, the soft sounds coming from the space should've alerted me to her presence.

Emory is lying in the bath, soapy bubbles barely covering her as she reads a book.

She gasps when I walk in, but she doesn't move or shy away. She just stares back at me. She *has* always liked men who worked with their hands and got dirty.

And I definitely should not be thinking about that right now. I am not for her.

But she looks heavenly.

Her legs are half propped out of the bath so the water is trickling down her smooth skin. My gaze is lead straight to the bubble infused water that covers the treasure ground.

My gaze slowly racks up over her barely covered breasts, toward her wet neck, and all I can think about is how desperately I want to lick her clean.

That chest is rising and falling, tempting the bubbles that hardly cover her to move, and fuck, am I praying to the lords that they listen.

I grit my teeth and force my eyes to move.

When I finally reach her face, her lips are slightly parted, and her breathing isn't coming out normally.

And when I finally reach her gaze, she's not looking at me. At least, not at my face. She's looking further south.

That's when I realize I'm so hard right now that my cock is straining against my jeans, and she can see the indentation of what I have to offer.

Her gaze is heated when it shoots back up to mine, and I know one thing for certain—I need to get out of there.

I slam the door shut behind me and lean against it to catch my breath. If Darius had walked in at that moment, he'd have killed me if for nothing else than the enormous hard-on I had going on in front of his sister.

I walk to my bed and sit on the edge, letting my head fall into my hands as I try to control my cock and remind it that she is the one person that is off limits.

But buddy is as persistent as the logical side of my brain and continues to remind me of everything that was Emory Aabeck since the moment she arrived back in town.

The way she smiled at me at the BBQ. The way her eyes dilated when I took that burger from her fingers *and* when we stopped at the drive-in. The way her heart raced when she cuddled into me in the canoe. The way she traced her name over my heart over and over and over again.

And those aren't even the dirty thoughts.

My cock also reminds me of her naked body in the bath, the water gliding over her skin. The way her chest rose and fell for me. The way her breath invited me in. I can feel the pre-cum ready to drip out of my cock as every picture passes through my mind.

The door opens, and I snap my head up to find her in a short white silk robe that barely skims her thighs. I bet if she turned around, it would just be covering her ass, probably not even that.

And because she's just been in water, that robe sticks to her every inch, and I can make out just how hard her nipples are underneath the material as she leans into the doorframe and crosses her arms—perfectly accentuating her breasts for me—and stares.

Buddy down south adds those hardened beauties to the list.

"Didn't realize you two were home already."

She sounds like she's trying for nonchalant, but I can pick out the undertones of desire in her voice.

I really hope I'm making that up. Maybe it's just embarrassment, and because my cock is up and feral, I'm hearing desire. Because I'm barely controlling myself as it is.

I try to keep my voice calm. "Yeah, we're back around six every day. Tried making sure we were on time today since we have dinner at your parents."

I try to force my gaze to remain on her face—her breathtaking face—as she stands before me.

She just nods in response. "Right. I'll let you shower then."

I don't say anything as I watch her walk out of my room, her scent hitting me as she passes, and I have to physically restrain myself from reaching out and throwing her onto my bed.

I was right too—the robe barely covers her ass.

I'll have to get her a longer, fluffier, less attractive robe. There is no way she will be wearing that around her brother; worse yet, if we have friends over.

"I'm gonna head out. Meet you guys there," Darius says as he walks out the door.

I nod and watch him leave as I sit back on the couch and wait for Emory to walk out.

She steps out five minutes later, and as I look up, I feel my skin burn from top to bottom. She's so fucking stunning in an ivory dress that hugs her torso in a corset and lightly flows around those perfect hips and thighs. The straps fall down her shoulders, enticing me to kiss the revealed skin. And the gladiator sandals that snake up her legs to her thighs make the whole enchanting look ferocious.

Her dark locks fall in waves down her back with two small braids clipped together and out of her face. It's that small detail that really does it for me. How it all frames that face. That stunning face.

She is a goddess from the myths. Breathtaking.

I can't move. I don't want to. I'd die a happy man just sitting here and staring at her for the rest of my days.

She stops in front of me and makes a slow spin. I let my gaze drag up every inch of her before she's facing me again. "You like?"

I have to clear my throat and rub my hands—which are now shaking with the need to throw her on this couch and take her—down my thighs as I rise to my feet and look down at her. "I love, baby girl."

Her lips tug up, and I know that even though she knows she's beautiful, hearing it still makes her feel special. And the tinge of a blush coating her cheeks tells me she especially likes my new little nickname for her.

That flush adds to her beauty.

So much so, I'm scared I might come in my pants if I continue staring at her.

"Let's go." My hand is at the small of her back because I won't survive the night if I can't touch her at least a little, and I'm leading her out to the car.

Her breathing hitches, which the cocky part of me knew it would.

We're out front, and I'm about to open her door when two of my favorite people come walking up the sidewalk.

They're in their late seventies but still walk about like they're merely in their fifties. And they're everything I aspire for in a relationship.

"Ahh," Nana smiles, tangled in Papa's arms, "what a beauty you've found, Thomas."

My body turns toward Emory, and I can't help the wide

grin at hearing her referred to as mine. "Nana. Papa. This is Emory, Darius's little sister." They should be able to figure that out based off the million pictures we've shown them. "Em, this is Nana Isla and Papa Atti from across the street."

Emory beams at them, and I'm caught again by her beauty. "Oh, yes. Darius told me all about how you tease him about his habits."

"Someone had to while you were away, little lady," Nana says through a smile as she glances between the two of us.

Papa is even less discrete as he eyes us. "Darius's baby sister, huh? And he's okay with you two going on a date?"

The blush fills Emory quickly. "Not a date, Papa Atti. We're going to my parents for dinner. They don't know I'm back yet, so Darius is making sure they're both home before we get there."

"Not a date?" Papa quirks a wrinkled brow at us.

Emory gives a slight shake of her head, her face heating up and causing the grin on mine to grow as my gaze latches down on her. I can't help it; the embarrassed smile she gives them is adorable.

And it's too difficult to tear my gaze away from her.

"Does Thomas know that? The way he's holding you, there isn't a man on this planet that would believe you single," Papa says.

And that's when I realize I have my hand wrapped around her waist and her form pulled close into my side.

I relax my hold, but don't let go. "We have to go."

Nana crinkles her forehead. "But I'm just meeting the girl."

Emory smiles at the couple. "I promise I'll come by. I've just moved back, and I'll be living with the boys, so I'll be yours to do with as you please, Nana."

Nana's smile grows. "I like you."

I do too. Too much.

"Mhm," I grumble under my breath and lead Emory toward the car again. I open the door and wait by it as she stops before me, and we turn back to Nana and Papa. "I'll see you two later."

Papa winks at me as the two of them walk onto the small street and across to their house directly diagonal with ours.

Emory watches them go until they're inside then turns to me. "Should I have told them we went on a date yesterday?"

"I thought it was a fake date," I tease because we both know what it was, and everything about it, about us, is real.

Her brows furrow in mock surprise. "Oh? No. I'm quite certain it was real."

I bite my bottom lip to keep my smile contained because fuck, she's so cute when she's like this. How I hadn't noticed before still baffles me. "Good. I needed to be sure you knew it."

Her gaze drops to my lips, then latches onto mine again as she leans in close. "Don't tease me, Buttercup."

She drops to her seat before I can process her statement, and I have to strain to keep myself contained. To keep buddy down south contained because he's persistent and begging, *begging* to play.

I slam the door shut and walk around the car, get in and start the engine without looking at her.

We're on the road when she speaks again, "I love yours too."

My heart stops, and I almost swerve us out of our lane. "What?"

She's smiling, but this one isn't teasing. It's almost shy. "What you chose to wear tonight. It does to me what I suspect this," she plays with the bottom of her dress, "does to you."

I glance down. I'm only wearing dark denim over nice

boots—the ones I only wear for nights out—and a nice button down. It's absolutely nothing compared to her dress.

But she likes it.

No.

She loves it.

I don't know how to handle myself at the thought that she may be feeling half of what I am right now, but my knuckles whiten around the wheel as my free hand scratches at my neck like an addict trying to fight the need.

CHAPTER 4

Emory

I DON'T KNOW what it is about Tommy, but I find every bit
of confidence when I'm around him. Maybe it's the way he's
been looking at me. Or maybe it's that I've grown up with
him and know that I'll always be safe around him.

Either way, when we step out of the car at my parents'
house and he starts walking, I reach out my hand and he
takes it without hesitation.

Maybe it's a mix of the two because he's definitely not shy
around me either.

Feeling him intertwine our fingers and turn to look at me,
I know that this is definitely not a stupid crush that'll go
away soon like the one I had when we were kids. This one is
strong and here to stay.

We walk into the house, and he calls out to let them
know we're here. He's walking right in front of me as we
turn the corner from the foyer into the dining room where
my family is waiting. Darius is sitting back in one of the
dining table chairs with a wide grin, and I know by the
spark in his eyes that they can't see me behind Tommy's
larger frame.

But from the squeals, I think they see our interlocked hands.

"Tommy," Mom calls out, "oh, sweetheart, I'm so excited to meet this girl. You've never brought a girl for us to meet."

Poor Mom, she sounds genuinely excited.

Tommy squeezes my hand, and I know without looking at him that he feels bad for getting my parents so excited. Though seeing me back would surely be a better surprise.

"Now," he teases, "I never said I was bringing anyone for you to meet."

"Tommy, what are..." Dad starts but is cut off when Tommy steps aside and both my parents' gazes drop to me.

Their gasps are equally followed by elated smiles as they rush for me.

"Emmie!" Mom calls out as she brings me in for a hug.

Mom pulls me deeper into the room, then Dad is in front of me. He flicks my nose and pulls me in for a tight hug. "Rascals. All three of you."

When I finally pull away, Mom has turned accusatory eyes on Darius. "You said Tommy was bringing home a girl!"

I move back to Tommy's side and wrap my arms around his bicep as a leg hitches up. "But he did bring home a girl."

Dad looks over all three of us. "All of you, pieces of shits."

His smile is so wide though that I know he's trying not to laugh too much at being fooled.

Tommy takes my hand again and he's leading us to the table Mom already has prepared. "It's not our fault you assumed I was bringing home a girlfriend."

My heart stutters, heartbroken. He hasn't brought home a girlfriend. Or anyone he would consider so. Because I'm his best friend's little sister, and that's all I'll remain to him. I was foolish to allow myself to think otherwise.

"No, you're right," Mom says as she takes her seat at the head of the table, opposite Dad, "it's my fault for birthing two morons and letting them befriend and take you down with them."

"Oh." I feign a blush and flick my wrist. "Stop being so sweet, Momushka."

She flips me off, and we're officially back together, the five of us. Tommy may not be related by blood, but my family practically raised him. He's been having dinner with us every night for as long as I can remember. Hell, he slept over half of the time, and we'd take him on vacations growing up.

Then the loud conversations begin. We can't ever talk without someone screaming over someone else and I realize I missed this more than I thought. Just being back and having Mom's food again, listening to their benign arguments, and feeling the love from every inch of this room, it's unbeatable.

Tommy glances over at me as he declares himself winner of the argument he was having with Darius and Mom and smiles, leaning into my ear. "Everything good?"

Our eyes meet, and my heart skips a beat, both because of his proximity and the happiness of being back. "Amazing."

His brows furrow slightly as he kisses my temple, and I have to remind myself he's only doing it the way Darius would.

He pulls out his phone and is playing with it in what I hope isn't him messaging a girl as Mom brings the conversation back to our little ploy.

Dad's moved to her side by now, just like he always did at our dinners, and she leans into his side as she angrily looks out to the three of us. "I still can't believe you lied to your mother."

Our mother. Because they've always considered Tommy one of their own. Darius's twin, they called him.

Darius tsks. "We didn't lie, Moman. I said Tommy would be bringing home a girl. You assumed it would be someone you didn't know."

She narrows her gaze at him as the speakers at the corners of the house activate and scare the crap out of me. Tommy's hand is on my leg, calming my jump, and when I look up, he's beaming down at me.

So that's what he's been doing.

"I also thought it would be a romantic partner," Mom mutters, but I'm too engrossed in Tommy to care.

An oldie song begins to play, and Tommy is out of his seat and pulling at my hand to join him.

Before I'm in his arms, I hear Dad mutter to Mom so low, I don't think either of the boys hear, "It still very well might be."

Mom sends a baffled look at Dad before turning back to us, but by then, I'm in Tommy's arms and I don't care enough to turn and see her reaction. Tommy wraps my arms around his neck, then slowly slides his hands down my arms until they meet at the small of my back so he can pull me in close. Shivers follow every inch of skin he touches.

And I can't help but match his wide smile as I look up at him.

He leans into my ear. "Everything good now?"

He's pulled away to look at me, and our faces are so close, I'm surprised Darius isn't jumping up and pulling us apart. "Perfect."

Then I remind myself there's no point in breaking us up because Tommy doesn't see anything in me. And this isn't the first time the two of us have danced.

Nothing we've done since I've been back has been new. It's all things we did before I left for London. The problem is back then, I didn't realize how romantic all of it was.

He winks. "That's my girl."

It would really help convincing myself that he's only Darius's best friend if he stopped talking about me like that.

But I hadn't been lying. This night was perfect.

And before long, it's over. We say our goodbyes to our parents, and I wrap my arms around Darius's waist as we walk down to the two cars parked back-to-back. "I could ride with you if you want."

I don't want to make my preference for being around Tommy so blatant. But that's not something I have to worry about because Darius seems blind to it all. Understandably so, considering none of our behaviors are any different than they were four years ago.

Darius throws his arm around my shoulders and brings me in for a kiss on the crown of my head before pulling away. "Thanks for the offer, princess, but I won't be home for a couple of hours."

I shake my head at him, and he winks back with a wide grin before getting in his car and driving off.

I turn back to Tommy, my head still shaking. "Douchebag."

He winks. "Guess you're stuck with me."

I get in the car as he's starting the engine and try to ignore the jump of excitement at being alone with him again. At the prospect of getting the house to ourselves for a few hours even though I know nothing will happen. He's Darius's best friend, and he wouldn't push that boundary.

It's a silent ride home, and the darkness gives me the opportunity to watch him as he focuses on the road. His cropped brown hair looks so soft. I can remember the feeling of the ends against my fingertips while we danced, and I just want to run my fingers through his hair again. He'd let me if I did, but I know it'll be too much for my hopeful heart.

He's handsome in a masculine way, the smile that he always seems to have for me lightening his features.

He's not wearing it now though.

He looks contemplative as he drives home staring out the

windshield though I catch his glances in my direction every so often.

He breaks the silence when we're only a couple of minutes from home. "Did I mention how beautiful you are?"

In the darkness I can't see his expression, but it doesn't matter; the words are enough. "Your looks spoke volumes."

And they did. Which is why it's so hard to convince myself that he doesn't see me the way I do him. Because when he looks at me, I swear it's electric. But then he turns around, talking about me like there's no way anything romantic will happen.

I guess I don't mind in the sense that it keeps us private, and I've always needed to keep the things I adore most private.

But I also don't know if that's why he said it or if it truly was because there's nothing behind this thing I'm feeling.

I can just about see the quirk of his lips as he stops before the house and turns in my direction. "You're so beautiful, Emory. Not just tonight either."

My heart's not skipping any more beats. It's racing now. A sprint.

I bite down on my lip to control myself and watch his attention fall there, hovering as his body leans forward.

He's out of the car and slamming the door without another word, and I know that even if he feels something, he won't break the boundary because of Darius.

I sigh. Damn Darius.

Tommy and Darius are both gone by the time I wake up the next morning.

After a quick breakfast, I go to the final room left in the house. This'll be my room, and it's time to begin clearing it. It's small, but perfectly sized for me.

It's technically their office now, but since they're in construction, it's really more of a storage room. There's so much crap littered everywhere.

We agreed to move it all to the garage so I can bring in a bed. And since I'm an easygoing girl—the thing that made living across the world so easy for me—I won't need much more than the bed. And maybe an armchair in the corner.

I decide to leave the desk as is because the boys could just move it to the garage without having to disrupt anything in or on it. It would be a lot less work, and I won't end up messing up any paperwork they may have.

The majority of the work is gonna come from the rest of the room. How they ever find anything in here is amazing.

I've just turned to a heap of wires lying on the ground with three small containers, ready to separate them based on color, when I get a call from Darius.

"Hey, douchebag," I open.

"Hey, princess." He's not being cute, just typical big brother.

"What's up?"

"Can you go to the office, first drawer on the right, is there a paper there? A list of supplies, like an order sheet?"

I turn and crawl to the desk, pulling the drawer open and taking the paper out. "Yes, sir."

"Damn," he curses. "Okay, thanks, Em. We can't leave now, but Tommy or I'll be back at lunch for it."

"Doesn't your buyer leave by lunch?"

"I'll see if I can get him to stick around. I gotta go, sis."

I hang up and stare at the sheet.

It's still early morning and from what I know about their buyer, the man normally comes by around eleven and is gone by noon. And the boys normally take lunch at one.

I don't drive. If I did, I'd be able to take the keys to one of their cars—they have their normal life cars and their works trucks—and drive it over to them.

And Darius knows that which is why he doesn't ask me to take it. He knows the anxiety I have when I get behind a wheel is too overwhelming and though I hardly show it, in my head, I'm having a full-blown panic attack.

So he doesn't ask for it. Wouldn't, no matter how important it may have been.

But they're also only working a few miles from here, so it wouldn't be too long of a walk. And I really don't want to be in the office right now, especially if there's a possibility I'll see Tommy sweaty and dirty as he's working.

I leave the house not two minutes later and am on my way.

It takes an hour and a half to walk to the site, but it's still early when I get there.

Tommy and Darius both see me at the same time as I walk up and neither one looks too happy about my presence.

"Emmie, what the hell are you doing out here? It's hot as fuck," Darius reprimands me.

I roll my eyes and hand over the sheet. "You needed it, and I wasn't doing anything important."

He takes it with a smile I know he's trying to suppress. "Thank you." He rolls it and smacks me with it. "But next time, when I say I'll come get it, I'll come get it."

I furrow my brows in submission. "Yes, Mr. Tough Guy."

Tommy doesn't say anything. He's still pulling pieces of material apart, when I look up toward the sun, shielding my eyes as I think about walking home. I throw out my hand between the boys. "Keys. I don't wanna walk home."

Darius rolls his eyes at me and throws the keys my way.

But hey, Tommy looks delectable, and if I can sit back and enjoy the show, there's no reason I should suffer the walk home.

I'm sitting in the truck—which is thankfully under a shaded tree—windows down and feet hanging out of the passenger side for a couple of hours when the driver's side door opens, and a heavily pregnant woman gets in. She's gorgeous with her tanned skinned and curly hair that's different shades of brown that mix beautifully together.

My brows shoot up. "Hello."

She gives me a warm smile that says she knows this looks weird but she can explain. "Hi. I'm Lynette, Octavio's wife." She points to the man helping Darius and Tommy fix a piece that's supposed to go into the house by the end of the day.

"Oh?" I don't know what else to say.

"We live pretty close by, so I normally go on walks and Octavio drives me home, but he looks really busy right now and I saw the truck open, so I got in." She looks me over. "You must be Darius's sister."

"Must I?"

Her smile is so inviting. "I've seen a million pictures, though there's definitely been a bit of a change in the years since you guys have been together."

I finally smile back. "I'm Emory. Or Emmie." I turn back to watch the men out of the window.

"Your brother is an amazing man."

I feel the chuckle at the back of my throat, but I don't turn around. "Douchebag Darius? I think you're thinking of someone else."

There's a twinkle in my eyes as I look at her, and she knows I'm teasing. "He's just a good big brother to you. And he's the reason I have my Octavio."

"Oh?" I haven't heard this story. All I know is that Octavio was the first hire the boys had when they started their business.

"Mhm." She settles back into the seat like she's about to tell a tale, her hand rubbing circles on her swollen belly.

I look back out the window, ready to listen to her as I watch both my brother and his best friend work.

"Octavio didn't have a great start to life. Grew up about an hour north of here. Mom was a whore; Dad her pimp. He spent half of his life locking himself away from the men that came in and out of his house and the other half hiding so he wouldn't get caught up in the drugs they were pulling. Somehow, child services never took him away. His parents only kept him anyway because of the money the government provided for low income families with children. And when he was finally eighteen and not bringing any more benefits, he was given the proposition—become a whore like his mother so his father had two sources of income or get out. Obviously, he chose to get out."

My gaze flickers to Octavio as he carries materials into the house, the sun beating down on him. He's got the latino charm that I could imagine being attracted to in another lifetime, one without Lynette or this connection to Tommy. All I know about him is that he's a damn hard worker and an even better friend. And now, that he had a damn tough start to life.

"He barely graduated high school. With everything going on at home, he wasn't entirely concerned with his grades. He loved to learn, but surviving clean was his priority. So with barely an education, he was only able to get a whatever-barely-making-anything jobs. But he did what he had to and rented out a room from someone he'd found online. He saved the money that didn't go to rent and food to buy a car. He got a truck, one of those bigger ones that also has a backseat. It was old, but he loved it. Still loves it. It's sitting in our garage."

I smile. I've barely met Octavio with the common greetings from time to time when I was on a call with Darius, but he's always seemed like a nice guy.

"Things were looking okay for him until his father got

nailed for a rap sheet a mile long, and he claimed Octavio had been helping him. The asshole has always been trying to ruin Octavio's life for not sticking around and becoming his whore. Apparently, a lot of people had been interested in Octavio."

Understandably so; he was fucking attractive. Dark hair, tanned skin, muscles, shy, but oh so cute smile.

"When he was finally released from the police station because hello, assholes, he wasn't part of it, the impact was already there. His room was month to month—if you're wondering why he would do that, it was crazy cheap—but when the guy heard about Octavio's arrest, short as it was, he booted him. Was too scared to keep him around. It was already the end of the month, so he really only had like two days to clean up and get out. He was fired from his job because again, people didn't want the trouble his father could bring. And somehow that background plagued him. No one wanted to hire him. He was out on the streets. He found out after a while it was because one simple search on him had his parents popping up, and no one wanted anything to do with them. Not to mention, it wasn't a large town, so word got around."

He may be years older, but all I can think is *poor kid.*

"He was lucky he'd bought a used car, didn't have any payments on it, just had to worry about gas, but at least he had his shelter. And with the wide backseat, he could lie back to sleep too. Anyway, he had just hit twenty-one when this happened, so for two years he lived on scraps. Barely got any showers in, used any money he had to pay for his gas and his food, lived off whatever he could make."

"Was he begging?" My gaze flickers to Octavio. No judgement, but I just can't see him begging.

I've just looked back to Tommy when Lynette answers, "No. He'd go to the sights where guys were picked up for projects, mostly construction. That's where he met your brother."

"He pick Octavio out for a project and decide to keep him?" It doesn't sound right. When Darius and Tommy started their business, they were barely making enough for themselves and definitely no projects so big, they'd need to hire out.

"No."

I can't help but whip around to look at her.

"Octavio was there everyday. And some days, very few and far between, but some days, he'd get picked out to go with them. At these sights, records aren't normally checked, so names aren't normally researched, but word *had* gotten around. It was normally the days when everyone else was taken or no one was there when he was chosen. But those few days would get him enough money for at least a couple of weeks usually. One tank of gas, he didn't have many places to drive, so he wasn't using much of it, and just enough food every day."

I turn back to watch the guys. It's easier to listen to the story when I can glaze over and blankly stare out.

"Darius and Tommy got a job not too far from where the men would wait, and they liked to get food from a truck that would stop up that block, so they saw Octavio practically every day. He'd asked for a job, but the boys were still in college, only doing things part time and whenever they could, so they didn't have a job to offer. Octavio would thank them and walk away. That was the first few months of being out there, maybe six months. By the two-year mark, the rumors around him had gotten really bad, almost like his father was purposefully sending people out to ruin Octavio's chances. No one wanted to hire him."

I remember that. The boys going off to do the the random jobs here and there while they were in college. They've always said they did college because it was free education—since we'd all gotten full scholarships—and could come in handy in the future, but what they really wanted was to get down and dirty.

"Tommy and Darius got another job with that same family, and again, Octavio asked for a job. But this time, their company was new; they didn't have the money for it, so again, Octavio thanked them and went back to trying for the odd job here or there."

So how did Darius come out the hero here?

"One of the days of this job, I don't know what they were doing, but apparently it was like a ten-day job, I think they were like half way through when Darius went to the convenience shop that Octavio would park his truck at to get some drinks for him and Tommy. I know most of this story from Octavio's perspective, but this part Darius told me. I asked him once at the beginning, why he took Octavio in when he couldn't afford it. That brother of yours, I love him." She chuckled beneath her breath.

I did too because Darius was the best brother in the world. She'd have to be crazy not to love him. He was my best friend.

"Octavio was in the store when Darius walked in; didn't notice him the entire time they were in there. Darius was scanning the isles when he glanced over and saw Octavio by the drinks, counting out the money he had left in his hand. He was whispering to himself, but Darius still somehow heard him. Four dollars and twenty-three cents. That's all he had left for food for...until he could find more work. Word around town was getting so bad that he'd been thinking about moving to a new location, maybe even a new state, to start over, but he didn't even have enough money for food. There was definitely no money for gas. And it was the middle of summer too, crazy hot temperatures, but Octavio dealt with sweating it out as he slept in his truck."

I glance back to Octavio, my heart going out to him.

"He had four dollars and twenty-three cents, so he bought a large water and a crappy sandwich with it. Barely made enough to pay for it. Darius said his heart went out at that moment and when he left to go back to the site with Tommy, he passed Octavio at his truck." She chuckles. "The man still didn't see him. I've asked him, and he has no recollection of seeing Darius that entire day. But Darius saw Octavio take a sip of his water even though it was blazing out and any sane person would've drunk half the bottle. Then he pulled out half the sandwich and put the other half away, like he was trying to ration so at least he'd have food the next day too. Darius says that's when he decided Octavio would be their first hire."

My smile is back as I glance back at my brother as he helps Tommy and Octavio work at some wood with all their force.

"He went back to the site, looking Octavio up on his phone to find out what it was that made him the black sheep of hires. His father was caught up in a lot of shit, shit no one wanted to acquaint themselves with. So when he got back to Tommy, he just sat him down and told him everything." I could hear the smile in her voice. "And this is why I love Darius *and* Tommy. Tommy didn't even hesitate. Before Darius could suggest it, Tommy was trying to come up with a way for it all to work. They went home that night to really think something through that would help Octavio in the long run and not just those next few days. It would help no one if they bankrupted themselves out of work."

And I'm back to staring at the sweat dripping down Tommy's muscles. As hot as it is out today, everyone is in wifebeaters showcasing those muscles entirely to the female species.

"At home they decided that Octavio needed more than a job and money. He needed shelter and a shower and real food. The next day, they went out to Octavio's truck early in the morning, woke him up, and asked him to breakfast. They took him to a diner. Darius says he still remembers how frustrated he got when Octavio didn't want to order anything because he didn't have the money for it. They basically force fed him through the growls of his stomach. Then they gave him their offer: room and board for his help."

A laugh bubbles out of me at the picture of the three of them arguing about getting Octavio to eat.

I hear her return the laugh. "Basically, they were offering a spot for Octavio to live with them. They had a two-bedroom, one bath at the time, and they were offering the couch. He'd have a real place to live and sleep, a shower and bathroom to use at any time, and loads of real food to eat every day. In return, they didn't have the money to pay him for his work, but as the business grew, they would begin to pay him. And they kept their promise too. Any extra profits that the business made went into creating a salary for Octavio. By the time their lease for their apartment was up, the boys were looking for a three bedroom, and Octavio was earning a real wage. He was making real money. He still put in his cut of the living expenses, but he also had money for himself. It was a completely different experience for him."

"All great, but where do you come in here?" I ask not to be rude, but to understand how she ended up knocked up beside me.

I can hear the smile in her voice. "I lived across the hall of the apartment the three of them got. Darius flirted with me at the beginning. I think we met like a week after they moved in. When he saw I wasn't interested, he backed off, but he become a good friend. Like I knew he was a playboy, but he didn't try with me anymore, and I felt safe to be around him. It was comforting. I think they were like two months in when Darius invited me over for dinner with the three of them. It was like love at first sight with Octavio. Darius saw it instantly and started making every innuendo in the book, and Octavio blushed so bright, I still think of it sometimes. That's when we learned he'd never even kissed a girl before. He'd spent so much of his life running and surviving, it just never happened."

My heart is melting for him. I'm falling half in love with the man; he's so sweet.

"Darius got us on our first date, kinda tricked the two of us into getting together for a group night out and cancelled last minute. It's kinda history from there. About halfway through their lease, mine ended and I moved in with them. By the time theirs was done, we were engaged, married not long after, and Darius and Tommy were looking into getting their house."

They got the house a year and a half ago, so Lynette and Octavio are basically still newlyweds.

"So yes, Darius is the reason we're together. He's an asshat, but he's also one of the best guys I know. You know, I'm sure he'd be okay with you and Tommy."

I'm about to agree when the comment processes and I whip my head around to look at her. "What?"

She scoffs. "Please. You've had your eyes glued to him this entire time. You're basically drooling."

A hand subconsciously flies to my face. "It's sweat. It's a million degrees out."

"Mhm." She looks me over, then her eyes are on the men. "He keeps glancing at us too. I've been coming on these walks for months. Plenty of those times, I've sat about to wait, and he's never looked over as much as he has today."

"You're ready to pop! He's looking out for you," I argue because somehow, I feel far too exposed.

"Oh, I know, but like I said, never so many times as today. It's like his eyes are magnets and your body is the pull." She looks pleased with herself.

I roll my eyes and turn away. "Whatever."

She laughs from beside me. "They're brothers. I think Darius would be pretty happy about making it official."

"Exactly. They're brothers. Which makes me his sister."

Lynette scoffs. "Please. The looks he's throwing your way are *far* from brotherly."

I don't respond, but damn, does my heart flutter at the thought.

It's not long before the boys are taking a break and Octavio comes over to the driver's side window, leaning into it and giving his wife a kiss as a hand flies to her stomach.

I smile as I watch them, and when I turn around, Tommy is leaning into my window, just shy of touching my feet still propped out. His fingers do graze over my shins though, and a tingle shoots up my entire body as I stare at his mischievous grin.

And fuck, do I just want to lean over and kiss him the way Lynette did Octavio.

"We're almost done. Maybe another half hour," Tommy tells me almost like he's sorry it's taking so long.

I nod though those fingers on my shin are far too distracting. "I'll be waiting."

He inhales deeply as he pushes away from the window then takes a swig of his water and winks at me before turning away and walking back to the house.

My glance drops to the black smudge his fingers left on my shin, and I feel myself get wet at the thought of him marking me everywhere.

I turn when I hear two bodies laughing from my left. "What?"

Octavio speaks now, his accent a little too sexy, and it's obvious Lynette told him of my rebuttals to any romance. "You two live with Darius, and you're telling me he doesn't see it?"

I roll my eyes and turn away.

CHAPTER 5

Tommy

EMORY'S GETTING DINNER READY.

She hadn't been doing any work out there with us, but her stomach growled just as loud as ours when we were driving home, and that's when I realized that Darius and I had lunch, but she hadn't eaten the entire time she sat watching us.

And that's exactly when I feel like a major ass.

But she pushes aside any apologies I attempt with a light squeeze of my jaw and that beautiful shine of her eyes on mine as she calls me by that insufferable nickname.

The moment we step into the house, she sends Darius and me to get cleaned up as she heads for the kitchen.

The thought that dinner will be ready for us when we get out is actually a really nice one. Not to mention the thought that Emory is the one making my food.

It still astounds me how Darius hasn't picked up on our flirtations because I know the way I look at Emory is nowhere near discreet.

And Darius hasn't picked up on it.

Darius was always the first to pick up flirtations, sometimes even before the parties involved realized it.

But now, he doesn't see it.

I scrub the sweat and grime out of my hair as the thought comes to me—is it less obvious than I think or is Darius subconsciously turning a blind eye?

I don't know the answer, but I do know one thing—as much as I want her, Emory is off limits. I will not ruin my relationship with the Aabeck family just because my cock has decided to jump at every sighting of her.

Another really important thing to remember is that Emory cannot continue to come watch us work. I've never been so distracted on a job in my life. Every instinct in me wanted to glance over at her every other second. And most of the times, I wasn't able to fight it. It was infuriating.

I take my time in the shower. Partly because I know there's no rush—she'll still be here when I get out—and partly because I need to settle my body before I spend the night with her *and* her brother.

I know I should turn the water so cold, my body shrivels up, but instead, like the pig that I am, I let my hand find my cock. Emory's giggles fill my mind before my eyes close, and all I see is her. I groan because fuck, I've never seen anyone so beautiful.

The way she looked at me when I turned around at the BBQ to find her in my yard.

The way she hugged me just a little tighter than I remembered our hugs.

The way she turned to find my eyes when Darius took her around to introduce her to our friends.

My hand is pumping wild, applying just that bit of pressure, and I have to slam against the wall to keep myself standing and silent.

The way she looked in that black shirt and those dark shorts.

The way she felt against me as we lay in that canoe.

The way her cheeks had beet red at the drive-in movie.

I need to open my eyes, get her picture out of my head, but I can't do it. I bite down on my lower lip and feel the sensations beginning to reach the base of my spine. And I keep pumping, basically humping my hand like a teenage kid.

The way she looked like a true goddess in that dress.

The way she leaned into me and took my hand that night.

The way she held me as we danced, a little too close. A little too tight.

My fist slams into the wall as the water beats down on me and I pump into the final sensations. I'm biting down hard to keep from calling out her name and letting the entire neighborhood hear how much I want her.

Then I'm coming, and all I can think is Emory, Emory, Em...

I hold myself against the wall for a couple of minutes to let my body enjoy the moment. But not too long. If I let myself stay like this, I'll be hard for her all over again.

I clean up and push out of the shower, throw on some sweatpants and a T-shirt and head out to the kitchen. The smell that's filling the house is amazing.

Emory is just pulling the mac and cheese from the oven, and the smell turns overwhelmingly delightful.

Darius is already there when I head in. He looks at me with a wide smirk, and I already want to punch him for whatever is about to come out of his mouth. "If you'd just come out with me from time to time, you wouldn't need such long showers."

Emory's blushing. Light, but there.

Douchebag Darius is his nickname for a reason.

"I'm not interested in your nights out."

"No? Your hand do it better?"

"Sure does." I grin at him.

"Oh? So we shouldn't worry about finding you any little friends? You've got your hand. What else could you need?"

Darius is pulling drinks from the fridge, giving me the opportunity to watch Emory's reaction. She's already staring at me.

"Oh, I'm sure there's one woman out there that could win out over my hand."

Her breath catches, and that blush is deep now. She's no longer looking at me, and I can't help but smirk. Maybe that makes me the douchebag now, but damn, does she look beautiful flushed like that.

Darius scoffs and turns with the drinks. "Please. Don't start with that soulmate crap."

"Afraid someone will take your spot as his soulmate, Brother?" Emory jokes, and my heart jumps at that giggle she gives at the end of her question.

Darius flips her off as I say, "I'm not starting with anything. I'm just saying, none of your little friends would help when I've only got one woman on my mind."

We're sitting around the island because the dining table is only for family dinners or more formal ones, and Emory is filling our plates with the baked mac and cheese that looks so good, my mouth is watering.

And some salad. Because adding vegetables to our meals is important and Emory is well aware that Darius and I don't necessarily always do it.

The salad looks good though. A true mix rather than some lettuce and tomatoes thrown onto a plate.

"Oh? And who's that?" Darius looks at me with a cocky grin.

My eyes flicker to Emory for only a second, so I know she's watching me, but I don't allow them to stay there. This is Darius's little sister and as much as he jokes with me now, if he finds out it's her I'm speaking of, I'll be skewered and the next meal.

But I won't lie. We never lie. We omit truths.

"A special little lady that pops into my head when I close my eyes." I smile at him because I know he's going to assume the little lady is a figment of my imagination.

"Oh, Em." Darius turns to his little sister, and now I can look at her without being obvious. "What are we going to do with him and his *little lady*?" He taps his head with the final words as if indicating I've lost my mind.

Emory frowns at her brother. "He won't tell you? But you share all your secrets."

Darius spins that finger by his head again. "Not this one."

Emory locks her gaze with mine, and there's a spark there that makes my hand time in the shower a lost cause.

"We can find out easily. Simply tie him down until he gives in to everything we desire to know. Sound good, Buttercup?" she says it as a joke to her brother, but her eyes tell me something entirely different.

My cock jumps and screams and tears at my sweatpants to get out.

Sounds better than good, baby girl.

Yeah, shower time was a total lost cause.

Darius laughs, and I try to steer the conversation to safer topics. Ones that will get my mind off Emory and curb any desires.

Darius and I are driving to work the next morning, and I can't help but think back to the night before. After dinner, we all huddled up on the couch in the living room to watch a scary movie. Well, they watched it and I watched Emory. Tried not to, but honestly *could not* help myself.

Especially with her tucked into my side like that.

We laughed and talked afterwards, and it was just like old times. Except I never spent so much of my time telling myself to stop staring at little Aabeck before.

But other than that, just like all our nights growing up together. And it wasn't until I was going to bed that I realized that this life with my two best friends—because Emory is definitely a best friend—was all I needed to be happy.

"You're chipper this morning," Octavio says as we meet him in the foyer of the house we're working on.

I shrug. "I had a really good night."

He wiggles his eyebrows. "Oh?"

Darius scoffs a laugh from behind me. "Yeah right. We hung out with my sister. It was like old times. Tommy Proper here wouldn't be having that kind of good night if you killed him."

Octavio's eyes shoot to me at the mention of Emory being there, and a smirk grows on his face as his eyes shimmer. "You hung out with Emory? Like you hung out with her the other day? On a date, right?"

Darius is laughing as he smacks my back. "Well, when your kid sister asks for a date, you give her a date. Gotta admit, last night was a fun one. It was nice going back to the old days."

The smile falters on my face. Kid sister. Because Darius sees us all as siblings. Sees Emory and me as brother and sister.

Octavio's smile drops slightly too, but he recovers faster. "I'm sure it wouldn't take killing to convince Tommy Proper to have one of those nights. Say, a certain woman..."

I punch him because knowing Octavio, he cannot be discrete. He will give it away in two seconds. Somehow, I've come this far without Darius seeing it in the looks I send his sister. Octavio will not be the reason I perish.

Darius ruffles my hair like I'm a child then moves to begin

pulling tools out.

I turn dark eyes on Octavio, and he smiles at me like he hasn't done a single thing wrong.

"He's going to find out, Tommy. Shouldn't you just tell him?" he whispers to me.

"I don't know what you're talking about." I try to move past him, but stop when he speaks so only I can hear.

"So you wouldn't mind if I asked him how he feels about the way his kid sister and best friend look at each other? If I put into his head that there could be something between you two and he sees it in an instance? You know the only reason he's blind right now is because he sees you both as family, and he thinks you do the same. How will he feel having his kid sister and best friend sharing a house when every time they look at each other, it's like they're already going at it?"

I control my breathing so I don't punch him and turn dark eyes on my closest friend outside the Aabecks. "Shut. Up."

Octavio smirks. "Don't know what I'm talking about, do you?"

Darius interrupts before I can get another word in. "C'mon, jackasses. We do have a business to run and shit to get done."

Octavio turns to the material, and I'm left standing in the foyer, watching them as our men begin to fill the space and everyone gets to their jobs.

All I can think is that Octavio is right. I'm lucky Darius hasn't noticed yet, but that's only because he trusts me so much around Emory that he wouldn't even consider it an idea. I don't deserve his trust like that. Not when all I can think about is getting that kid sister of his beneath me.

And her smiles as she talks about the things she loves. I could go back to lying in that car in front of the deli over and over and never get tired of it.

Yeah, her smiles are all I can really think about.

56

CHAPTER 6

Emory

I COULD EASILY WALK to the guys' job again and sit back in their truck, watch the sweat glisten off Tommy's skin as he works. But I don't want to be a distraction.

And I promised a certain neighbor couple that I would visit them.

I saw them through the window on another walk last night and came to the conclusion that Nana Isla and Papa Atti —short for Atticus—were adorable. And as I learned from Tommy and Darius this morning, they saw my family as their own. Which only favored them to me.

I hope they like brownies because that's all I have, and I cannot go empty handed.

Nana Isla opens the door, and her eyes twinkle with joy at seeing me. It's nice. This happiness at my presence. Especially from her old eyes, it's the perfect substitute for the grandparents I've never had.

"Oh, Atti, look, she's come," she calls out to her husband as she motions for me to come in and takes the plate of brownies from my hands.

Papa Atti is sitting in the living room with a cup in hand and a football game on. True Southern man.

Nana Isla walks me to the table connecting the family room to the kitchen and sits me down, placing the brownies on the table before me as she moves to the fridge for milk.

"I was almost sure you wouldn't show up." She places two cups on the table and sits beside me. "Then I remembered you are Darius's little sister, and that's not in your blood."

I smile, glad Darius has made such a great impression. He's a douchebag, but he's also one of the best people in my life.

Papa Atti walks over to us, grabby hands ready to steal a brownies or four. "I never doubted for a moment you would show up."

I quirk a brow. "No?"

He shakes an old finger at me. "You know how much those boys care for us. You wouldn't want to do anything to disappoint them. Not to mention, Thomas would never fall for anyone who didn't regard us as royalty."

I snort, and that gleam in his eyes tells me that was the intent. "Tommy hasn't fallen for me. We've always been close. He's just…missed me."

He looks to his wife with disbelief written on his every feature, and Nana Isla is smiling with that knowing look.

"He doesn't. I'm Darius's little sister. The baby. That's why he's always given me whatever I want. That's it," I insist because the more I say it, the more I'll be able to believe it and throw that hopeful jump of my heart away.

Nana Isla's old hand takes mine softly. "I know you are saying that because you are scared, deary. But I can assure you, that boy's eyes shine for you."

"And that hold he had on you was like yelling it to the

world." Papa Atti is moving back to his spot in front of the TV.

I'm blushing. I know I am, but it's not something I can control.

"Hey," Nana Isla calls my attention back to her. "Forget about what you think Thomas feels for you. What do you feel for him?"

Okay, so the blush is a deep, deep crimson now.

"I don't know," I stutter. When she gives me an unconvinced look, I try to explain my thoughts. "He was always like a brother growing up, and when I was in London—or anywhere in Europe —and thought of him, it was like thinking of Darius. Yeah, I mean, maybe not exactly like thinking of Darius since Tommy has always been way too easy on the eyes, but it wasn't romantic. So when I walked into their yard to surprise them, I didn't think anything of it. Even when I was staring at their backs, all I was thinking was that the three of us would be back together."

Nana Isla's eyes are twinkling like she's excited and even Papa Atti has lowered the volume of his game.

"Then he turned around, and it was like a firework show in my chest. Weird. And I was stuck like what the *hell* is going on. I pushed it aside, then I hugged him, and I didn't want to let go, but I was like that before too. I always used to want to cuddle up and hug Tommy, so again, I pushed it aside. But then the night progressed, and he came to me, and all I wanted was to *kiss* him. It was so weird, and it's still weird, but we went on a date…"

"I knew it. You little liars," Papa Atti calls out.

I laugh. "The day before we met, Papa Atti. We weren't lying."

"And you're trying to tell us there's nothing romantic?" Nana Isla looks like she wants to thwart me with a pamphlet. Or a shoe.

I shrug. "We did that growing up too. Dates. Darius and Tommy would take me out together, and we'd have a group date kinda thing, and other times they'd take me out individually. So it was nothing new for Tommy and me to go out." I look down at my fingers as they fidget together. "But this time, I wanted more. I wanted it to be real, and he kept insisting it was, and then at my parents, he said he hasn't brought a girlfriend. I know I can't be upset about that because I'm *not* his girlfriend, but the way it hit me...It felt like he was saying it wouldn't be a possibility."

I'm surprised I've just told them all that. I keep things I desire more than anything private.

But then again, they did ask and that's when the floodgates tend to open for me, and I spew out everything.

Nana Isla's hand is squeezing mine. "I know it's a scary thing, falling for someone. And I know it makes it scarier since it's not only your brother's best friend, but someone that's basically part of the family. But in this case, dear, I'm telling you to get rid of that fear. Throw it away because that boy looks damn near ready to drop to his knee for you."

I roll my eyes but smile at her too.

"Come," she says. "Why don't we make something together to feed our boys, and we can erase this anxiety from your system. You can tell me about some of these European cities you've been to."

I've never cooked with a grandmother before. It's something I've always envied when kids at school would talk about it or I would see it in shows and movies, but always thought it would be a joy I wouldn't experience.

"I'd love that."

. . .

It's six twenty-three when their truck stops out front. Exactly seven minutes after the baked lasagna comes out of the oven. Perfect timing.

Two large chunks are cut out for Nana Isla and Papa Atti and the rest is covered with aluminum foil before Nana Isla and I are heading out to meet the boys.

We stop in the middle of the street, and both boys meet us halfway. That's the beautiful thing about small streets; you can stop in the middle, and it's not a problem.

"Keeping promises, I see," Tommy says as they stop.

He looks so good, I want to lick him everywhere. Which should be disgusting because he's dirty and sweaty, and the shower is going to feel so nice on his skin, but it's all perfect for me. His hands especially are dirty, and that fact alone does things to my body I didn't know were possible just by looking at hands.

"Promises?" Darius asks.

Nana Isla plays with my hair. "Your dear sister promised to visit the other night."

"Ah, yes. Well, of course she kept her promise. The princess would be remiss to break her promises." Darius was sweet like that sometimes.

Tommy looks at the wrapped food in my hands. "Tell me that's for us."

"Hmm." I look at Nana Isla, then back at him. "I don't know. It could be. What would you give me for it?"

The look Tommy gives me tells me exactly what he'd like to give me for it and makes me think that maybe Nana Isla and Papa Atti were right about the way he feels about me.

Darius throws a sweaty arm over my shoulders and pulls me between the two men. "Princess, be kind."

I laugh. "Right. Well, let's go. You smell, and I'm also hungry."

"Before you leave," Nana Isla stops us, "tell me, are you busy this Saturday?"

"Yes," Tommy answers. "We all are."

Nana Isla's hopeful gaze drops ever-so-slightly, and I want to punch him for upsetting her, but I'm also stuck wondering what plans we have.

"Oh," Nana Isla says.

Tommy's smile is wicked and oh so delicious. "We have a barbecue for the family. That does include you and Papa Atti, of course. You didn't think we would skip out on a family barbecue the first Saturday Little Miss Sunshine is back with us, did you?"

I kick him because Little Miss Sunshine makes me sound like a kid, and I know he doesn't look at me like a kid. I know it because people don't look at kids the way he's just looked at me.

But I hate that ounce of doubt that's still around, telling me he still sees me as Darius's kid sister.

He laughs and throws his arm over the one Darius still has wrapped around my shoulders and pulls me in close to kiss my crown. I want desperately to tilt my head back and catch his lips with mine.

Nana Isla's smile is bright. "Tommy, you wicked child. I just might smack you."

Tommy winks at her. "But you love me too much."

Nana Isla looks at me. "Yes, I bet we're all a bit victim to fall just a bit in love with you."

My heart stops, and I'm thankful that neither boy seems to pick up on that look Nana Isla's sending me. "Right, well, if we stand here any longer, my shoulders will fall off with all this pressure."

Nana Isla's smile says she knows exactly why I want to end this conversation. "See you three later," she calls as she turns back to her house.

It wasn't a lie; their combined weights on my shoulders is too much.

We watch Nana Isla enter her house before Tommy drops his arm as we turn for our house, and Darius pulls me in a little tighter. "Good job, princess."

"For making you food?"

Darius smiles down at me. "Yes. But also for going to Nana Isla and Papa Atti."

"I really like them."

He kisses my head. "Me too."

CHAPTER 7

Tommy

BBQS like the one we had last week were nice. Having friends over and really enjoying our twenties with them rather than going out to the clubs. It's what Darius and I both prefer.

But BBQs like this Saturday? With the entire family—the people I chose as my family rather than the ones given to me by birth? Nothing could ever beat that.

I don't know what I would've done if I hadn't found them when my parents shipped me off to live with the aunt and uncle who never wanted kids so they could sail the Mediterranean. Can't imagine a life without them.

And if Lynette wasn't so big and tired all the time, she and Octavio would be here too. Then it would truly by my entire family.

Even without them, I have Darius, my life brother. Calvin and Lynn, my parents for all intents and purposes. And Nana Isla and Papa Atti, our grandparents since none of us ever truly had grandparents and their families were thousands of miles away. Add Octavio and Lynette, and we had these family BBQs at least once a month.

But now Emory's back, and there's a space filled that I hadn't realized was missing. I thought of her every time we had a family function, of course I did, but I've always figured she was happy in London, so I've never really considered she would be our missing piece.

Had anyone asked me a month ago—hell, even a week ago—about Emory, I would've said she was my sister for all intents and purposes.

But not anymore. I can't.

Can't wrap my head around how I had ever seen her as a sister because there's nothing brotherly about the way I reacted when I saw her last week. There's nothing brotherly about the way I've reacted every moment since then. Nothing brotherly about the way I think about her now. All the fucking time.

But this week has also shown me that she isn't family the way the others are to me. She's more. I can't even come to comprehend how in only a week, she's booted her brother for the most important person in my life. She's become my life, and all I know is that she was meant for me. *She's mine.*

And she looks gorgeous walking outside with a bowl of her everything-but-the-kitchen-sink salad in hand. Her summer dress flows in the breeze of the hot summer day, and I fall a little deeper watching her smile at something her father said to her.

We're making burgers again this week because that's what Papa Atti wants. It isn't long before everyone is seated at the outdoor table, and Lynn is telling Emory about the one BBQ a year ago when we put out a children's pool in the backyard. We did it to throw water balloons inside so we could have a water fight. Problem was, Calvin and Darius started before the water balloons were made, wrestling all around the back-yard. It ended with Calvin fireman-carrying Darius into the kiddie pool. Funniest fucking day.

And somehow, one Emory hasn't heard about.

"Yeah, yeah, yeah," Darius interrupts. "I like how everyone seems to forget that I let the old man win. I wasn't going to beat on my own father."

Nana Isla throws a carrot at him. "Sure, boy. Is that what you tell the girls to make them want you?"

Darius's eyes narrow on the old woman, but there's mirth there. "And they wouldn't want me for my charming personality and good looks?"

Papa Atti scoffs from beside his wife. "Women aren't so dumb, child."

"And yet I still get them."

"By telling them you're so sweet you let Daddy win in a fight?"

Darius is used to Nana Isla's teasing him.

I join in because it's our favorite pastime. "Please. He tells everyone we're brothers, and since they can't have me, they jump on him. Figure the genes must have it all. If only they knew."

Now Darius is affronted.

Lynn and Calvin agree with me, and Darius goes into fighter mode. If there's anything Darius wins at, it's being the whore of the family. And he needs no help with it by telling any stories. Women do naturally go to him.

But it's also the funniest thing to make fun of him for. Because making it sound like women couldn't possibly want him is so absurd to Darius that he will start World War III just to prove everyone wrong.

We haven't made fun of him like this in some time; it was long overdue. And it's not just me either; everyone is jumping in. This *is* how it usually goes.

I'm laughing so hard when Lynn tells Darius her grand-children are going to be from pity fucks that my chair almost breaks.

But then my entire form is on high alert.

Emory's been quiet the entire time, so no one gives it much attention when she gets up for the bathroom, but it's all I notice.

I watch her and can't help but know she's not leaving for the bathroom. She's upset.

I wait a moment, allow some time to pass between our departures, and laugh with the others though now I can't be sure why we're laughing. Then I follow her inside.

I head to the guest bathroom—because somehow Darius and I have been lucky enough to get private bathrooms and a guest. Maybe she really was just going to the bathroom.

But I was right; she's not in there.

I turn toward my room, figuring she could've gone into that bathroom, but pause when I see the office door open. She's leaning against the desk inside, staring at the mess in the room.

"Don't know if you're aware, but the bathroom is one door down," I open.

She jumps and turns to face me, and there's a sadness in her eyes that cripples me inside.

I push inside and stride right to her. "What is it?"

She turns to look at the room again. "If I hadn't gone to London, you think I would've moved right into this room when you guys got the house or would I still be with Mom and Dad?"

"No, you wouldn't have gotten this room."

Her shoulders deflate. "So, Mom and Da…"

"You would've gotten one of the rooms with an ensuite. Darius and I would've fought for the other."

Because she definitely would've moved in with us. Even the me from four years ago who wasn't interested in her in the slightest would've made sure of that.

She turns back to me, and her eyes are almost watering.

I step up and take her face into my hands. "What is it, baby?"

Her eyes close, and it's like she's trying to keep from crying. It kills me to watch. And not just because I suddenly have the hots for her, but because I've always been protective of Emory Aabeck.

Her eyes are trained on me again, and she finally answers, "I missed so much while I was away. I…"

"Em, no. You can't regret going to London. You loved it there. You had great moments there." Even if I didn't speak to her often, I knew that much.

"I don't regret it." Her hands circle my wrists as I hold her face. "I just wish I would've come back from time to time, on breaks. Taken the time to come home. I've missed so much, and now you guys all have family stories, and I'm not a part of them."

"Baby." My forehead falls against hers. "You are our family. You are my family. Above all else, Emory. You're mine."

I don't know what possessed me to say those words out loud, but I can't take them back. I don't want to.

She pulls back to look up at me, and there's a furrow between her brows. So I technically shouldn't have said that she was mine when we were talking about the family, but it's true. Since she came back, she's all the family I see, the first person to pop into my mind. The only person I truly need in my life.

Her thumbs rub circles on my hands as her gaze drops to my lips, then back up. "Yours? Like your kid sister?"

"A far cry from kid sister, baby girl." I know Darius will kill me for it, but she has to know.

She steps up so our bodies are flush. "Good."

It's like that one word is the fuel because I'm looking down at her and I'm no longer controlling myself.

I lean into her slowly, making sure she has time to pull away if she wants, and press my lips to hers. It's soft, but she doesn't pull away. She leans in.

I lied earlier. This was all the fuel I needed.

My lips press firmly to hers, and I'm tasting her, and it truly is what dreams are made of. It's what my dreams and hopes and needs are made of.

Her hands are around my waist, pulling me closer, and it's only the faintest bit of control that stops me from digging into her hair and pulling her head back for better purchase.

I still do it. Just softer.

And slower.

My lips are still tasting hers when my fingers move from her face and into her hair, nails scraping at her scalp and causing a moan I didn't know I needed for survival.

Another moan escapes the back of her throat, and I follow closely behind with one of my own.

And it's in that moment that my tongue slips into her mouth, and I know she's all I need. She's all mine. Like an assurance that's settled itself into my heart and will never move.

I pull on her hair just enough to tilt her head back and relish in the light moans that escape her.

And it's only when I hear the bout of laughter from outside that I remember her entire family is out there, and I'm a dead man if we're seen.

She smiles up at me when I pull away, then we're both laughing, and her head is falling to hit my chest.

"I can't believe that just happened," she whispers against me.

"Me neither." *In the best way possible.*

She's looking back up at me with all the trust in the world, and I know I never stood a chance of resisting her. It never would've been possible.

My hand lingers at her back as I turn toward the door. "Let's go before your brother comes looking for us."

Part of me wishes Darius had come looking for us and found us together in the office.

But only part of me.

The other, much more rational part knows I need to break this to him softly. Need to explain what's going on.

But that would also mean I need to be sure Emory and I are on the same page.

I want to do this right and take Emory on dates that everyone knows are dates. Hold her close to me without people thinking I'm being brotherly the same way Darius is when he brings her in close to him when he hugs her.

And if Darius wasn't currently snoring his life away in his room, I would go talk to him.

But that's a good thing too because first I need to talk to Emory.

She's in the kitchen, sitting at the island with a cup of hot lemon water in hand as she stares into space. For someone who lived in London for four years, it's shocking how much she doesn't like tea.

"Hey you." I walk to the kettle and place it on the stove. I like tea.

"Hey, Buttercup." She smiles at me.

I turn to look at her, and her eyes fly up to meet mine. I feel the smirk come on but allow only a grin. "Staring at my ass?"

The blush colors her cheeks, but she doesn't back away. "In those sweatpants, I'd be stupid not to."

"Yet if I did it to you, I'd be a pig."

She acts like she's thinking about it as she drinks her water and I watch her lips hug the cup. I breathe in to relax myself and watch her as she smiles at me. "You can stare at my ass. I have no problems with that."

I know she can see the desire blooming in my eyes. "Turn around, baby girl."

The blush is deeper as her breath hitches, but her gaze challenges me. She pushes her stool back and drops to the ground, leaving her cup on the table as she walks back so her full length is in my line of sight. Then she takes her time turning around, giving me a perfect view of her every curve, including that delectable ass covered by the tiny fucking robe.

I groan, and there's a giggle that escapes from her, and it takes all of me not to rush toward her and take her right there in the kitchen.

No.

Darius needs to know first!

She's facing me again, and the grin is wide on her face as the kettle whistles.

I turn to it and give myself a break from her. It's intoxicating to watch her like that, happy and with me. But it's also torture to watch her and not touch her. Not taste her.

Unlike Darius who likes his tea bland—the healthy way—I add a spoonful of sugar. Or two.

I leave the tea on the counter to cool while I talk to Emory about…everything.

I'm glad I chose to leave it on the counter because when I turn around, she's sitting on the island right in front of me, and I definitely would've dropped it.

Her legs are just slightly parted, and in that tiny robe that covers nothing, it feels like a glimpse of heaven. I can even see her nipples peaking through the silky material.

My eyes rake up her body, and when they finally reach her eyes, there's a wickedness there I didn't think her capable of.

"Come here, Buttercup," she says in an innocent tone.

I groan and push toward her because I am at her mercy.

Those legs slip farther apart as I step up to her until my hips are just centimeters from being pressed into hers. Until my cock is just about pressed against her center.

I growl as my hands grab the edges of the island counter on either side of her thighs to stop from touching her. Then, like she's trying to torture me, her thighs wrap around my waist and kill me a little inside. She only pulls me in a little, not enough for our centers to touch, but closer.

I grip the counter tighter because *goddamn.*

Her hands crawl up my arms and wrap around my neck, those fingers playing with the tiny pieces at the nape of my neck. Our faces are so close, breaths mixing as we stare at one another. Her lips are parted like they're inviting me to kiss them, slip my tongue between them and ravish her.

"I'm telling Darius tomorrow," I blurt out because if I don't, I'm never getting it out.

She pauses and leans back. "What?"

"Darius," I say again, able to breathe just a little better with her leaned back like that. "I need to tell him. He needs to know I'm not just looking for some fuck, that I want this, us."

I pause as I realize she may not want this. Now I push back, but stuck between her thighs it's not far.

"Do you want this?" I ask because if she doesn't, if all she was looking for was a fuck, then all of this has to end. Immediately.

It's like she reads the uncertainty in my features because her smile is reassuring as she pulls me in toward her again. Our breaths aren't mixing again, but that just means I can concentrate.

"I want this." Her gaze doesn't leave mine, and I read the sincerity behind her look. "I don't know what it is, but I saw you at that barbecue, and I haven't been able to think of anything else since."

I close my eyes as I take it in. "Good."

It's the same thing she said to me before I kissed her. And apparently, it's like fuel to her too because now she's pulling me in close and pressing her lips to mine.

And I'm kissing her again.

My best friend's baby sister.

My Emory.

She tastes amazing, but I pull away before I get carried away. My forehead leans against hers when I breathe out, "I'm telling Darius in the morning. He's gonna be mad, but he has to know."

She pulls away again and leans back to watch me. "We don't have to tell him. We don't have to say anything."

I know she knows I'm confused because there is literally nothing else I'm feeling at the moment, so it must be shining in my eyes.

"I just...you know how I like to keep things private."

That was true. Emory was known to keep things to herself. We learned pretty early on that the only way to find out about those important things was to ask her about them directly. Which was difficult when you didn't know about them in the first place. Especially the things she really cared about—private. So private, I'm sure there're still things I don't know about her because I haven't thought to ask about them.

"You want this to be a secret?"

That's not what she said, but that's what I heard.

"No, not secret. *Private*. If he doesn't ask, there's no reason to say anything." Typical Emory.

And as I look into her eyes, I know she's genuine. She's not trying to keep this a secret.

I know because the fear is there. The fear she always had telling anyone a very private matter. One of those things she cared for so much, she didn't want others to know about them and possibly destroy them. She called it sending the evil eye.

And it breaks my heart a little that she's scared of anything happening with us.

But it also makes my heart sing because that means I'm up there on the important things list.

And private means I can continue touching her and taking her out, keeping her to myself, in front of everyone. And a very large part of me knows everyone will see what this is between us.

Darius though?

That is a different question because now that I think back to the way Em and I grew up, I realize just how romantic *everything* we did together was. And they're all things Darius is used to seeing between us.

"Okay." I release my grip around the counter and cradle her face in my hands. "But I'm taking you on a date and calling it a date."

She smirks. "You already took me on a date."

"Oh, so now we're admitting it was a real date?" It was most definitely a real date.

She shrugs. "It was kinda the best date."

"I think so too, baby."

CHAPTER 8

Emory

NANA ISLA OFFERS to show me some recipes around the kitchen on Monday while the boys are at work, and I'm excited because I've always wanted a grandmother to teach me to cook. But I should have expected her intentions weren't so innocent.

She's taking out a pot and two pans when she turns a cheeky smile on me.

I narrow my eyes at her. "What?"

"That was quite the barbecue the other day, was it not?"

"Quite," I answer and take the vegetables out to begin chopping.

"Very exciting. Memorable." She's being far too coy for an old woman.

I cross my arms over my chest and narrow my eyes deeper. "What aren't you telling me, Nana?"

"I'd flip that question on you, darling?" She smiles with an equally narrowed look.

"Papa Atti," I call out to the man out in the back garden through the kitchen window, "am I meant to be following her line of questioning?"

His laugh comes to us as Nana Isla whips me with a spatula. "You're not going to say anything?"

"About what?"

"That kiss you shared with Thomas!"

I freeze, and a whisper escapes me, "What?"

It can't all be falling apart now. I've just gotten him. I can't let go now. She's going to say it's a bad idea, that he's a part of the family and if things don't work out, then I'll ruin the family. That I should've stayed in London so the family unit remained unharmed.

But I know things will work out.

And that's when the naivety comments will come in.

I can't lose Tommy. I can't.

I can feel my breathing shifting as my mind clogs with all the possibilities of how this beautiful thing I've found with my brother's best friend could fall apart, how all the prying eyes could send us crashing.

"Unlike you, I was truly headed to the bathroom," Nana Isla explains. "Passed the office on the way to Tommy's room. I thought you must be in the guest one, so I'd go there." Her smile is still cheeky, but there's a happiness in her eyes, my heart flutters at seeing.

And though my heart notices that cheeky smile and flutters at it, knowing she encourages my relationship, my mind can't seem to catch up. Swirls of uncertainty, of fear, of the need to protect this relationship, swaddle it up and keep it hidden.

"You saw us?" I ask again to give myself time to calm down.

She's smirking now. "I heard you first."

Now the blush is definitely beating down on me.

Papa Atti is at the window. "Calvin will be excited about calling Tommy his son for real. Why haven't they mentioned it?"

I know by looking at him, he knows the answer.

"Did you guys tell anyone?"

No one else. If they knew, then the questions would start, and the opinions would get thrown in, and I cannot handle something happening to us because of someone else's opinion.

"Is there a reason we shouldn't?"

I know by her tone, Nana Isla isn't trying to intimidate or blackmail me, she's truly curious.

"I like keeping my matters private. I just don't want my relationship to be everyone else's business. Especially since it's with Tommy. Everyone will think they have a say because he also grew up with us and Mom and Dad boss him around like he's theirs."

"So it is a relationship then?" Nana Isla asks in a sweet voice.

I'm about to answer when my phone rings. Speaking of the devil.

"Hey," I say, and I know by my own tone that Nana Isla and Papa Atti can figure out who I'm speaking to.

"Hey, baby," he says, and his voice calms all the dread clogging my mind.

"Her nickname is princess. Or kid sister. Stop calling her baby. She's not that much younger than us to be a baby, and it feels too dirty when you say that," Darius calls out from beyond Tommy's side.

I roll my eyes and smirk. How Darius can truly be so blind to it all is astounding. It just goes to show, if you truly put your mind to one thing, it is difficult to change. Like Darius seeing Tommy and I together as anything but brother and sister.

"*Baby*," Tommy emphasizes, and I can basically hear Darius's eye roll, "what're you doing? Busy tonight?"

I hear Darius's yell fade away in the background and I

know he's gone to instruct his men on the job, officially ignoring the call.

"Well, right now I'm with Nana Isla and Papa Atti learning some recipes. Tonight," I turn away from the old couple because my cheeks are beginning to burn, and their looks aren't helping, "whatever you have planned."

"Good, baby girl." His voice drops to almost a whisper, and my skin prickles with goosebumps as I feel myself growing wet. "Then I want you in a little dress. I'm taking you dancing."

"Dancing dancing or dancing euphemism dancing?" I ask in a whisper, so I'm not heard because I want it to be both, and the way he said it to me in that low raspy voice makes me imagine the latter.

He chuckles. "Dancing dancing." His voice drops again. "I'm trying to control myself from the latter, baby. We've just started going."

I want to tell him I don't want him to control himself, but Nana and Papa are right behind me. So I take a large breath that effectively tells him how frustrated I feel with his decision and listen to that beautiful chuckle.

"I'll see you tonight, baby girl."

"Tonight," I whisper.

He hangs up, and I close my eyes to wash away the feelings talking to him brought up before I turn back to the lovely, cheeky old couple.

Nana Isla's smile is sweet, Papa Atti's knowing.

Nana Isla speaks. "Look at that smile. Even if you're not caught kissing, I expect your family will figure it out soon enough."

My smile falters because Nana Isla is right. Everyone will be able to tell, and then this relationship won't be mine anymore, but the entire family's.

I try to push the panic aside. I need to think positively

about this. Tommy is mine, and there's only so long we can go before we're asked about it. But I was definitely hoping on enough time to at least figure *us* out without everyone else's opinions.

"I'm here to learn some recipes, Nana Isla."

They laugh, and Papa Atti goes back to his garden as Nana Isla drops the topic and turns to the recipe she wrote out for me.

I walk out to the living room in a red halter dress that flows as it ends right above my knees and a pair of black dancing heels. My hair is slightly curled, and pieces are clipped back and out of my face. I feel beautiful.

"Look at you," Darius takes my hand and spins me as Tommy walks out, dressed in black jeans and a black button down. Darius looks between the two of us with a quirked brow. "Are we going somewhere?"

Technically, Darius is dressed nice enough to go out as well.

I step away from my brother and move to Tommy, wrapping my arms around his waist and turning to face Darius. "*We're* going on a date. You can go wherever your dick desires."

Tommy's arms are around me, and he's trying to hide his laughter in my hair. Everything about him makes my heart flutter.

Darius smiles at me. "Yeah, yeah. Where're we going?"

"Darius, you're not coming," I say again.

Darius's gaze shoots up to Tommy, then back to me. "Seriously? I can't come?"

"Nope," I say because there's no way I'm leaving any room for argument.

Darius looks annoyed as he throws himself on the couch.

"Fine. Miss one date, and you're never allowed on another." He turns to Tommy. "Make sure the kid has fun."

Asshole.

Tommy stiffens, and I hold him just a little bit tighter to let him know the comment doesn't bother me.

"Em and I will have plenty of fun." He looks down at me. "Right, baby girl?"

There's a humor-filled furrow between my brows. "Right, Buttercup."

Darius makes vomiting noises, and we laugh as we head out, Tommy taking my hand and leading me.

He presses me against the car and cages me in, his breath hitting my ear and sending flutters through every inch of me. "You looking fucking stunning, baby."

I'm caught off guard, struck with need for him, so he's already on the other side of the car when I clear my head enough to respond. I turn a grumble at him and listen to that enticing chuckle as he gets in but doesn't start the car.

Instead, he just stares at me.

"What?"

His smile is wide. "I love that you mean it when you say private, not secret."

I know the look I'm giving him tells him I don't understand.

"We agreed," he clarifies, "but I was still worried you would try to hide it. Be extra cautious not to touch me or talk about being alone with me."

We've always touched and been alone. It wouldn't be anything to get suspicious over. Might actually be more so if we stopped touching.

My hand cradles his cheek softly, and I lean in to give him a chaste kiss, then don't pull away. "You're mine, Buttercup."

His nose dances with mine in an eskimo kiss, then he's pulling away and starting the car.

The dance bar is in the next town over, but it's still a short ride.

There're couples of every legal age spinning around the dance floor, hanging by the bar, flirting at the small round tables. The dance floor couples are my favorite, and it's evident by the wide smile on my face.

"I'm guessing this date is a win too?" He leans into my ear, his hand clutched in mine tightening a little.

I scoff through my smile. "Well, Mr. Cockypants, how about we let the date happen first?"

He winks and pulls on my hand so we're on the dance floor.

It's a slow song, but the one right before was a faster oldies one. I'm really going to like this place.

He brings me in close, and I'm transported from the dance bar to all things Tommy. His arms wrapped around me, his chest pressed to mine, his scent filling my every breath.

"Tell me, Mr. Cockypants…"

"Mr. Cockypants now, no more Buttercup?" He smiles as he leans down so our faces are only inches apart.

The furrow is between my brows again to show the semblance of anger. "No. You're only Buttercup when I like you."

He laughs. "And why don't you like me now?"

"I haven't decided yet. That's based on your next answer."

He gets serious, but there's joy sparkling in his eyes.

"Brought any girls here?" I truly don't care about the answer because it's not like he's never dated before, and it's unreasonable to think he would steer clear of every place he's gone on dates before. But I am curious.

The joy slips a little from his eyes, but a smirk replaces it on his face. "Your brother and I had a double date here."

"One girl?" That's kinda hard to believe.

He smiles. "The girl was kind of a psychopath; made me

never want to come here again. I decided that I wanted to change my memory of this place."

I quirk a brow. "She was a psychopath, or you made her one?"

He leans in just a little bit more. "I met her that night when we went to pick them up. When we got here, in the middle of a dance, she got down on one knee and proposed. I thought it was a joke, so I laughed, but she didn't like that. When she told me she was serious and I rejected her, she stood up and yelled at me that she was pregnant and how was she supposed to bring our child into this world without a father."

I bite my lip. "See, not a psychopath. You made her one. How was she supposed to bring your child up without you?"

His smile is wide as he pulls my body in even closer so there literally is no space between us, and he drops the hand he's holding behind his neck so that he can wrap both arms around me. "Picking up asshole lessons from your brother?"

I tighten my hold around his neck, so our faces are closer now. I stand on my tip toes because even in these little heels, he towers over me. "No, I think it's the genes."

His laugh mixes with mine, and he kisses me. It's soft but passionate. It's telling everyone in the room that he's mine, but not being disturbingly PDAish about it.

When he pulls away, and we stare at each other as the song hits its end notes, I can feel the smile growing on my face, and my cheeks are beginning to hurt from how much bigger my smile wants to be.

CHAPTER 9

Tommy

THAT SMILE HAS the power to kill me.

I try to lean in for another kiss because they're intoxicating and I've become an addict, when the song changes. This one is faster, one of those songs couples danced to in the fifties movies.

Emory pulls away, and she's now moving like those characters in *Grease*. She's beckoning me to join her, and because she holds the power to my heart, I'm unable to resist her.

Her dress flows up as she spins, then she's back in my arms and back out. Her movements are fast, and mine are behind her every step, ready to catch and lead her when necessary. All I care is that she's having a good time, which the smile on her face and twinkle in her eyes tell me she is.

And I am too. This dance bar will forever have this new memory ingrained for it.

Then she's spinning again, and an elderly man catches her in his arms, spinning his wife to me. And we've switched partners.

Emory and I look at each other and laugh, then we're paying attention to our partners. I never catch the name of my partner, but she's sweet, and her smile is as wide on her face as it was on Emory's. Suddenly, I'm getting a vision. One of Em and me coming here in fifty years and being this old couple that's still dancing and laughing. It's the most exhilarating vision I've ever had.

Right before she pushes away from me, the old woman pulls me in close and screams into my ear past the music, "She's a keeper, that one."

I don't have time to tell her I know, but I'm sure she can see it in my eyes.

Then Emory is back in my arms, and she's laughing so much that I feel my own laugh bubbling out.

Then the song changes again. Another fast-paced one.

It's another three fast ones before a slow one is back on, and I can pull Emory in close to me and breathe her in.

She kisses me, then against my lips says, "I want to say this is the best date ever, but that first one was also the best date ever." She kisses me again, then pulls back to look me in the eyes. "You're my best date ever."

"And you're mine." I pull her in again. "You're my best everything."

I'm kissing her again. Out in public and for all to see. It's soft, but it tells her everything. Tells her the vision I saw of us growing old to be that couple we danced with; tells her she's it for me; tells her I think I might be falling in love with her.

And I know it's too soon, but I think I read the same things as she kisses me back.

It feels nice, kissing her in public. I know it's not the same, know that the same anxieties that eat her up don't apply to the general public, but to those closest to her. The general public will see us one minute, and we'll be out of their minds the next. Emory's anxieties have always come from those she loved the most constantly having an opinion.

We're staring at each other, and again, we say nothing. We

let our eyes do the speaking. Mine are telling her exactly what my kiss had. And again, I swear I read the same thing in hers.

All I know is that I've always called Darius my brother, but soon, even though it might be too fast, he's truly going to be my brother.

We're out of the house and at the job site before Emory is awake the next morning. I know because she texts me when she wakes up with a grumpy face emoji and a *I wanted a good morning kiss.*

I text her back. *Next time, I'll wake you up for one before leaving.*

A smiley face comes back to me.

We're getting out of the truck, Octavio leaning against his with three coffee's in hand, when Darius says, "You're chipper this morning. Fun time last night on the date I was not allowed to go on?"

He sounds bitter, and that makes me enjoy the date just a little bit more.

"Amazing time," I respond honestly.

Octavio quirks a brow. "Date?"

Darius sighs as he brings the coffee to his lips. "Yeah, he took the kid on another date last night."

Octavio's gaze shoots to me, and there's a question in his eyes whether I told Darius.

"And I wasn't allowed to join." Darius grumbles under his breath, and Octavio's question is answered.

He turns to Darius. "Why would you be allowed to go? A date is for the couple."

Darius rolls his eyes. "Poor Emmie."

"Why poor Emmie?" he asks before I can.

"I think the poor kid is so lost on romance, she's living her fantasies out on Tommy Proper." Darius laughs, then turns to me. "How am I going to get you laid if you're always stuck taking her on these little dates?"

I want to tell him that Emory's mine, and the only person my cock will be touching is her. But Emory doesn't want us talking about it, and I know it's not her fault that her mind won't allow her the ease of letting everyone know about us. And that's the only reason I shrug. "I'm not getting out of spending time with Emory for your dumb ideas."

He rolls his eyes. "You know, I remember always choosing to spend time with Em. But that was both of us spending time with her. Why am I kicked out all of a sudden?"

Octavio's wearing a smirk that tells me he knows exactly why. He doesn't have a lifetime of watching me baby Emory and be her pretend boyfriend to get guys to stop talking to her. If the roles were reserved, I don't think I'd see it either if I were Darius.

But I also won't lie to Darius. We don't lie. "Because I'm taking her on a date, douchebag."

He rolls his eyes. "You're right. Show her what a real date looks like so she doesn't spend the time of day with any losers."

"And if they're not losers? If they're Tommy's?" Octavio asks, and though I want to punch him for it, I really want to know the answer.

Darius's smile is wide. "Tommy is *my* best friend, and that's how I know he's not good enough for the princess."

My breath hitches, and the fear of having Darius find out redoubles inside me. Maybe Emory had a point to keep this to ourselves, at least for this beginning stage.

"Is anyone good enough para la princessa?" Octavio asks.

Darius tilts his head. "No, but there are men who can provide her everything she needs and spend their time with her. Be clean and smart and protective."

"I'd argue Tommy is all those things," Octavio says, and I could just kiss him for sticking up for me.

"Tommy's gone ten to twelve hours a day, comes home dirty and tired, and doesn't like going out. Makes good money but at the cost of time. Plus, he's friends with me, and I don't need anyone with the princess okay with my whoring."

"Emory doesn't like going out either." I don't realize the argument is coming until I've said it, but now that it's out, I add another. "And I've been all those things and am still taking her out." I ignore the whoring because I know he threw that in as a joke; even Darius makes fun of himself.

Darius rolls his eyes through the cocky grin. "I'm not haranguing you, Brother. Emory just likes adventure. I mean, she left for four years, and on her vacations, she went to other countries instead of coming home. She needs someone who makes good money without having to be gone all day. Someone who can take care of her and travel with her."

"So you wouldn't be happy if Emory ended up with Tommy?" Octavio asks because I can't.

And my heart is breaking in fear for the answer.

"Guys like Tommy are great guys. But no, I wouldn't. She deserves better, deserves all there is and more."

This time Darius isn't being a douchebag. He's just the typical older brother who sees his baby sister on a pedestal. And it's a pedestal she deserves. But it breaks my heart that to him, I'm not able to keep her up there.

Octavio looks at me with sincere eyes, and I have to push aside the pain of the moment and pretend things are all right. But this just means exactly what I've feared—Darius is not going to be happy with the outcome of this relationship.

Darius turns back to me with a shine in his eyes, and for a second, I think he's put it together. He's fought through the blindness that a lifetime with us has created, and he sees the truth.

But then he says, "On the topic of the princess, I'm spending the weekend with Laura. Make sure Emory has a great time."

"Always," I say because it's true, and that much he knows for a fact.

CHAPTER 10

Emory

TUESDAY NIGHTS ARE takeout nights at the Aabeck house. Always have been.

We didn't do it every Tuesday growing up, but most. It was Mom's way of giving us takeout so we didn't complain about only having home cooked meals—because takeout night was Tuesday night!

And it was her way of helping local businesses.

I've always loved Tuesday nights. Especially when it was my turn to choose the cuisine.

Or Tommy's.

Tommy always took my wants into consideration when choosing. Sometimes, he even chose whatever I wanted even if it made everyone else complain because that was us. I've always had him wrapped around my finger.

This time around, it's my turn, but mostly just because it's the first takeout night since I've been back because they didn't have one last week.

And I'm going with Chinese because I've missed MuShu's, and it's the perfect excuse. And though I've never really cared about pleasing them, it's also a place everyone else loves, and Darius happened to be craving. So win-wins all around.

We're sitting on the plush rugs Mom has thrown all over the living room, and my crisscrossed leg is lying over Tommy's thigh because I have an incessant need to touch him. And it gives me perfect range of his food so I can steal a bit. He'll be stealing too, but he's always been the one person I didn't mind it from.

Maybe that's because it's sort of like atonement for being wrapped around my finger.

Now that I think back to the way we grew up, I seriously cannot believe how romantic every part of our relationship has been. Like every single aspect. Inconceivable.

Music is playing in the background so low, it's barely audible, but I sway along with it anyway. Also giving my shoulder an excuse every other second to touch Tommy.

"You know what you want to do now that you're back?" Dad asks as we're enjoying our food.

I shrug. "I haven't really thought about it." My goal before arriving was just to be with my family again. I thought I'd have all the time in the world to think of it when I moved back home. I didn't realize Tommy would take up all the time my mind had.

"You should do what I did," Mom says proudly. "We just need to find you a husband."

Mom was a stay-at-home mom and housewife, and honestly, sometimes it was like she did more work than Dad. She's always taken pride in having every aspect of the house in top condition while she cooked and made new recipes. While she helped the neighborhood with any local events and took care of the kids when other parents had an emergency.

I smile as I raise my orange chicken between my chopsticks as a salute. "As long as I have someone like your old man as a husband."

Dad throws some broccoli at me. "Who you callin' old, you rascal?"

"You, you ancient artifact," Darius teases before turning to me. "Besides, you're not getting married *unless* you have someone like the old man. I'm not giving you away to anyone who doesn't worship the ground you walk on."

"Who said you're giving her away?" Mom instigates.

Darius's eyes narrow on her. "I did."

Dad scoffs. "I'm giving her away."

They go back and forth, and Dad smacks the back of Darius's neck, but still, the argument doesn't end. I'm laughing so hard, the food might come out my nose.

"And why should it be either of you?" Mom's only doing this to instigate because she finds their arguments amusing. "Maybe I want to give her away." Both Dad and Darius argue, but she's not done. "Or Tommy."

Tommy and I stiffen, but make ourselves relax before it's noticed.

Tommy gives a cheeky smile. "Trust me, my role in that wedding will *not* be to give her away."

"Thank you," Darius turns back to Dad. "I win."

Dad argues again, but all I can focus on is Tommy at me ear. "It will be to receive her."

I flush, push him away, and turn to my family. "Enough. How about you argue about this when I'm actually engaged?" Then under my breath, "Even though there's really no argument."

The others are changing the subject, but Tommy heard me. "Your dad?" He whispers.

I wink. "Darius'll be busy walking you down."

He laughs into his chow mien, and my smile is wide as I steal a spring role from his plate.

Then we're talking about random things, but none of that really matters to me because all I can do is focus on Mom and

Dad. The way they lean into each other sitting across from Tommy and me. The way Dad keeps finding excuses to touch her, even thirty years into their relationship. The way he pokes fun at her and kisses her temple. The way he turns to look at her like she's the only thing in the room while she's arguing with Darius and Tommy—because in the Aabeck household, we're always arguing. The way he simply exists to make her happy.

No question about it—if I don't have everything Calvin Aabeck gives to Lynn Aabeck, I don't want it.

Then he interrupts their "conversation" because *Can't Help Falling in Love* comes on the speakers, and Dad has always had a need to dance with Mom when this song comes on.

So now I'm watching them, mesmerized all over again.

The way Dad spins her into him. The way she smiles up at him. The way his hands soften when they touch her. The way she clings to him. The way they're completely googly-eyed for one another. I should be disgusted as their child at all the displays of their ooye gooye love, but I'm not.

Tommy is at me ear again, but I don't take my eyes off my parents. I have a feeling he can't take his eyes off either. "You know, I've always imagined my first dance to this song because of your parents. I figured if I was ever lucky enough to find someone like Lynn, I'd *have* to commemorate it to this song."

My heart warms as my head falls onto his shoulder. "You're making me fall harder for you, Buttercup."

He chuckles but says nothing else as we all watch on.

They don't break away as the song ends and another begins. It's obvious that they're so enamored with one another and whatever benign conversation they're having that they don't even realize that they should break away and reengage with their children.

They're perfect.

CHAPTER 11

Tommy

THURSDAY NIGHTS ARE BOYS' nights.

Usually that means the guys show up to our place because we don't have any nagging women about. That's not the case any longer, but I wound't classify Emory as *nagging*.

The poker table is brought out and set up at the edge of the living room and all six chairs are placed around it. Emory even makes us dips for the night because she's always loved to cook for other people and wants to do this little gesture.

It's the first Thursday night since we started this little tradition that I don't want to be here.

Octavio's the first to show up, as per usual, with a large pack of beers. He's dropped Lynette off with Nana and Papa like he always does because this gives his wife bonding time with the couple she also considers her own grandparents. We are just a mess of wayward kids who found family in the old couple.

"What're you planning tonight, princessa?" Octavio asks Emory with a smile on his face. He's started calling her that since it's what Darius always calls her.

She flushes and shrugs. "A bath and a book, I think."

"One of those dirty books?" he asks with a smirk.

My gaze shoots to Emory's because I need to hear the answer, but she doesn't reply. Instead, she just flushes deeper. Bingo.

Then I remember she'd been in the bath with a book the other day when I walked in on her. Every fiber of my being knows it was a dirty one by the way she won't meet my gaze.

I lounge back in my seat, and the grin spreads wide across my face. "What do you think about when you read these books?"

Her eyes are black as they give me a once-over, but Darius interrupts whatever snarky comment she was thinking about making as he's placing the dips around the table. "Hey, hey, hey. That's my sister! Dirty and Emory do not belong in the same universe together. She's going to be reading a whole-some story."

Octavio snorts. "Yeah, with the shower head within reach."

I punch him before Darius does because I don't care if he doesn't see her as anything but a friend. I don't want anyone else thinking of her in *that* way.

Octavio's usually not one to be cocky, but the smirk he gives me is a little too knowing.

"I'm gonna go." She takes a jug of water with her. "Have fun you big idiots!"

"Thank you, princess," Darius singsongs after her.

Luke, Mikey, and Drew show up not much later.

Everyone's chips are before them, and Octavio is handing out cards for the first game when Drew says, "Everything looks the same."

I quirk a brow, and Darius asks, "Why wouldn't it?"

"Wasn't your sister moving in with you? Girls like *changing* things." He throws two chips into the middle.

Darius laughs. "Nah, she helped pick out half the things in here through FaceTime, so she's got nothing to change."

Luke grimaces as he shows his losing cards. "How is it? Having her back? Have to kick anyone's ass yet? Heard she's hot."

Darius's eyes narrow on him, and I have to physically restrain myself from glowering when Darius asks, "Heard from who?"

Luke's gaze hovers to Drew as he smirks. "Unimportant."

Darius rolls his eyes, but we all hear it as he kicks Drew under the table. "It's great. I've missed her more than I thought. I figured the weekly calls were good, but now I see her every day, and I know she's safe and it makes every-thing...calmer."

"I agree." And I haven't had the weekly calls.

"That's right," Mikey laughs. "She's got *two* brothers."

I grimace and say, "I am *not* her brother," at the same time Darius says, "He is *not* her brother."

They all quirk their brows. Even Octavio. "Oh?"

"I am the sole owner of that crown, and I refuse to share it," Darius says smugly. "Plus, he used to pretend to be her boyfriend to get her out of dates with weirdos, so he can't be a brother."

Mikey's wiggling his eyebrows because he obviously wants me dead. "Just pretend?"

"Yes," Darius barks and places his winning hand down. He's always been the best player.

Octavio smirks and mutters under his breath, "Maybe before."

I kick him beneath the table and am glad he's across from Darius.

But also, not. Maybe Darius should hear it, should find out about us now. Maybe with the others around, they can hold him back from beating me to a pulp.

"You didn't answer, though," Drew says as the next round starts. "Have to beat any asses yet?"

He sounds like he's checking. My leg is shaking beneath the table as I refrain from reaching across the table and killing him.

"No," Darius answers. "And don't even think about it, asshole. She's too focused on us right now anyway. Spends all her time with me or Tommy or the family. I mean, it's been four years."

"She's allowed to be alone with Tommy and not us?" Mikey asks, his eyes growing a little darker. And he hasn't even seen what she looks like yet.

"Yes," I growl, my leg trying to cause an earthquake.

"Can we stop talking about my sister, please?" Darius takes a swig of his beer. "This is supposed to be guys night."

"We talk about girls on guys night," Luke argues.

"*Not* my sister." Darius glowers at him.

They move the subject to the game that took place the other day, and my leg can finally settle as my heart stops racing. Octavio looks at me with a small shrug as he mouthes, "Tell him," and I grit my teeth at him to tell him to fuck off.

"I'm just refilling my water," Emory calls out as she passes by us for the kitchen.

Her voice is like heaven to my ears, and I'm smiling as I glance over. Then I have to do a double take.

She's wearing that *fucking* robe.

I'm out of my seat just as the fuckers around the table notice her barely covered ass and the dampness of her hair, which is making the white silk almost see-through.

My body's covering hers, my dick fitting perfectly against her ass as I use my body to push her into the kitchen. "What the fuck do you think you're doing?"

I can tell the push and my rough tone startle her as she turns confused eyes on me. "I told you. Getting more water."

"In that?" I grit out.

Fuck, I can see her nipples poking out at me, begging to be sucked. My cock stirs, but I force my gaze back up to meet hers.

"What's wrong with it?"

"What's wrong with it is you damn near showed your entire body to the guys, Emory." I'm seething, then my voice drops. "I don't care if you weren't mine, you do not show your body to fuckers like them." I push her against the counter and cage her in as I grip the edges. "But since you *are* mine, I definitely will not have you walking around in *that*."

She swallows, and I can tell by the dilation of her pupils that she's not angry about the way I'm bossing her around. "You've seen this robe before, Tommy."

"And I hated it then too."

"But I love this robe."

"And you can wear it in the privacy of our room. If you insist on barely wearing anything, I'd rather have you coming out here in one of my shirts. At least, that would cover more of you." *And it would tell the fuckers at the table that you're mine.*

She perks up. "You told me six years ago that I wasn't allowed to wear your shirts anymore."

Six years ago, she was sixteen, and wearing my shirts had been giving girls my age the wrong idea about our relationship.

My index toys with her cheek. "Well, baby girl, unlike six years ago, I'm yours now. Everything I have is yours, so I'm going to take you to our room right now, and you're changing."

She rolls her eyes, but the pleased grin is still there. "I can go to the room by myself, Buttercup."

"I'm not letting those fuckers get another eyeful."

She bites her lip, and my cock twitches again. But I have

to push the need aside, take things slow, show her she's the most important person in this world to me.

"Fine." She pushes me away. "But I'm getting water first."

"Everything good in there?" Darius calls out.

I adjust myself so the major hard-on isn't calling for attention, then move to the opening to the kitchen and lean against it as the boys continue the game without me. "She's changing out of that fucking thing."

"Good." Darius takes a swig of beer. "I barely saw anything, and it was too much."

"Can you guys not talk about me like I'm not here?"

Emory's body hits my back, and I'm glad she's at least using me to cover herself because all three—Luke, Mikey, and Drew—are looking at her with too much lust in their eyes.

"Look away, assholes," I bark, and even Darius looks at me with raised brows at the possessiveness in my tone.

Emory pushes against my back and moves past me. "I'm not waiting around all day, Buttercup."

Even as quick as I move to cover her with my double-her-size body, I know the guys got another look. And one of her front this time, with her nipples hard and almost peaking through the silk and her legs completely bared to the tops of her thighs.

"Ugh, princess, please don't wear that around me," Darius complains as I shove her into the hall.

She's giggling when I hiss into her ear, "What fucking part of 'I don't want them seeing you in that' did you not understand?"

She pulls away from my body when we reach my room, and I miss her touch already. She's at my dresser, putting down her water, and pulling out a large shirt I wear sometimes on the job. "You were taking too long."

She pulls on the belt of her robe, and I turn around faster than the speed of light. If I saw her naked right now, there's no way Darius won't know exactly what is going on between us because I'll have her screaming so loud, her voice will be hoarse for days afterward.

"I'll see you when the guys leave, baby," I throw past my shoulder then move back for the living room.

I stop right before turning out of the hall to adjust myself again. Then I'm back in my seat and waiting for them to start a new game before joining.

Mikey smirks at me as he nods back to my room. "You're quite...protective, Tommy boy."

The glint in his eyes tells me unlike Luke and Drew, he knows exactly what's going on with Emory and me.

Good. Let him be the one to know it because outside of Darius, he's the biggest whore in our friend group. Bigger even. And Darius isn't a problem since Em is his sister.

"He's always been like that with her. Made my life easier," Darius speaks around his mouthful of dip.

It's true. I've always been a little more actively protective of Emory. We're both protective—Darius even scarier than me at times—but normally, I'm the only one showing it. And that means Darius can trust me to take care of her. It means, in situations when people don't know she's his sister, he doesn't have to explain to girls why he is so protective over her because I would take care of it. It means I can threaten anyone for even thinking about touching her while he gets the green light to screw around with whomever he pleases.

But I've never minded. I loved being her protector.

And now, I love it even more. Require it to function properly.

Octavio eyes me, and I read it in his gaze—I can't hide behind how normal this all looks to Darius for too long. Eventually, he has to know I have it bad for his baby sister. The one I'm meant to be protecting.

I sigh and look down at the new set of cards in front of

me. I'm not hiding it from him. Everything I do is telling enough in its own right. It's not my fault Darius isn't thinking about questioning me about it.

I scoff at myself because even I know that's utter bullshit.

Luke throws his losing cards down. "She *is* hot."

Darius and I both kick him under the table, mine harder by the way he leans into his left side.

"Fucker," I mutter under my breath.

"Em said you needed your shelves fixed?"

Nana Isla gives me a warm smile. "Yes, the big oaf went and knocked a shelf off those beautiful bookshelves you made us a few months ago and can't fix it."

Papa Atti grunts. "That shelf weights as much as he does. I'm not the lifter I once was, old woman."

I laugh at their bickering. It's always done with a glint in their eyes. "I'll have it fixed in two minutes, Nana."

"Yeah, yeah," Atti grunts again. "Show off, why don't you, Thomas? You know Isla is mine."

I smirk at the old man, then send a winning smile to Nana Isla. "I don't know. I think I can win her over."

Nana's hand flutters to her heart. "You already have, Thomas."

I laugh as the couple follow me to the back room, which they've turned into a small library office. The shelves have all been built by me, Octavio, and Darius. Nana Isla had a certain design in her head that was difficult to find and we'd preferred to build it anyway. We work in constructions, so it'd have been more of an offense than not to not be the ones building it.

The middle shelf on the case by the window is completely cracked in two and jammed out of its hinges. "Damn, Atti. What did you do to it?"

I meet his gaze just in time to see the wiggling eyebrows. "Nana wanted to play, and I got a little too excited."

My brow quirks in amusement. "You old man. You still violating the poor woman?"

"Every. Day," Atti says with a proud smirk. "And it's not violating if she's just as thrilled by it."

The thought of Nana Isla doing anything sexual is off-putting since she *is* my grandmother for all intents and purposes, but I love hearing that they're still hot for one another. Love the image it brings up of Em and me in fifty years, clawing at each other while our grandkids make vomiting sounds.

My heart flutters at the thought of such a future with Emory. Of any future with her. Of the fact that I'm actually considering futures with her.

"Yeah, yeah," I throw him the same amused phrase he's just thrown me and move for the closet at the end of the room. When we'd made these bookcases, we'd cut a few extra shelves in case of anything like this.

"It's quite attractive watching you work with your hands, Tommy." Nana Isla's tone is almost seductive, and I know she's teasing Papa Atti as much as she's teasing me.

I throw her a smirk over my shoulder as I pull at the broken shelf. "I've heard the ladies love it."

Papa Atti grumbles. "You shouldn't pay attention to what the ladies love."

I place the broken pieces of wood off to the side; they could come in handy when building something small later. "You do remember that I like girls, don't you, Papa?"

Papa Atti's smile is cunning now. "Don't be smart with me, boy. I'm just reminding you that the only one that should love it is Emory."

I freeze as I'm going to pull out the nails from the old shelf in order to have spots for new ones, and I'm glad my back is to them. "Why do you say that?"

"Oh, calm down, boy." I hear him take a seat in the armchair at the other side of the room. "We didn't have to catch you kissing to know you two have the hots for each other."

Emory *did* mention they'd caught us kissing. But still, a big part of me didn't think they'd bring it up.

"Emory sounded keen on keeping the relationship hidden." Nana Isla's using her 'trying to not be obvious, but nosy' voice. She thinks we don't know what it sounds like, but it's too obvious.

I pull the last nail free and grab a new set and the new shelf. The thing is quite a bit heavier than a normal shelf, so it's no surprise that old Papa Atti couldn't hold it up on his own.

"She's always been protective of things she cares about."

I crouch to my knees and hold the shelf with my shoulder so it lines perfectly with where I need it as I move to place the first nail.

"Still, Son," Atti says in less of a joking manner. "I think Darius will be happy about the outcome. You know, once he gets past the fact that you're sleeping with his little sister."

I'm glad I finished nailing the shelf in before those words left his mouth because I definitely would've jammed my thumb from the shock. I move on to another nail and only speak when I'm near finished with it. "I'm not sleeping with her."

"In the same way that I didn't break that shelf?" The teasing is back in Atti's voice.

I move on to another nail. "No. In the way that we've only kissed."

"That is so sweet, Thomas." Nana Isla's comment sends another flutter through my chest.

Does Emory think it's sweet? Does she realize the only reason I haven't taken her yet is because I want us to work so desperately, I'm terrified of ruining it?

I don't comment as I hammer in a few more nails to hold the shelf up and rise to my feet. I play with the shelf to make sure it's sturdy then turn around. "All done."

Papa Atti knits a disbelieving brow, obviously not trusting the words coming out of my mouth. "You've only kissed."

I stare into his crinkled eyes. "Yes, Atti. That's it."

"Well, I'll be damned. You have quite the control on yourself, Thomas."

Nana Isla smacks him then pulls on his shirt to stand. "It's sweet, Atticus."

The old man makes a throaty laugh. "I'm just saying, if we'd been living together when we first got together, Isla, I would not have had the control to stay away from you."

"That's because you're a pig, Atti. And you also didn't have to worry about your relationship with my brother, old man." Nana Isla looks at me. "You're doing the right thing."

Papa Atti rolls his eyes. Nana Isla doesn't need to turn around to see it; she just elbows him in the gut.

"Thank you, Nana," I say because I truly hope this is the right thing. Taking it slow to show everyone, but especially Emory, that I'm serious about us. Not telling Darius only because Emory's anxieties don't allow for it at the moment. I hope they're all the right decisions.

"Don't be so proud, Isla. He'll be in that girl by week's end. I saw the light in her eyes when she spoke of him. She wants him as much as you wanted me when we broke that shelf." Papa Atti is already leaving the room as if his word is final.

I laugh as I pick up the broken shelf and follow Nana Isla out as she reprimands her husband for being so crass. And I'm completely split in two. Half of me wants what he's saying to be so true, it's unbearable. I want her to want me to fuck her as much as I want to fuck her.

But the other half—the one that insists that if she doesn't want to be with me sexually at the moment, it will make controlling myself easier—is incessant and demands to be listened to. I need to take this slow.

CHAPTER 12

Emory

FRIDAY NIGHT IS a special Darius-Emory night because of his plans with Laura over the weekend. And though I missed him in Europe and should be mad that I've just come back, and instead of spending time with me, he's ditching me to get some ass, I'm glad. This means Tommy and I can do things without his annoying comments. This means Tommy and I can do *things*.

So naturally, the things Tommy decides he wants to do is go on a long ass hike. He chuckles when I grumble, but I stroll along after him to the car. We'll park at the end of a small forest scape, hike it up at a slight incline then back down. Yippie.

Realistically, I am excited because I've always liked hikes and checking out new areas, and I want to spend all this time with Tommy. But it's almost five miles each way, and I've never been excited about those types of hikes. I've only ever been on a couple of these long ones and those were when Tommy and Darius dragged me along years ago.

But at least now when Tommy walks ahead of me, I can check out his ass.

We begin the hike together, but it's not long before he's ahead. I can't really have a problem with it since his legs are as long as I am and he's pacing himself so he's only about five steps ahead.

It was always like this before. Darius and Tommy would stroll ahead, talking and joking, and I would follow behind.

But now Tommy doesn't have his best friend to talk to, so he calls out to me.

And we talk.

He tells me about work and the next client they have lined up. About how excited and nervous Octavio is getting now that Lynette could pop at any moment. He tells me how much he loves the nature around us and the fact that we can do this little adventure just the two of us.

And I agree on that point. I've always loved traveling and doing new things. Checking out new areas and being one with nature. I loved my time in Europe where I got to do and see so much, but there's something about being home and doing these little things that's almost more exciting. Maybe it's just because I'm doing them with Tommy.

We're about three miles in when I'm thankful that Tommy remembered to grab our baseball caps before heading out because the sun is beating down hard. I've never been too big of a sweater, but I definitely feel the heat.

I don't care when Tommy turns around every so often to wait for me to catch up, when he sees me gross and sweaty like this. He's seen me like this—worse than this—so many times that it doesn't bother me.

I love that.

He bites his lip when he turns to wait for me at the four-mile marker. "You know, you're really hot all sweaty and breathing all accelerated like that."

There's a darkness in his eyes as he says it. Pervert.

"Yeah?" I stop beside him and bring the water to my lips.

"You know if you agreed to stay home instead of going on a whole ten-mile hike today, I could be sweaty and accelerated breathing for an entirely different reason."

His pupils grow to take over all the color in his eyes, and I smirk as I walk past him and continue the hike. There's only a little less than a mile left until we reach the meadow at the top and we can stop to eat.

"Your ass looks delicious, baby girl," he calls from behind me this time.

I turn and give him a wink. "As does yours. That's why I choose to walk behind you all the time."

He chuckles. "Yeah? Is that what you did when we were teenagers too?"

I laugh as he reaches my side. "I wasn't into you like that when we were younger, but yeah, I did. Not all the time, but sometimes when you and Darius would be talking sports and nothing I understood, my gaze would just...hover. And I wasn't gonna be staring at Darius's ass. Plus, yours has always been nicer."

He laughs as he throws his arm over my shoulders and brings me in to kiss my crown. "Mine has never been nicer, but I'm glad you think so."

His gait slows down so we can walk together for the last half mile, and it's so nice to be out in nature with Thomas Rutherford's arm over my shoulders. Even in the blazing heat when I normally wouldn't want anyone touching me, I love that he's holding me.

The meadow is so beautiful when we arrive that I'm rooted to the spot for a minute, only able to stare.

At the wildflowers growing haphazardly all over. At the little splotches of greenery everywhere that make great spots to throw a blanket and have a picnic. At the little bees flying around. At the birds chirping away.

It's unimaginable how much I've forgotten how beautiful

it is up here. It'd been the second reason for agreeing to come with the boys when we were younger. The first had always been to spend time with them, but this view was definitely right up there.

Tommy has a blanket thrown over a patch of grass when I come out of my reverie and walk up to him. He's pulling Tupperware filled with food out of his backpack and putting them down next to two huge bottles of water. I'm grateful for those two bottles; my water is almost out.

I made sun-dried tomato pesto pasta and my infamous little salad, and he made—stole from Nana Isla—cookies and fruit and some of her little meat pies.

I take my shoes and socks off and let my feet fall into the grass, already feeling the rightness of it all, and Tommy follows me. We both walk a couple of laps around the blanket to allow our feet the acquaintance with the earth before sitting for our lunch.

Mmm! I'm so hungry.

There's no need to pour them onto separate plates. We just take out two forks and dig in. Always have.

When the food's consumed and put away again so the bees don't harass us, we lie back and look out at the blue skies. With the tree positioning here, the sun isn't an issue, and the breeze is always around, another reason I loved this spot when I was younger.

I'm cuddled into Tommy like old times, but this feels nothing like old times. Now I'm thinking about how much our bodies are touching and how much I want to kiss him. More than just kiss him.

Now I'm thinking about how content my heart feels to have him at my side and how much this feels like I've always dreamed happily ever afters would feel like.

"What're you thinking about?" he asks through the serenity of the birds chirping around us.

"Getting you naked," I answer because it's true.

He barks a laugh. "And they say men are the perverts."

"We're just better at hiding it." I hug him tighter.

He breaths in the fresh air. I'm also grateful for that. With his job, he needs days like this to clean out all the dust he's always taking in.

"I'm thinking about kissing you," he says.

I wait a moment but when he says nothing more, I lift to my elbows and rest on his chest. "And?"

"And nothing. I'm thinking about kissing you." His hand plays with my hair, and my heart jumps at how sweet this is. "Is that childish? I feel like I'm a teenager, but honestly, I just want to kiss you."

I trace his face until I reach his lips. "Then kiss me."

His hand plays with my hair another few seconds as he smiles up at me before stopping and holding my face. He leans up and kisses me, and he's right; it feels like I'm a teenager again.

He flips us so his body is pressed above mine, but his hands don't wander, and his hips don't thrust. Just his lips. His lips are doing all the work.

And there's an intimacy to this that I have never fathomed. To just holding him close as we make out, as his mouth presses to mine and our tongues meet. As we share breath that tells the other how we feel.

When he pulls away, I knock my head against his.

"What was that for?"

"For making me feel like a pervert," I say because he's being so sweet, and he was so right to just want to kiss right now.

His gaze jumps from my lips to my eyes several times as he smiles. He doesn't say anything in response; instead he just leans down and continues kissing me.

And it truly is just another best date ever. I think I'm

coming to realize it's more the spending time with Tommy rather than the dates that are the best thing ever.

We only spend about an hour lying there—mostly kissing —before it's time to do the whole five miles again. Yay!

We're two and a half miles into the walk back to the car when I slip on some mud. Thinking it's only that little bit and I'm going to catch myself in a patch of dirt, I don't really care. But then, I smack into full on mud.

Tommy hears my yelp and turns wide-eyed. And instead of running to me, he laughs.

"Picking up douchebag traits from your best friend, I see," I mutter as I try to make my way up but slip back down.

And his laugh only grows.

I keep the eye roll from happening and instead take a fist full of mud and throw it at him as hard as my nonathletic arm can muster. And because he's laughing and not really paying attention, it actually hits him.

And almost on the face too! I got his neck and jaw.

His smile immediately drops, and he looks over at me like I'm in big trouble.

"Not so funny now, is it?" I say as I actually pick myself up from the mud this time, completely stained on my right side.

"I don't know." He drops the backpack and slowly walks toward me.

My eyes widen a little too late, and I'm about to turn and run when he catches me around the thighs and throws me— somehow softly—back into the mud. This time my entire back and ass gets it.

I screech but don't let him wiggle out untouched. My knees lock around his waist, and I pull him in as much as my strength allows. And again, because he's not fully paying attention, it actually works. Then I'm flipping us so his back and ass are now fully submerged.

I'm doing my evil laugh, straddling his hips, when two handfuls of mud come flying at my face. Then it's war.

I jump off and grab for some more, and I'm throwing as much and as fast as I can. He's almost entirely covered when he finally picks himself up without slipping and grabs for me again. I run out of the way the first two times, but eventually he has me. And he throws us both into the mud.

He hovers over me so I can't get away and makes sure I'm as attacked as he is.

We're laughing so much, I snort which only makes us laugh even harder. Then he's falling off me, and we're both lying in mud, and this is so gross, but so amazing all at the same time.

I turn to look at him, and he's already watching me.

"At least there's a two and a half mile walk to let this dry before we get in the truck."

Of course he's worried about his car. No matter how much it dries though, he's gonna need to get the inside cleaned.

I laugh and lean in to kiss his mud-covered face. "I hate you, Buttercup."

He throws me on top of him and hugs me tight. "Liar."

We kiss through our laughs, and all I can think is that I'm so glad we came on this little—big—hike today.

Tommy takes Darius's shower so I can take his when we get home. It takes two run throughs of shampoo and body wash to completely scrub myself clean, but finally, I'm pristine.

When I'm washing out the conditioner from my hair, Tommy yells through the door that he got a call from the family they're contracted for and needs to deal with it. Darius and Tommy don't normally get calls like these, but when they do, it normally takes a while. That much I know.

And that much is the reason I decide on a bath after my shower.

The water is steaming, and I decide against adding any bombs to it. I just want to feel the heat on my muscles and wipe away the strain after using muscles not used to such long ass hikes causes.

It feels amazing, so I close my eyes and let a small moan escape my lips.

Only to be surprised by the door flying open and Tommy strolling in. "Turns out, nothing to worry ab…"

And freezing.

I have a feeling when he heard the shower off, he probably thought I was in that tiny robe again because the shock on his face tells me he definitely wasn't expecting to see me naked in the clear water. Or the moan that passed my lips.

I should probably be embarrassed, but I'm far from it. I tilt my head and attempt to keep myself serious. "This is becoming a habit of yours, isn't it, Buttercup?"

I give him a second to process what I said, then as gracefully as I can manage in a slippery tub, I stand before he has the chance to take off and shut the door.

Now I'm standing naked before him, water gliding down my skin, and his gaze is locked on every inch of me. His tongue juts out to wet his lips, and I feel myself shiver with the need to feel that tongue on me.

I step out of the tub in as graceful a manner as any human could ever manage and tip toe up to him. The pointed toe will make me look more graceful, more elegant, taller and more predatory.

He swallows hard but doesn't move.

My hands are damp when they land on his chest, but neither one of us cares. "Buttercup?"

He's looking at my breasts, my nipples are peaked with

the chill of stepping out of the steaming bath. And he looks hungry.

I let one hand slide up his chest until my index is at his chin, and I'm tilting his head so his eyes meet mine.

"Baby…" his voice sounds pained.

"Yes, Buttercup?"

My finger plays with his lips, and his tongue comes out to taste it.

I smile and push him so he's out of the bathroom and back in his room.

I follow, letting my hips sway with each movement as we make our way to his bed. When his knees hit the edge of the bed, I stop. He doesn't fall over, just stands there and watches me.

But that doesn't matter because my job's done.

His move.

CHAPTER 13

Tommy

I **KNOW** I need to control myself, but fuck, is she making it difficult.

I'm not strong enough for this. I'm going to give in. My every fiber knows I'm going to give in because she's mine and it's time I marked her.

My hand slowly raises to graze her skin, her breath hitching as my fingers skim her torso, making their way up to her breasts. I let my fingers circle a nipple, but nothing more, before I'm skimming up and cradling her face.

My thumb runs over her lips, and I'm a lost cause to her.

I step up and kiss her. Soft and slow.

But the moment our tongues touch, I can't keep the pace. My kiss grows rough, my tongue clashing with hers in a need to taste more.

When we pull away for breath and I look into her eyes, I know she's sure about this. Her fingers cling to the sides of my shirt, and she's waiting for me to make a decision. It's hilarious that she thinks I could ever resist her. That I could ever say no to her.

I turn us so I'm facing the bed, and my hands reach down

to the backs of her thighs. I hike her up and our lips are together again.

Her hands are messing through my hair, and I can tell she's growing more desperate by the way her hips thrust in the air. She's trying to get closer, rub herself against me, but I don't let her. I don't let her legs wrap around me.

Instead, I break the kiss and throw her onto the bed.

She bounces then stops and looks up at me on her elbows, her legs just slightly parted. My mouth waters at the prospect of what's before me.

My hands are at the back of my neck before I realize what I'm doing, and my shirt is ripped off.

Now she's licking her lips in anticipation. *Good, baby girl, good.*

I drop to my knees on the bed, and she crawls backwards.

"Where're you going, baby girl?" I drop to all fours and prowl over to her. "I thought you wanted this."

Her chest rises in a deep inhalation, and her legs spread a little more. So she likes when I speak to her.

"Do you want this?"

She doesn't say anything, but I can smell how much she wants this.

"I need you to tell me what you want, baby."

Her legs are spreading again. Just a little more, but her glistening center is opening to me, and it takes every ounce of self-control to pace myself.

My gaze latches onto hers, and I see the black eyes of desire mirroring mine. "Baby girl."

"I want this," she whispers in a raspy voice.

A low chuckle escapes me. "Good."

I drop to get a deeper smell and watch as her legs open for me, but I don't touch her. Just bask in the glory of her scent.

She whimpers on her elbows as she watches me.

I look at her through my lashes and know the Mr. Cockypants smirk is there. "What exactly do you want, baby?" My voice is raspy and so full of a desire I've never known possible.

"You," she whispers.

I chuckle. "I'm going to need more."

She's growing red, and I'm sure that's partly from her body heating up with desire and partly from embarrassment. "I want you to kiss me."

I let my brows furrow. "Kiss you? Where?"

She smells so good as she grows wetter, her legs as open as possible, that my fists have to dig into the sheets to keep me still.

Her voice is barely audible now, but the desperation is all there. "On my lips."

Those words go straight down my spine and through my cock. Fuck, I want to come hearing her speak like that.

But I play with her instead.

I lift higher and press my lips to hers, my tongue playing with her mouth until hers is joining in the dance. When I pull away, I ask, "Is that what you want, baby girl?"

She shakes her head, and I see from my periphery that her fingers are digging into the sheets, her hips almost bucking in desire. "Wrong lips."

I smirk. "I don't know what you could mean."

There's a defiant look in her eyes, and I know in that moment that I'm definitely falling in love with this girl.

"I want your tongue on my pussy." There's nothing shy about the way she says it, but her cheeks flush a darker red.

I bite down on my bottom lip as I take in every inch of her face. "That's my girl."

I slide back down and take another inhalation of her scent, closing my eyes to bask in the glory, when I feel her move on the bed. I open my eyes to see her hips writhing in anticipation.

My hands move to her thighs and press them back. "Stay still, baby."

I kiss the apex of one thigh then the next, and she's trying to push against my hands so my mouth is at her center. I chuckle, look at her through hooded eyes, and finally give her what she wants.

My tongue licks her from entrance to clit just once, and one of her elbows drops, but the other is still holding her up to watch.

"Is that what you want, baby girl?"

"Yes," her answer is breathy and just shy of a moan. My favorite sound to exist.

"Good." I lick her again. "Because it's what I want too."

Then she's my feast, and my lips latch around her clit, and she can no longer hold herself up. I suck, and the moan that escapes her almost ends me right then and there.

But I hold on and lick around her clit, down the slit between her folds, and into her opening. My tongue fucks her, and her back arches off the bed, legs pushing against my hands. I have to press down on her thighs so hard to keep her still, there'll be bruises for sure come morning.

That thought makes me want her more. Makes my tongue go on a frenzy as it relishes pumping into her, then sliding up her folds, circling her little nub before giving it all the attention it desires.

"Come in my mouth, baby girl." My tongue tastes down her folds before reaching my new little best friend. "I want to taste all of you."

Her nails are scraping into my scalp as her back arches impossibly deep, and her thighs fight me again to press together. I know she's about to come when her legs begin to shake at my sides, so I redouble my efforts on that beautiful nub made solely for her pleasure.

When she comes, the taste is so delicious, I'm ready to

drown in it. I'm ready to kill myself gorging on it until my body can take no more.

And the sound.

Her moans as she calls out every curse word in existence, throwing my name in there every few words, it pushes me to the edge. I feel the pressure at the base of my cock telling me it's almost time for me too.

It's because of that fact that I pull away from her center and drop her thighs. I watch her finish quivering and close my eyes to restrain myself.

When I open them again, she's staring up at me with a contented smile and hooded eyes.

I swipe her cum off my face and smile back. I lick my hand to get all of her taste before I drop down and slowly crawl over her body. I kiss her stomach, my tongue circling her navel before continuing upward.

I stop at her breasts, the beaded nipples staring at me, begging to be tasted. A request I am unable to resist.

My hands are caressing every bit of her skin when my mouth latches around one nipple. She arches off the bed as a hand finds its way to my hair again while the other rakes down my back. My hand reaches for her other nipple and plays with it.

Her moans are growing again, and when she calls out my name, I switch, giving the other breast my mouth's attention. I bite down on her nipple and pull, my gaze latched on her because I need to watch her. Need to see the ecstasy on her features.

My hands move to cup both breasts as I say, "These girls. These are mine, baby girl."

She shakes her head at me. "No," she breaths out. I'm about to argue when she continues, "it's all yours. Not just the girls. I'm all yours."

I smirk up at her. "That's my girl."

I kiss upward again, and she bites down on her bottom lip as her head rolls back. I leave a lite bite mark at the base of her neck before continuing up and reaching her ear. "My tongue can spend all night between those legs, but my cock is getting jealous."

Her hips thrust up, and I know she likes the sound of that.

I push off the bed and love the sound of her whimpering for me. It's that sound that makes me take my time, knowing she wants this as much as I do.

I walk to my dresser and am thankful Darius feels the need to throw a few new condoms in there every few weeks even though I never use them. I take one and move back to the front of the bed so I can watch her laid out before me.

I throw the condom on the bed and reach for my sweatpants, push them down, and strip out of them. Emory's eyes widen, and she's wetting her lips and biting down on the bottom one as those fingers dig into the sheets again.

If she feels even half of what I did when she stepped out of that tub, I sympathize with her because it was torture watching her and not touching her.

Her gaze remains fixed to my hard cock until I drop to my knees on the bed again. Then they shoot up to meet mine.

I prowl over to her again, this time letting my tongue enjoy a taste of her every inch before making it to her mouth. Her calves, thighs, another glorious taste of her cunt. Her stomach, breasts, neck.

Then my lips are on hers again, and our tongues are clashing.

Her fingers are in my hair, pulling on the small strands and telling me how much she wants this. But again, I ask, "Do you want this?"

We've done a lot so far that would put me on Darius's dead man list, but this would put me up on the number one spot. And more importantly, I'd put myself as first on the dead man list if even an ounce of her was hesitant.

She looks almost annoyed with the question which makes me even happier to have asked it. She's cute when she's annoyed. And angry. And happy. And horny. Always.

"Buttercup," she pulls on my hair a little harder, "put your cock in me. Now."

I know my brows shoot up in astonishment, but I can't help it. I wasn't expecting that language.

"Yes, ma'am." My voice is husky as I kiss her again and reach for the condom.

It's opened and sliding down my dick in a matter of seconds. I don't have much more patience. I need to be inside her.

I angle myself at her center, but catch myself and pause before pushing in. "Is this your first time?"

Her lips droop a little when she shakes her head. Like she wishes it were, wishes I were her first.

"I wish the same, baby girl. For you to be my only." I push inside her and inhale deeply to keep still as she arches off the bed, our lips pressed together as I say, "But you'll be my last."

Her nails rake down my back, and I can no longer keep still. In a way, I'm glad it's not her first time. I don't have to be gentle.

I pull out and pump into her hard, needing this to be rough, unable to control myself enough to make it slow. "Fuck, baby, you feel so good." A little deeper this time.

And again.

And again.

Going so deep, there's no way we're not meshed together for a split second every time. Our breaths mix as our lips remain pressed together, moans and groans filling the house, the loveliest of sounds to exist.

"Please never stop, Tommy," she moans out, "you feel so good inside me, never stop."

I lied before. That's the loveliest sound to exist.

She's so wet around my cock, the sound fills the room past our moans, and it's all bringing me so close to the edge. I drop a hand to her pussy, my thumb finding that glorious best friend of mine and rubbing it in slow circles.

Her hips buck at the contact, and the skin on my back breaks as she digs her nails down into my flesh. "Good, leave marks, baby. Show the entire world whose I am."

Her head falls back with a moan so long and incomprehensible, I push into her harder and just a little bit faster to make it last longer.

"I can't wait any longer." My lips fall to hers, so our breaths mix again. "Come with me, baby girl. Come all over my cock, Emory."

I think the name did it for her.

She's writhing beneath me, her body shaking as she comes again. And finally, I allow myself the release.

It's a release so hard and long, I truly think I died and came back.

When it finally stops and I can pull out of her, I roll over before I drop and crush her with my weight. I allow myself the moment to bask in the glory of it all before going to the bathroom.

The condom is fuller than I thought possible. Considering I came harder than ever before, it's not surprising.

I throw it out then grab for a small wash cloth, dampen it with warm water, and move back into the room.

Emory is still lying in bed, dead to the world as her chest rises and falls. Her eyes are just barely open to slits as she watches me.

I move to clean her because even though I didn't come

inside her—no matter how much I want to, which is a fact I'll have to think about another day—she deserves this.

When I discard the washcloth and join her in bed again, her eyes are fully open, and she's smiling at me. I bring her into my chest and hold her like that.

At least an hour passes, but I know she's still awake by the drawings her fingers create on my chest. And as my fingers dance across her back, I think back to what Darius said at work.

Guys like Tommy are great guys. But no, I wouldn't.

She needs someone who makes good money without having to be gone all day.

She deserves better.

I know all of it is true, but that doesn't stop me from knowing that Emory is mine, and I will do it all, give everything up to make sure she's happy. I will live in Hell to make sure she's in Heaven every moment of every day.

Darius should know me well enough to trust that much.

He's not going to like it, but I really couldn't care less. She's mine, and I need everyone to be a hundred percent clear on that.

"I don't want to keep beating around this relationship with your brother. Him thinking it's a joke. I have to tell him it's real. Tell him I've had you," I tell her in the quietude of the night.

She freezes over me. "What?" She lifts and rests her arm on my chest so she can look at me. "No. What do you mean you're going to tell him you've *had* me?"

I quirk a brow. "Baby girl, you know exactly what I mean."

She rises so she's holding herself up with a hand and my gaze immediately latches on a luscious breast. But my gaze shoots back up to hers when she speaks, "You can't tell him that!"

"Why not?"

"Because what we do is private. It's none of his business."

"Oh, I think it's plenty of his business that I'm fucking his baby sister," I argue because I don't understand why she's so upset about this.

"Regardless of whose sister I am, it's no one else's business what we're doing."

I narrow my eyes at her but give in because she's kinda right about that bit.

"Fine. I won't say I've had you. But he's going to guess it when I tell him we're together together."

She pushes straight up, so she's fully sitting now. "Why? There's no need to bring anything up."

That suspicion that this is a secret starts creeping in. "Why not? I want him to know."

"I don't."

I scoff as I sit up too. "So it's exactly like I thought before. This *is* a secret, not just private."

"Tommy, you know I keep things to myself. Important things especially!"

That much was true, everyone in the family knew it.

"And I tell Darius all of my important things," I argue. "Do you know how much worse it's going to look if I don't tell him now? He's going to think you're not important to me, think I'm just fucking you because we live together."

"Tommy..." she begins.

"Emory." I control the anger rising in me and let a harsh breath out. "Are you ashamed of this?" Maybe Darius has been right. "Ashamed I have to physically put in the hours for my money? That I come home dirty and don't stroll around in expensive suits?"

Her brows furrow in horror. "Absolutely not, Tommy. You know I like guys who work with their hands, guys who get dirty."

"So it's me then? Something about me embarrasses you? That I don't have a real family like you? That my parents would rather jet around the Mediterranean than be with me? That I don't even get a fucking happy birthday or Merry Christmas from them?" I push out of the bed and stalk across the room to let the anger out.

"No!" She turns on her knees, and watches me; the pain in her eyes killing me.

"What is it then?" I ask through gritted teeth.

"Everything you are is everything I've ever dreamed of, Tommy."

"Then why hide me?"

"Because I finally have all I've ever dreamed of. I won't let anyone destroy that!"

"So instead, you'll destroy my relationship with your brother?"

She doesn't answer. Water begins filling her eyes, but still, she remains silent.

I scoff and snatch my sweatpants off the ground and leave the room.

CHAPTER 14
Emory

TOMMY ISN'T SPEAKING with me past clipped answers. It's obvious Darius can tell something is off, but he doesn't push for more when we both answer *nothing*.

Instead, like the amazing brother he is, he steals me away for our own little date. His theory is we got into a fight while hanging out—something that had happened in the past, though not often. And he isn't too far off from the truth.

He's taking me to the batting cages to hit some balls because he can see I'm frustrated, and this was always something we did when we were frustrated. Another thing I missed in my time away in London.

Plus, this happened to be one of the only things we ever did without Tommy. Darius has always insisted that this was something only the two of us would do and Tommy has never pushed that line. There were things only he and Darius did, and things that only he and I did so he understood the boundary. The same way Darius understood the boundary when we insisted it would only be me and Tommy for a night. It's how we've always been, and the guilt is beginning to eat into me that Darius thinks it's still like it used to be.

The guilt redoubles, thinking about the fact that Tommy was probably right, and this may destroy his relationship with my brother. So when Darius hands me the bat and stands off to the side of the cage so the machine can throw the ball at me, I convince myself Tommy has been right and Darius needs to know. But when the balls flies past me and I don't hit it, Darius's worried eyes meet mine, and my heart races. I can't tell him.

I just got Tommy. I can't lose him.

"Princess? You all right?" Darius's tone is too soft.

I swallow and turn to the machine as another ball comes flying at me, and I swing. "Fine."

He relaxes back into the fenced cage, and I try not to pay attention to him as I stare the machine down and another ball flies at me.

"You still mad at Tommy?"

"I was never mad at Tommy," I grit as I hit the ball. Hard.

"Really?" He smirks at me as I hand the bat over, and we switch positions. "Cause I swear we could've frozen Hell over with the amount of tension in the kitchen this morning."

"We had a disagreement," I finalize. "I'm not mad at him."

"Mhm."

He swings, and his hit is so much more graceful than mine. I can see two girls off to the side staring at him swooningly.

Thankfully, he doesn't pay them any mind. The last thing I want is to stand around while he flirts with some girls. And since he and Laura are only fuck buddies, and as long as they're honest about it—for safety purposes—they can sleep with whomever they please. There's a chance it could be more than just flirting. So I'm extra glad he's more focused on me because the last thing I want is to stand around while he gets *flirty* with them.

Instead, he looks at me and changes the subject. "Your hit is still pretty spot on, Sister. Did you practice across the pond?"

Baseball is a minor sport in England. And I didn't exactly have my brother around, and this was something I liked doing especially with Darius. "No. I'm just that talented."

He rolls his eyes with that cocky grin and swings as another ball comes flying at him. "Good. We need that talent when Mom and Dad get here. They always wanna get competitive even though we'll definitely win."

Dad was a huge baseball player growing up, so his swing is better than mine and Darius's combined, but Mom sucks so it gives us a winning chance. "Mom and Dad are coming?"

He rolls his eyes. "They insisted. Even when I told them this round is just for us. Dad was super excited."

Other than coming here with Darius alone, the family trips were my only other excuse to be here. Dad and Darius's competitiveness make it especially amusing.

I smirk. "I bet."

We switch positions again, and Darius spends the next twenty minutes we wait for Mom and Dad telling me about the current house they're working on. Apparently, they're adding a whole section of the house, and it's almost done. They're just hoping to have it finished before Lynette gives birth.

Then our time of just the two of us is disturbed.

"Hey, Buttercup," Dad calls out to me with a smirk.

Darius punches him in the arm. "That's not funny. They're fighting right now."

"Oh?" Dad turns a feigned worried look on me. "Does that mean you're distracted?" He turns to Mom. "We're definitely winning."

I gasp, and this time, I'm punching him. "Shouldn't you be threatening anyone I'm in the middle of a fight with?"

Dad rolls his eyes. "Between you and Tommy? Please, I won't waste my breath. You two love each other too much for me to even consider it a problem."

I fight the smile because of course he's right. "I'm gonna kick your ass."

"Mhm." His eyes twinkle down on me. "Buttercup."

I raise the bat at him. "Stop it, Father. I am not afraid to use this. That is *my* name for Tommy, and no one else is allowed to use it."

I don't care if Tommy's mad at me right now and technically no one—other than Nana and Papa—knows about us; he's mine.

Mom's eyes twinkle now. "So possessive."

I know they're trying to rile me up so I do poorly and they win. I inhale a large breath rather than falling for it. "I hate you guys."

Dad pulls me in and kisses my crown as we all settle to the side of the cage, and the competition between parents and kids begins.

We got home late the night before, and Tommy was already crashed out on the couch since I'm sleeping in his room. More guilt hits me because it's his room, he shouldn't feel the need to sleep on the couch. Especially after what we've done together.

But that's my fault too. I'm the one who insisted we don't tell Darius.

But Tommy should've slept in his bed. Next to me. Because I want him there and because it wouldn't have been the first time we slept next to one another. Darius wouldn't have been suspicious.

But he's a deep sleeper, and he looked so peaceful last

night, I didn't want to wake him to tell him that much. Especially considering he was still angry with me.

Sleeping in the sheets that still smelled like our night together was also nice—because even though it's sort of gross, I didn't have time to change the sheets and I sort of love that I didn't. Love that it plagues me with the memory of what we'd done.

In the morning, even though he's still visibly angry, Tommy keeps his promise. He wakes me by rolling me onto my back and kisses me a few seconds longer than I would've expected. "Good morning," he whispers before leaning in for another kiss as I come out of sleep.

Then he pushes away and is out the house before I can process any of it.

The kiss doesn't mean he isn't angry with me. It simply means he never makes promises he doesn't keep. But fuck, I wish he would've stuck around so we could talk about this.

It's about a half hour later that I'm fully dressed in a flowy summer dress and my white Vans. I'm finally throwing the sheets into the wash and placing a clean set onto the bed. Then I down a bowl of oatmeal mixed with berries and cinnamon before I'm ready to leave. Because I'm not going another moment of allowing Tommy to be angry with me.

It's another hot day out and another hour and a half's walk to get to the job site. I purposefully didn't do my hair, knowing it would get messed in all the sweat from the sun beating down on me anyway. At least I'll have a killer tan with all this walking.

When I get to the site, the men are all drenched in sweat, and half of them have their shirts off. Tommy is still wearing his, and I have a feeling that's to hide the marks I left on him the other night. Even though he wants Darius to see them, wants Darius to know. I love that he's angry with me, but still respects my wishes.

Then I hate myself a little more because he has to suffer beneath the shirt just to keep my wishes safe.

Darius isn't here though.

A quick question to one of the men tells me he's out back. Perfect. He won't see me. At least not until I have the opportunity to speak with his best friend.

I walk right up to Tommy, the dust and dirt all around him, and finally catch his attention.

"Emory." He pulls his gloves off, lets them fall to the floor, and moves to me. "What are you doing here? You'll get dirty. You shouldn't be breathing this in."

He has stains all over his face, undoubtably from when he went to wipe the sweat, and the dirt from his arms marred his face. And this look—this utter show of masculinity—is turning me on way too much. I need to focus on apologizing first. Then I can taste him the way he tasted me the other night.

"Where's the bathroom?" I ignore his question.

His brows narrow, but he points behind me and I take his arm and move.

The men aren't really paying attention, and even those who do see us don't bother me. Darius has made it so known that the three of us grew up together that I don't think they'll think anything of it.

Or maybe they will, and they just won't gossip about it to their boss.

When we stop in the bathroom, which is thankfully further away from the working men than I'd originally thought, I lock the door and turn to him.

He still looks confused. "Emory…"

"I'm sorry," I blurt and step up closer. "I'm sorry that I'm making this so difficult on you, and I'm sorry that you hate me for it."

"I could never hate you, baby," his tone softens.

"Figuratively, I'm sorry you hate me. But I can't." I don't know how to talk about it, since I've never really had to. "I can't lose you, Tommy." I take another step closer. "I'm sorry if for whatever reason you think you're not good enough because trust me, you're the best man imaginable." Closer. "I'm sorry you think your parents being assholes makes you less desirable, but I need you to remember that they're not your family; we are." A final step so I'm less than a foot away from him. "And I'm sorry that you think I want a man in an expensive suit at some corporate job. I'm sorry that you think I want anything other than what I'm looking at right now."

He doesn't move for long moments as he stares between my eyes and lips and back again like he's trying to figure something out. "I want to tell him."

I know he can see the sadness fill my eyes. "I know."

He lets out a breath. "But I won't make it an ultimatum. This is our relationship. If you're not ready to share it with the world yet, I'll deal."

"But I don't want you to *have to deal*."

He moves to cradle my face but pauses when he remembers his state at the moment. Even with the gloves on, sweat and dust cover his hands.

I take his wrists and move his hands to my face. "I like dirty, Buttercup."

He tries to struggle away. "If I stain you, the others will know."

I quirk an amused brow at him. "I'm on a construction site. I could easily have done this to myself."

He struggles with himself, but finally he lets his hands cradle my face. His thumbs rub smooth little circles on my cheeks. "Emory, baby, I'll give up my life to make you happy." I go to shake my head, but he stops me. "I'll do it all to make you the happiest person to exist. That's why I want your brother to know. Because this is it for me." My heart stops, and I know he can see the joy of his statements in my eyes. "But I can wait to tell him. Nothing about us is going to change."

Hearing those words from him, that assurance in us, makes me want to make *him* the happiest person in the world. Coupled with the fact that I'm ridiculously wet from seeing him sweaty and stained and working, I can finally give in to my desires.

I push his chest so he slams into the wall behind him. He looks flabbergasted, but the look quickly changes as I push a rag left on the ground before him and drop to my knees. "Then let me make you the happiest person too."

My hands are at his belt, unbuckling, when he says in hushed tones, "Emory, your brother is out there! You just said you don't want him knowing yet!"

I smirk up at him as the belt comes undone and the button pops open under my fingers. "Then you'll just have to be quiet."

His zipper falls, and I'm pulling his briefs with his jeans straight down so he springs free, cock already growing harder with each passing moment.

I lick my lips because wow, does he look delicious.

"Emory," he breaths down to me.

I look up at him as my hand reaches for the base of his cock. "Shh."

His hands slam into the wall and sink on either side of him as he watches me. Watches my hand slide up his shaft and my mouth kiss its way down. Watches my tongue lick the veins up the side to the very top before taking just the tip into my mouth.

He's breathing hard, but he's quiet. *Good Buttercup.*

I suckle, then pop him out licking back down then up. I watch him through my lashes and love the sight of him barely controlling himself. But now, play time is over. I want to taste him.

I take him in my mouth again—as much of him that I can fit—and let my hands play with the bit that's left over. Then he's mine. All. Entirely. Mine.

Through my lashes, I see he's biting down on his bottom lip to keep from making noise; his fists slam into the wall and sink to keep still. He's really doing his best to make sure we're not caught. Though I know from the sounds I'm making alone, if anyone passes the bathroom door, they'll know exactly what's going on in here.

And part of me doesn't care. I'm enjoying this far too much to care. I really wish that part was alive in me more often.

His hand reaches for my hair so he can lead me, and I whimper at the control he has on me. A moan escapes his lips which only makes one escape mine and vibrate over his cock.

His head slams into the wall, and his breathing is becoming labored, and it all drives me to please him more. The feel of him filling my mouth is so good, I cannot understand how anyone doesn't enjoy the act.

My hand slips to his balls, and I give the boys some attention as I take him as far back as I can and choke on his hard cock. Anyone passing by the bathroom will definitely know what is going on in here.

He groans and his hips are thrusting in time with my head, so he's fucking my mouth. Just the taste of his pre-cum is amazing, I can't wait for the full thing.

I push my mouth off him and gasp for air, and he seems to come alive with the act. There's an animalistic look in his eyes as he stares down at me while I lick down his shaft. "I want to taste you, Tommy."

I lick his balls and allow my teeth to lightly graze over them as my hand pumps his cock, and his hips roll with it. "I was so jealous when you tasted me the other night, and I didn't get a turn." I suck on his balls again then go back to playing with them as I make my way back to the tip. "Come in my mouth, Tommy. I'm drooling at the thought of tasting you."

I take him into my mouth again, and Tommy gives me what I asked for. He's always been like that, giving me what I want when I want it.

I pull him out just enough so he doesn't shoot into the back of my throat. I want his taste on my tongue. I want to relish in it.

Then he's finally coming, and I'm rewarded for my good job when I taste him on my tongue, all over the inside of my mouth, dripping down the sides of my lips. He's delicious.

His head slams the wall again, and as much as he tries to keep quiet, a groan leaves him, and his breathing is too labored to be silent. But I can't be any more bothered at the moment because I'm too busy lapping up every bit of his seed. I want to swallow every last drop.

When he comes back to reality and looks down at me, I smile. My hand is at his hips, playing against his skin, and I kiss one hip. "I'm kinda hungry for more."

He groans and pulls on my hair to lift me to my feet. "When we get home, you're getting more, baby girl."

I don't have time to smile before he's kissing me, our tongues fighting.

He pulls away when there's a knocking at the door. We both hold our breaths until we hear Octavio on the other side, "You two may want to get out of there. Darius is coming in."

Perfect timing.

But. Wait.

I turn on Tommy. "You told him!"

He scoffs, buckling his belt. "I didn't have to say anything. He knew it the moment he saw the two of us together."

I blush. I knew it was too obvious. Exactly why we don't need to go around telling everyone.

His hand is at my back, and he leads me to the door and opens it. Octavio is standing on the other side, a smirk so big on his face, I know he heard every little sound. I snuggle into Tommy's side to shrivel away from it, and both boys laugh.

I hide my face in his side and punch him lightly. "It's not funny."

"Hey, baby girl, you came to me." He's definitely not shy about what we just did or that his best friend just heard us.

"Let's go, princessa." Octavio nods toward the front where I can already hear Darius laughing with a couple of the guys.

CHAPTER 15

Tommy

FAMILY BBQS HAVE to be my favorite days.

Closely followed by Tuesday takeout nights, but topped only because this one includes Nana, Papa, Octavio, and Lynette.

And today, Lynette isn't too tired to join, so everyone is over.

We're not having any grilled meats. So I guess technically, it's not a BBQ. But the family is together on Sunday afternoon, and we're sitting out at the outdoor table. A family picnic.

Emory made a caprese board and grilled some bread to make mini sandwiches.

Nana Isla made southern sweet tea and sausage rolls while Lynn made focaccia sandwiches.

Even Lynette made cookies—both snickerdoodle and chocolate chip—because even though everyone insisted she didn't have to make a thing, she wanted to be included in the cooking.

The women wanted full control this week, and who was I to decline them that? Though, only this time around. I love grilling for our BBQs, so I couldn't give that up completely. Plus, I feel that same inclination to feed them that they do to feed us. Love being the one to take care of them in that manner.

Emory's sitting across from me at the table, but I can feel her foot sliding up the inside of my leg, from ankle to thigh and back again. She switches legs often, but all of it is the same amount of torture.

And she knows what she's doing too because as Darius tells the others about the next two jobs we have—ones Octavio won't be joining on since Lynette is so close to due— she eyes me with a glint in her eyes. And her fingers dance across her lips as she eats a sausage roll, effectively hiding the cunning smile from the others around the table.

But I know the smile is back there.

There are so many things I'd like to do to that mouth. And those tits. And her pussy.

Especially her pussy.

I adjust myself on my seat, and her foot grazes my hard-on, sending an extra jolt of sensations through me.

She laughs at my discomfort, and all I can think is how badly I want to get her somewhere private and make her pay for this. Bend her over and ingrain my handprint on her ass.

She's doing a great job of being inconspicuous though because even Octavio isn't giving me his knowing look.

Then she pulls her phone out as Atti and Calvin begin talking about some fun projects we boys could do for Nana and Papa.

Then my phone vibrates, and I'm so glad no one is paying attention to me or looking over my shoulder when I read her message.

If I spread my legs even a little bit, the wind will pick up how badly I want you. Quite inappropriate with my family around.

I close my eyes to try to control my urge to jump over the

table and drag her inside. When I finally peel them open and look up, Emory's not even paying attention to me.

At least, it doesn't look like it. But that smile that's wide on her lips tells me she's picking up my every reaction.

But it's also a grin that could easily be passed off as being happy to be around the family.

I put my phone back down and choose to ignore her.

Her foot plays against my thigh, and my hand reaches down to stay her. This is torture, but also way more fun than I've expected. Maybe keeping us a semi-secret wasn't such a bad idea.

"You don't need a chicken pen," I argue because now Papa Atti is coming up with ludicrous things for us to build. And I know it's only to stand over us and boss us around.

Another vibration. *You think if I go to the bathroom and touch myself, you'd be able to lick it off my hand without the others knowing?*

My hips jerk involuntarily on the chair, and I try to cough in order to mask my reaction. Again, so glad the others are too distracted with all the projects they're stacking for me and Darius. Even Octavio is joining in the fun because he's going to be on paternity leave, and he's using it as an excuse to not be able to do a damn thing. Even though we all know he'll get restless and need to build something. Like the crib we've helped him build from scratch.

I'm imagining you taking that beautiful cock in hand and jacking off while you stare into my eyes.

A growl leaves me, but luckily, it's soft so only Lynette hears it beside me, and I'm hoping she's guessing I'm dealing with business emails on my phone.

Stop. It.

But if I make this fantasy a clear one, we can reenact it later.

I take a deep breath and put my phone into my pocket. If I leave it on the table and it continues to vibrate, the others will ask why I'm ignoring it. Darius will try to take my phone and look at the messages. And as much as I want my best friend to know about us, this definitely isn't the way I want him finding out.

My pocket vibrates, but I ignore it.

"We're not building you a chicken coop, old man," I get back into the conversation around the table.

It vibrates again. This time I take the leg she has stretched out between mine and play with her calf, teasing it beneath the table.

"Why not?" Atti asks indignantly.

"Because we all know you're afraid of chickens. You won't be taking care of a damn thing." Darius laughs at him.

"Not to mention, you're not stinking my yard like that," Nana grumbles with a humor-filled glint in her eyes.

"Our yard," Atti argues, but the same glint is in his eyes.

Two more vibrations before Emory finally throws her phone down and glares at me. She even tries to pull her leg away, but I don't allow it. I like touching her.

"Emory." Atti turns to her. "What do you think? Should I get the chickens?"

Emory peels her eyes off me, and a light blush fills her cheeks at being the bearer of all the attention. I'm guessing that has more to do with where her thoughts are at the moment than because she doesn't love attention.

She stutters for a moment as my fingers graze the back of her knee, and I know she's getting wetter without having to smell or feel it. "I'm on Nana's side. Whatever she said."

Atti grumbles. "Knew I should've asked Lynette."

"You should've." Octavio laughs. "She would've definitely been on your side. I won't let her get chickens."

Papa Atti tries to turn on her, but Nana Isla is already laughing. "No, no, no. Too late, sucker."

Emory laughs, and that sound fills me with so much joy.

The look in her eyes as she glances my way is the beginning and end to my source of happiness.

CHAPTER 16
Emory

WE GO on a date with Darius the next day because he complained after everyone left last night and Tommy and I were making plans without him. So finally, we feel bad enough to give in and allow him to come.

Darius and Tommy are showered and ready within half an hour of getting home, and the three of us are on our way.

We stop for dinner first because the boys still haven't eaten, then we'll be on our way to the fair arcade. It's a place that was made by a couple who wanted to take their children to the fair whenever they felt like it, so they made an arcade with all sorts of fair games.

They even had a few of the smaller fair rides.

We used to go as kids and the boys would fight over who could win the most points for my prize. I was one lucky girl.

We're at a Thai restaurant that Tommy and Darius both swear by. I order a cashew noodle but am so ready to steal from Tommy's fried rice and lomein noodles. Maybe even from Darius's drunken noodles and Khao pad jungle beef.

We're at a round table, and it's only noticeable if you really pay attention, but Tommy is definitely sitting closer to me than he needs to. His leg touches mine with every bounce, and I have to stop myself from playing footsie with him.

"Did you see what Octavio sent earlier?" Darius asks.

"The video of him carrying Lynette? Yeah. She's huge," Tommy responds, and I smack him for it.

"She's not huge. She's pregnant!"

"Pregnant and ginormous. That stomach of hers is swallowing her whole," Tommy defends himself.

Darius throws Tommy a warning look. "Ooh, Tommy, you don't say that to women."

"You don't say that to pregnant women. I didn't say it to Lynette. I'm saying it to Emory." His smile says he thinks he's right, and we can't do anything to change that.

I narrow my eyes at him. "So if I were pregnant, you'd call me huge?"

"What? No. I just said you don't say it to the pregnant woman," Tommy says.

"So you'd lie to my face and talk behind my back?" I cross my arms, and he knows he's in trouble.

He looks to Darius for help and only gets a smile in return. "Told you."

"Emory…" he reaches out for me, but I lean back.

"Don't you mean big fat whale?"

He grabs my arm and forces me into him, hugging my reluctant body close. "Stop it, baby. You're not pregnant, and when it does happen, you're going to be fucking beautiful, not huge."

I look up at him, indignant. "So Lynette's not beautiful." I have my mom's love of instigating too.

He throws his head back. "You've got to be kidding me."

"I told you not to do it, man," Darius says though his smile shows he's enjoying watching his best friend get in trouble.

He looks back at me. "Of course she is."

"Hm." I eye him up and down. "These the types of compliments I should expect when I'm huge?"

I pull away, but his arms don't release me. His eyes tell me that he's serious as he forces me to look up at him. "Baby girl, you're going to look so damn sexy when you're pregnant. I honestly can't wait. I think about it all the time."

My heart stops.

He thinks about it.

"Think about what?" My voice is soft and barely audible as I ask, and Darius kicks Tommy under the table with a "Dude, that's my baby sister."

A tiny smile grows on Tommy's face as he ignores Darius. "Your giant belly in an oversized button up as you try to make breakfast, all barefoot and beautiful."

He knows he's forgiven by the look on my face because that was so sweet, I'm melting.

Darius rolls his eyes but laughs anyway. "Good one. I'm gonna need to use that."

"Fuck off." Tommy smiles at his best friend.

"Yeah, Darius, fuck off," I say as Tommy finally releases me from his hold. "I am gonna be sexy all barefoot and gigantic. Just like Lynette is right now."

His smirk says he knows he's about two seconds away from being the one in trouble. "You're an Aabeck, of course you will be."

The food is placed before us with large cups of water, and we're all breaking chopsticks for our meals.

Darius turns the conversation back around. "But Lynette *is* huge, like can pop any day. I can't imagine how nervous Octavio is."

I smile because that's actually kinda sweet. "I think he's ready."

"Oh, he's definitely ready," Tommy says. "He hasn't shut up about it since he found out."

I smack him again as I mutter, "Asshole."

He winks at me, then takes a mouthful of noodles.

"Are you ready?" I turn to Darius, then realize I want to hear Tommy's answer too. "Both of you. Are you ready to become fathers?"

Darius laughs through a scoff, but his attention remains on his food. Tommy's gaze shoots to mine, and he just stares at me.

"Definitely not," Darius says at the same moment Tommy mutters a soft, "Yeah, I think I am."

Now Darius's gaze shoots to his best friend. "What? Since when?"

Tommy looks at him and shrugs. "Recently."

My heart's beating a million miles a minute. He's ready to become a father? He's recently made that decision? Recently as in thinking of me barefoot and in his huge button down with a nine-month belly.

This should be too much. Too fast. Too...scary.

But, surprisingly, it's not. Because he's thought of us having a baby. Of *us* starting a family. I can't breathe; I'm so awestruck.

"No, no, no, no, no, no," Darius interrupts my thoughts. "You cannot be having a baby too. Both of my best friends cannot become fathers without me. Plus, you're not married!"

Tommy smirks. "I can remedy that quickly."

Darius looks heavenward like anything could help him at the moment. "You've got to be kidding me."

I laugh because I know Tommy's not kidding.

"I think I might be ready too. Soon...ish." I say partly to drive Darius just that little bit crazier and because I haven't realized until Tommy said it, but the thought of a family with him fills me with so much excitement.

Now Darius's head snaps to me. "*You've* got to be kidding me." He looks between the two of us. "No. No, you guys aren't really thinking about this. Wait until Lynette gives birth and that kid tortures them with insomnia. Then you'll get your heads out of your asses."

I scoff. "Don't be an asshole, Darius. You're going to be an uncle."

He rolls his eyes to calm himself because he knows he's close to getting in trouble and doesn't want that. "You have to do things to become pregnant. Things that are not a part of your world, Emory."

I roll my eyes now. "I've had sex, Darius."

He yells, and his hands are covering his ears. "La la la… "

Tommy looks at me, and we laugh. And his eyes twinkle in a way that's just shy of innocent.

Definitely falling in love with this man.

I quickly get dressed to drive to the job site with the boys in the morning—after an amazing, want-to-throw-him-into-the-bed kiss from Tommy—because I want to watch them again.

And because I heard Lynette would be there, and I want to keep her company.

It's not nearly as hot of a day as it has been this summer, so when we sit in the truck, it's not horrible. Still bad, but manageable.

Plus, we're parked under a shaded tree, so there's nothing beating down on us.

And if pregnant Lynette isn't complaining about the heat, I definitely won't be. Though Lynette does start to complain when Octavio comes over every half hour to ask her again if she's sure she doesn't want to blast the air in the truck or for him to take her home.

Octavio doesn't stop though. I don't think he can. I think he's so obsessed with his little family, he always wants to do the best for them. Offer his wife the best. He was the best.

"You better watch out, Lynette," I say after she shoos Octavio away for the fourth time, and I'm feeling the baby in her stomach kick. "I might steal him from you."

She laughs as the baby gives a major kick as if to say, '*You better stay away from my daddy.*'

"Let me know now. I can tell Tommy he's gonna be a father before the baby comes."

"Hey." I shoot angry eyes at her.

She smirks. "You steal my man, I'll steal yours." Her eyes sparkle under the shining sun. "Especially after I hear he's ready to become a father."

"Octavio," I shout. "Lynette's ready to go home."

Lynette laughs at me, but my call was heard, and Octavio is opening the driver's side door and getting in beside his wife. Lynette had to take the middle of the long seat since her belly is too round for the driver's side, and she's now cocooned between us.

She doesn't even give her husband the chance to make a sound. "She's kidding. I'm perfectly comfortable. And enjoying watching you sweat out there. It's making me horny for when we *do* get home."

Octavio's normally a quieter guy and not too public about the things he'd like to do to his wife, but he smirks at her now. "Then let's go home now."

"Well, that's my cue to get outta here."

Lynette grabs my arm and stays me before turning to her husband. "She was kidding. And I can wait. Now go back to work."

He gives her a lingering kiss and obliges.

She turns a smirk on me while her hand lands on a kick I *see*. "I thought there was nothing going on between you two."

I roll my eyes and turn back to the site where the men are walking in and out of the house sporadically, so I can't actually see Tommy. "Your husband heard us in the bathroom."

She laughs, then after a bout of comfortable silence, she asks, "So how is it?"

"What?" I turn and instinctively reach my hand for her belly when I see another kick. It's such an exciting and thrilling experience, feeling baby Rodrigez even before birth.

"Being back. Leaving Europe. Your parents took us out to the shops the other day and were telling us stories of some of your adventures. They sound epic."

A warm smile reaches my lips. "They were epic." There's a light, insistent kick, like the baby is telling me to continue talking. "I spent a good amount of time studying because obviously I didn't want to fail out of the program, but I wasn't bent on being a top student. Just enough to get through and be able to explore. So most of the exploring was done on breaks—summer and winter holiday mostly since they don't have Thanksgiving or Spring break. Though we did have an Easter break, so I guess that was Spring break."

"Sounds like a pretty good excuse to not come back in my book." Lynette's gaze hovers past me, and I turn to see the boys walking out before quickly making their way back in.

That short sighting of Tommy, though, is invigorating. He's so sexy on the job. Too much so that I'm kinda glad they're inside for most of it.

Plus, they're inside where the AC can blast and at least give them a little break from all the sweat that coated their skin.

I turn back when they're completely out of sight. "It was. I don't regret my adventures. I just wish at least once I would've thought to use an Easter holiday or part of the winter or summer ones in order to come back. A week. But I don't regret it. I got to go to every European country. It's a once in a lifetime opportunity, and I'm glad I took it."

Lynette smiles down at her bump as she softly rubs it. "I

hope Baby also takes an opportunity like that. Though how we'd afford every country is kind of another story."

I laugh. "My parents mostly only paid for the living expenses in London. I was there on scholarship, and my flat was a uni one, so almost like a college apartment rather than a dorm. My parents paid for that and my groceries mostly. Sometimes they'd gift me with enough money for a weekend trip, other times I paid for those."

"I thought you traveled on holidays," she interrupted.

"Mostly," I answer. "But some weekends I would go to Scotland or the Cotswolds. Wales or just another city, like Manchester or Brighton. I wanted to see the U.K. too while I was living in it."

"And you paid for it?"

I give a cheeky smile. "Not all, but as much as I could. Most everything, but there were a couple of trips Darius and Tommy sent me as a present. My Christmas present two years ago was a trip to the Swiss Alps." I turn back to look at the site even though the boys are inside, and feel another profound wave of love pass through me for them. "And a few others over the years, usually the more expensive places. But mostly, I paid for my expenses. We were given opportunities at jobs, and I would use all the money to take my trips. I picked up some freelance work online for most of the other money, and I paid for my way through the continent."

When I turn back, she's smiling at me. "And being back?"

"Amazing." The baby kicks at my hand again, and my grin widens. "I miss the traveling, sure, but I can get the boys to go with me next time. We can check out the U.S., then Canada, or fly out together. It's just incredible to be with them again. There's a sense of safety and peacefulness I don't feel anywhere else."

Her hand lands on mine. "Maybe in a few years, when the

baby is a little older, we can take one together. Maybe to London, and you can show us your stomping grounds."

I laugh. "Sure. But how are we certain that'll happen?" At her furrowed brows, I wiggle my own. "What if you get pregnant again and again. Then we'll have to keep waiting for the next one to be older."

She pushes me away. "You sound like my husband. He's already talking about the next one. I won't blame him because he didn't have siblings, so he wants to give our child one right away, but not you too!"

I laugh again. "Don't worry. We'll travel no matter how pregnant you are or little the baby is, but right now, I'm just happy to be back in town. I think I needed this break from it all."

When I turn back around—because Lynette is looking past my shoulder again, which means her husband is out, and I hope that means my man is out too—and meet Tommy's gaze, my heart explodes. He's walking toward us, and in no time, he's leaning into the window. Octavio is at Lynette's side, so we get our little semblance of privacy as I lean into him.

"Thank you for keeping her company." His mouth is so close to mine, there's no hiding there's something going on between us.

"Don't thank me like it's a chore." I kiss him quickly because I can't help it, then pull away before any of his men come out and see us. "Anyway, she's got me reminiscing on my travels so we need to choose where we're going because I cannot wait to travel with you."

He smirks. "Africa, remember?"

"I thought that was our honeymoon?" I'm joking because it's way too soon to talk about marriage, but his eyes shimmer.

"It is."

My breath hitches, and I push him from the window. "Get back to work."

He pulls at my arm, and my face is flush with his as he kisses me then whispers against my lips. "I'm sending your brother out tonight. There are some things I'd like to do to that mouth that he doesn't need to hear."

I pull away before anyone else walks out, but my cheeks are flaming. I'm glad it's hot out, so I can just blame it on that.

I push at him again, but it's much weaker. "Go."

He winks at me and walks backward a few steps before completely turning around.

When he's gone, I turn back to see the wide grins on Lynette and Octavio's faces and have to hide my own giddy one. "Shut up."

CHAPTER 17

Tommy

DARIUS STOLE Emory away after work, and I'm bothered by how my skin crawls at not seeing her. I've spoiled myself with the sight of her every night.

I'm also annoyed I wasn't able to convince him to go with Laura, so I can't do those lovely things to her mouth.

But it's a good thing too because he deserves time with her as her brother. Even though I want to selfishly hog all of her time for myself.

And it means we can take things slower.

Which was something I told myself we'd do from the very beginning and lost the battle to immediately. Keeping her away from me at least helps with the slow part.

Though, not really.

She's still all I can think about. Still plagues my every sense with her scent filling my room and the memory of her flashing before my eyes every other second. The sound of her laughs filling my ears in the silence of the house. The feel of her on my skin even though I'm alone. The taste of her on my tongue.

It's all there, and none of it seems in the mood to leave me be. My mind's own form of torture.

I've jacked off twice now, but the memories seem insistent on keeping me hard as a rock.

I do what I'd done all those nights Darius would go out and I'd stay home before Emory came back—put some mindless sitcom on the T.V. and open my laptop. Except before, I would check on Emory's safety—news in London, weather, anything important we should know about. I may not have spoken to her much while she was away, but I never stopped thinking about her.

And when that was done, sometimes I'd spend time researching costs on different trips to see which ones Darius and I could afford to send her on. Those were the few times I'd actually get on FaceTime with her—to tell her about whatever trip I was ready to pay for. I still remember those smiles every single time I insisted and she tried to refuse me. It brought me and Darius so much happiness to create those smiles.

So, in a way, I understand why Darius won't question us even though I've seen his brows furrow in our direction a few times already. And that brings me back to feeling like an ass for not telling him.

I throw on a rerun of The Big Bang Theory and open my laptop. I don't have to check up on whatever city she's in because she's safe here with us, so I'm free to do whatever I want.

So I do the next best thing and look up houses for sale that we could possibly buy to flip or just invest in.

Darius and I have a pretty full schedule for the next couple of months, but considering it would take time to find a house we all loved and for escrow to go through, it's still something to think about. Especially since we've been talking about it for a few months now.

Plus, Emory is here now, and we can rely on her to help us with anything we need.

The thought brings a grin to my lips. When we were growing up and helping Calvin out with projects around the house—the way Darius and I found out we enjoyed construction—Emory would always insist on being part of the projects. Even if it was only catching us whatever tools we needed or holding up a plank of wood for ten minutes straight. She always did it with a wide grin on her face. She loved Darius so much, she always wanted to spend time with her older brother. Even when said older brother made her hold a plank of wood for ten minutes straight, and her little arms were shaking by the end of it.

Emory would always be dirtier than the two of us, but she'd always be so happy by the end of the project that we could never deny her the opportunity to join. That was around the time we'd become the three of us. She'd been around eight or nine; we were four years older, and instead of seeing her as the annoying baby sister, we saw her as the princess that deserved to smile larger than life.

My grin grows at the memory.

Emory will like the opportunity to spend some time with us during projects on a new house the way she did when we were younger. She can't do so now because they're actual jobs, and we're on schedules and don't have time to take it easy and goof around. But on our own home, I could teach her how to do every single project. I could teach her how to use every single tool—though from all the time she spent with us, she knows way more than the average person.

And most importantly, I could bring back that goofy laugh and those shining eyes every time she worked on a project with me and Darius. Calvin had always been fun on those projects too, so it could be some nice father-daughter time.

Plus, I think she'll enjoy some quality time with Octavio and Atti if they ever want to join.

Overall, the more I look at these houses that all need some fixing up, the more excited I get about the possibilities with Emory there. I think Darius will love the sound of it too, if only to make Emory happier. He was honestly such a great brother to her that I cannot fathom why she has such a large fear of telling Darius about us.

But the more I think about it, the more I want her by my side.

I don't want to bother them while they're having a siblings' night, but I miss Emory in this couple of hours more than I did the entire four years she'd been away.

I can't help but pick up my phone even though I know I should leave them be.

She's mine tomorrow night, I text to Darius because there's no way I'm giving up two nights alone with her.

He sends back an emoji with a tongue sticking out and a *She loves me more, loser.*

We'll see about that, I send back because I already know she prefers her time with me.

But I also know how I can guarantee she'll have a better night with me tomorrow.

CHAPTER 18

Emory

ALL I GOT out of him was to wear something casual. Tommy was real helpful like that.

But since he refused to give me any more information on what we'd be doing, I dress in similar shorts and shirt I wore on our first date.

"It's the lake, isn't it?" I might be a little too excited.

"It's a little dark out to be going to the lake right now, don't ya think?" he makes fun of me.

I roll my eyes. "We're going in the same direction."

He smirks at me. "And that's the only thing in that direction, right?"

I shove him and send a few choice words his way under my breath, but he only laughs.

We're in their work truck instead of Tommy's car, so it also makes me wonder why. I have a feeling though, as I sit pressed against his side; it's only because this truck has one long seat so we can sit together.

About five minutes later, he asks, "Would you trust me enough to close your eyes until we get there?"

My curiosity insists I don't, but I can see he wants me to,

so I relent. I hold the forearm of the hand he has on my thigh as it jitters against his leg. "I've always trusted you, Tommy. And I always will."

He smiles down at me as I relax against his side and let my head fall back as I go through every memory of Tommy.

And for some reason, one of when I was eight and he was twelve comes to mind. He and Darius were a little bit meaner at that age, but middle school did tend to be the worst time.

I had told everyone about the imaginary world I had created and all the adventures I went on in the backyard, and they'd all laughed at me for it, but I hadn't let it bother me. I spent that entire summer creating this fantasy in my head, all with costumes—made by Mom—laws—made by me—and little sets for the different parts of my fantasy—made mostly by Dad.

It was a couple of months before Dad started asking the boys for help doing odd projects—and in turn, a couple of months before I insisted on helping too. But it was the reason he got the boys started. I'd asked him to make me a little throne because as princess of my kingdom, I needed a throne. He'd made it, then decided this was the sort of thing I had an older brother for, so he started the boys into working with their hands.

But I had my imaginary world, and I was happy until the boys, being the assholes they were at that age, decided they were bored one day and began messing with all of my things. My laws that were meticulously written out. My costumes that I'd spent all summer with Mom making—a total of three dresses, a cloak, and simple armor, because I was a badass princess. And my beloved little set.

Mom and Dad had gone out for a few hours, and the boys were annoyed that they had to stay at home with me rather than be allowed to go out skating around the neighborhood. So they'd retaliated and tried on my costumes, which on their double-my-size bodies had ripped the already poorly made pieces.

They'd been careless as they'd flipped through the pages of the world I'd built and laughed as they recited some of the pages. Half of those pages ended up torn by how roughly they passed my little handmade booklet between the two of them.

And finally, they'd messed with my little set. Thrown the pieces around until they broke and took their turns kicking at my little throne. Since it was made of wood, nothing happened to it, but they'd enjoyed how much it had bothered me.

It was definitely the meanest they've ever been to me.

But I hadn't allowed myself to cry in front of them. I'd held my head high and promised myself I wouldn't show them weakness.

Then I told the only lie I've ever told my parents and said everything had gone perfectly and they had been the best babysitters. And promptly headed to bed and cried myself to sleep.

When I told my parents I was too tired to play in the morning, Tommy came to my room, and he looked so upset. I promised I hadn't said anything to my parents. He insisted he knew, that they weren't in trouble and my parents simply thought me past that stage. Then he took the seat beside me on the rug as I held my little doll and hugged me as he whispered how sorry he was.

I accepted his apology instantly because I've never been one to hold grudges, but I promised myself that day that I'd never tell anyone about the things I loved, lest they go and destroy them.

By the next morning, when Darius still hadn't apologized, Tommy had beat him so hard, Mom and Dad had had to pull them apart from each other. But eventually, Darius looked me in the eyes and sincerely apologized.

That's the day that comes to me as we drive to who knows where—Tommy after he got into his first fist fight with my brother. Because of me.

The scratches on his face. The ripped shirt. The dirt marring his skin. His clenched fists and determination. He didn't need to do anything, but he felt so badly for what he'd done that he'd done everything to make it up to me after that. Even as Darius went on to torment me for a few more months before it all stopped, and I solely became *princess*.

The car stops, but Tommy insists I keep my eyes close. I hear him talking to a guy but can't make out enough to know where we are.

Then we're driving again.

And stop. For good this time.

His breath at my ear sends shivers down my spine. "Open your eyes, baby girl."

When I open my eyes, I gasp and can't imagine how big they widen. Because I've been here before. *We've* been here before.

Except last time was an accident.

I turn sharply to him. "Tommy, what the hell are we doing here?"

His smirk is way too wicked for that charming face. "We're watching a movie, baby."

"No." I shove away from him. "No, no, no, no, no. I am *not* watching a dirty movie with you! With other people around!"

That smile is too cheeky. "Get back over here, Emory."

I push into the door of the truck. "No!"

His hand slithers across the space that separates us and coils around the belt loop of my shorts. He pulls me into him with no effort at all.

"Tommy!" I try to push away, but his hand at my waist makes my attempts futile.

"Settle down, baby girl." His hand slips beneath my shirt and is skimming by my shorts. "We always have fun on our dates, remember?"

"Tommy," I gasp because those fingers are very distracting.

He pushes me to sit beside him so I'm facing the screen. He's still facing me though, and his face is so close to mine, I feel his breath on the side of my neck. "Ready to watch the movie now, baby?"

I swallow and try to keep my breathing even. "We could've watched a dirty movie at home."

"But we're not watching a dirty movie." His lips tease my ear.

I turn sharply on him. "No?"

His fingers trail up to my jaw and force me to turn back to the screen. "No." He kisses the spot at the back of my ear. "You're going to watch and tell me what happens. What you want me to copy afterward."

I moan and no longer have any power over my reactions to him—the breathing, the sounds coming from my mouth, none of it. I especially lose control when he notices and chuckles against my ear. That sound sends shivers down my spine and makes my pussy throb with need.

I moan again because I'm at his mercy.

He's pleased and kisses my neck as his hand travels down my chest, lightly squeezing my breasts before continuing down slowly. "We're going to have fun on this date, aren't we, Emory?"

The screen brightens as I nod slowly. A few production studio names pop up before music starts thrumming through the speakers. At least they're setting up for a storyline. Even though porn storylines are always the worst.

I almost laugh when the storyline ends up being a construction worker over to do some work on the house.

"Talk to me, Emory." His breath hits my neck, and that hand is hot on my stomach. I can feel it burn through my shirt.

"Construction." My back arches as if that'll get him to move his hand, but it doesn't work. I lick my lips, imagining Tommy right when he gets home from work. "I like men who work with their hands."

"Lucky me." His breath tickles my skin.

My eyes flutter closed as the image of Tommy coming into the house after a long day of work filters through my mind.

"Eyes open, baby," he demands. "Or I stop touching."

My eyes shoot open, and I'm watching the barely dressed girl show the construction worker what she needs help with. I should have him stop touching me because we're in public, but I don't want to. I need his touch, crave it like I do air.

Tommy's hand finally skims the edge of my shirt and my core tightens and my pussy throbs at the sensation. "You're not talking to me, baby."

"She's...she's getting help with some damage she caused to the walls."

Those fingers continue skimming the edge of my shorts as his teeth nibble at my ear. "Is that something you need, baby? Fixing up a wall?"

I have a vague recollection of buying fixer upper houses and huff out, "Maybe when we get a place."

My eyes are latched to the screen, wanting desperately for something to happen between the two already so Tommy can touch me where I want him to. And surprisingly, I don't care that we're a parked car in a field of parked cars. Though it's dark and the light from the screen is the only illumination, I don't care if anyone sees us.

"He's fixing up the wall, sweat dripping off of him. He's

dirty from the work," I moan at the image of Tommy working again.

My thighs rub together for some friction, but Tommy's leg falls over my thigh and keeps my legs apart. "No cheating."

"She's offering some lemonade..." I mutter as Tommy suckles behind my ear, and my back arcs again to get that hand to slip lower. It works a little.

Then finally. Finally, finally, finally.

"She's sitting on the couch, watching him, and starts touching herself," I cry out.

His chuckle at my ear almost has me coming on the spot. "Yeah, baby girl? You touch yourself thinking of me?"

"Every day," the honest answer comes out before I have time to filter it.

But I'm rewarded with that sexy chuckle.

"Her legs are spread..." He drops his leg from mine and spreads my thighs apart. "Her hand is between her legs..." His hand finally slips beneath my shorts—when he unbuttoned my shorts, I'm unaware. "She's rubbing on her clit..." His fingers slip through my wet pussy and circle my clit as he moans into my ear.

That one sound in my ear is so much better than any of the sounds coming through the speakers for this movie. So much. So fucking much, my hips buck into his hand.

His fingers finally reach my clit and rub slow circles. The woman in the movie cries out the man's name the same moment I cry out Tommy's.

My eyes flutter closed at the sensations.

And instantly, his touch is gone.

My eyes snap open and over to him as he says, "Eyes on the movie, baby."

I grab at his forearm and pull his hand back to where I'd like it as I turn back to the screen. "Okay, just don't stop touching me. Never stop touching me."

"What's going on in that movie, Emory?" His tone is demanding, and I get wetter at the sound.

"She's fucking herself and…" Tommy's finger slips inside me, and I gasp. "And he's watching, moving toward her." Tommy's thumb is rubbing on my clit as another fingers slips in, and I clench around him.

"Tommy, I'm going…" I can't even warn him as I explode around his fingers. I hadn't even realized I was that close.

But Tommy doesn't stop. His fingers continue moving in and out of me, and that thumb continues its pressure. "Keep going, baby."

A groan mixed with a moan escapes the back of my throat as the man drops to his knees and starts eating the girl out. "He's licking her, sucking her clit, fuck," I exclaim. "He's eating her out!"

Tommy's chuckle is dark at my ear as his fingers keep their rhythm. "Is that what you want? For me to eat you out? Suck on that pussy, baby girl?"

"I want it now!" My hips are moving with his fingers as my body gets close again.

He tsks at my ear. "We can't be greedy, baby. I said we were watching for what we'll be doing later."

I groan, but I can't peel my gaze off the screen. "His fingers are fucking her as…" My pussy clenches around Tommy's finger as he continues his movements inside me. "As he…he sucks…fuck!"

My body bucks, and I hold onto his forearm for dear life as my pussy clenches around his fingers, and I cry with another orgasm.

The speakers tell me the girl in the movie is crying out too, but I'm too focused on my own pleasure, at the pleased sounds Tommy's making at my ear.

"Keep watching, baby," he demands, and I can hear the restrain in his voice.

But his fingers never stop inside me, that thumb never stops around my clit, and I know his entire hand must be wet now because I've completely soaked through my shorts.

"She's sucking his dick. Fuck, baby, I want to taste your cock," I moan out.

He growls into my ear. "You're definitely getting everything you want later, baby girl."

My head shakes involuntarily. "Now! I want your cum in my mouth."

He bites the side of my neck. "Watch the movie, Emory."

Thankfully, they're over that part rather quickly, and now he's fucking her. My pussy throbs at the sight, and I come again as I scream, "He's fucking her, Tommy. Please fuck me, Tommy, Tommy Tomm..."

My nails are scratching at the arm of the hand in my pants as I come, and Tommy growls at my ear. It only draws my orgasm out.

"I don't think my body can take any more," I whimper as his other hand joins the party and slips from my back, around my body until his free fingers are at my nipple. That other hand never stops pumping in and out of me, and it's all too much.

"Your body can take everything I have for it, baby girl."

I try to focus on the movie instead of his touch everywhere. "He's fucking her." But now I'm just thinking of Tommy fucking me, of his touch. "I want your cock stretching my pussy, Tommy."

"Give me one more," he demands. "Come for me one more time, then maybe I'll cheat at our little game and drive us somewhere more private to fuck you. We can play out this movie later."

I cry out so loud, I don't even hear the moans from the movie any longer as I come around his hand. I should be more annoyed that my body's ready to give Tommy everything, but not an ounce of me cares.

When I finally come down from this high, his hand slips out of my shorts, and I'd been right, his hand is completely soaked.

He brings that hand to his mouth and sucks it clean. The sight makes my pussy clench again, needing his cock now more than ever.

"You taste so fucking good, baby," he mutters as he sucks at his hand.

My hand involuntarily flies to the speakers of the car and turns them off because I want to hear Tommy, not the movie.

"Tommy…" I whimper.

He gets a final taste of his hand, then turns the car on. "I know, baby. I'm gonna find us somewhere a little more private."

I can see how hard he is and the moistness of his pre-cum through his pants. Then I look up at his handsomeness.

I'm so distracted watching him that I barely turn in time to notice a few people in the cars around us staring our way. And I can't find a bit of me that cares that they probably saw what was going on in our truck. Maybe even heard a bit of it.

CHAPTER 19

Tommy

EMORY IS AT MY BACK, arms wrapped around me while I grill steaks for today's family BBQ. I can feel her breathing in my scent and biting my back every time I make a joke about her. To be fair to her not wanting to tell her brother about us, she hasn't been shy about showing Darius.

He just seems blind to it all. Though I have caught a couple of suspicious looks our way this past week, but he keeps pushing them aside rather than acknowledging them.

I genuinely cannot imagine any action but kissing Emory that will convince him there is something more. And even then, part of me thinks he'd think we were joking. But at least it'd be enough for him to ask.

But would he? If he thought we were joking, he'd probably push us away from one another and punch me, but he'd laugh it off rather than ask any more. I don't know what to do to get him to move beyond the suspicious looks and ask already.

Because that's Emory's one rule—the important thing can be known by anyone as long as they ask about it first.

Everyone else seems to be very aware though. Nana Isla

and Papa Atti since Nana caught us kissing in the office. Octavio and Lynette since he heard us in the bathroom, not to mention both couples have been able to tell from the beginning. Which gave me the opportunity to kiss her in front of the latter the other day on the job site. I don't know why since I've kissed her plenty on our dates, but something about having people in our lives see us kissing excited me. Like its own form of showing off our relationship.

Now all I wonder is how bad it would be if Darius found out. Emory seems fine with the four of them knowing, so how bad could it be?

But then I remember that Emory has always insisted on keeping important things most private from those she is closest to because it is their opinions that matter most to her. Her parents, Darius and I—but especially Darius and I—are always last to find out about things because she actually cares about our opinions. Other people, she usually lets slide and doesn't think about twice.

And though she may really like, even love, the four of them, it's not the same as the relationships she already has with us.

I wonder if Calvin and Lynn can tell. I don't know, but part of me thinks they can see it. The other part thinks they see us the same way Darius sees us: just two kids that grew up together and are now very comfortable with one another.

I feel rather than see Darius smack Emory on the head with a rolled-up paper plate. "Leave the poor man alone. It's bad enough you have him taking you out on dates every other night. Let him at least grill in peace."

I smile because I have been taking her out basically every other day, but that's only because work has been cooling down this week. There'll be weeks when we hardly get one date in, so I'm taking advantage while I can.

My one hand is holding the tongs to flip the meat, but

the other reaches for the ones she has wrapped around me and holds them close so she doesn't let go. "I like her like this."

Darius rolls his eyes. "Of course you do. Any repellent so I don't take you out on a double date with sure things! You did the same thing years ago."

"What makes you think I'm not a sure thing?" Emory jokes from behind me.

Darius's face twists in disgust as Octavio and Lynette laugh from my other side. "Don't be gross, princess."

Lynette is sitting on a chair in front of Octavio since her belly makes her tired in seconds. Her hand plays with the ones Octavio keeps on her shoulders as she says, "It's not gross. She's an adult and very entitled to an active sex life, especially with…"

Darius doesn't let her finish, but I know she was going to say my name. "She's my baby sister, and she doesn't have a sex life. That's not even a thing in her world."

"Oh, behave, Darius," Nana Isla calls from the table where she's mixing a bowl of fruit salad. "The girl has every right to the releases she desires."

Darius looks sick with the comment, but its Calvin who interrupts. "All right, I think that's enough about my daughter's sex life."

Emory laughs into my back and gives it a small kiss before pulling away. "Steaks smell like they're almost done. I'm gonna help Mom bring everything else out."

"And you can go grab the cheesecake I left in my fridge, Darius," Nana Isla tells him.

Darius isn't going to refuse Nana Isla, but he exaggerates an annoyed hop as he leaves for the house across the street.

I laugh and watch Octavio help Lynette to the table with Nana and Papa. Then I'm placing the cooked steaks on a platter for everyone to grab from.

I'm almost done when Calvin steps up beside me and watches. "You're her best kept treasure, aren't you?"

I look up to him with a furrow between my brows. "What?"

"Emory. She keeps her most prized treasures private as can be. She's not talking about you, but she's also not hiding it. She used to do that about going to school in London too. She never spoke of it, but she made it obvious that's what she cared about most."

I remembered. She was too scared to jinx herself out of going so she never said anything.

I shrug because technically I'm not telling anyone until Emory feels comfortable with it.

He smiles. "I just don't see how Darius doesn't see it."

I relent to answering, "He's used to this. Em and I always used to cuddle and hang out just the two of us. It's more normal to him than anyone else to see us cozied up. Plus, I think he thinks the four years away are just making us a bit more affectionate, but that it'll go away in a few more weeks."

He nods. "You are his best friend and brother. Of course you would understand the lunacy behind his reasoning for being blind to it."

I laugh and I guess this is my way of confirming our relationship to her father. "Not like he's doing it on purpose."

Now I just need Darius to ask me some leading questions too.

Calvin laughs. "No, I suppose not."

I look at him and evaluate his expression. He doesn't look upset about the idea of my being with his daughter. About my possibly—definitely—being sexual with his daughter. His little girl.

I think he sees the uncertainty on my face because he says, "I've always seen you as a son, Tommy. This just means you're legally going to be part of the family. Plus, you know

Lynn is happy about it. She's been dreaming of this moment since the day Em started calling you Buttercup."

I smile. "Yeah, I remember her little insinuations that we would be cute together."

"She was right." He tips his beer to me, then takes a swig.

I don't say anything, but my smile says it all.

Darius is knocked out in his room, the snoring carrying into the hall. I shake my head as I move for my room, hoping for a good night kiss from Emory before heading to the couch. I was an ass for not waiting it out before we had sex, but I'm trying to be better about sleeping arrangements. I don't want to assume it's all right when it's only been a couple of weeks.

And when she's keeping us *private*.

She's sitting in the armchair in the corner of the room with a journal and pen in hand when I walk in. She looks at me for only a moment before saying, "Take your shirt off."

I know the smirk is cocky as I oblige her command.

She nods toward the bed. "Lie down. On your stomach."

I quirk a brow in her direction. "Excuse me? I kind of need my front half if we're going to do this."

"Do it," she says with an eye roll, and again, I oblige.

I hold myself up on my forearms as I turn to watch her disappear into the bathroom. What the hell does she have planned?

She walks out with a bottle of oil in hand. Then she's on the bed, moving up my body on her hands and knees. She bites my ass and I laugh. "Hungry, baby?"

She kisses the small of my back as she moves to straddle my ass. "You have a perky, beautiful behind, Buttercup."

She pushes the middle of my upper back so I can no longer hold myself up and fall straight down. I hear the bottle open and feel the oil hit my back.

"A massage?" I ask as I turn my head to try and look at her from my periphery.

"Yes, sir." Her hands are rubbing the oil all over before starting at my shoulder blades and pressing in. She applies the perfect amount of pressure.

I close my eyes and relax into it, feeling like the luckiest man alive. "Do I get to know what I did to deserve this?"

Her fingers dig into my muscles, and I feel a knot loosen in my shoulder. It hurts, and I groan to let it out, but it also feels amazing. "You're you. Sometimes I like doing these things for you as much as you like receiving them."

"You're telling me you enjoy giving me a massage with no ulterior motives?" It's almost too good to be real.

"Do I enjoy the opportunity to touch all up on you *and* hurt you a little bit? Yup, love it."

I chuckle. "You're an asshole, baby."

"In the genes, Buttercup."

She pushes into one particularly painful knot, and I have to fist the sheets to keep the groan low. She laughs but doesn't stop.

"Fucking asshole, baby girl," I grit out when the groan subsides.

She leans down, her hands gliding up and down my back, and whispers into my ear, "You can punish me for it later."

I bite down on my lip and pretend I didn't just hear that because now my cock is awake.

She grows serious, lips teasing my ear as her fingers continue to massage up and down my back. "You do so much, Tommy. You said it the other day. Physically put in the work, breathe in that smell, stain your skin in that dirt. All of it to be this successful. You deserve far more than a lousy massage."

"There's nothing lousy about this massage, baby, I can

guarantee you that." My muscles will be dancing in gratitude tomorrow.

She bites down on my ear and is sitting back upright. "You know what I mean. I like doing things for you. I always kind of looked down at housewives and stay-at-home moms, but what they do is a whole job too, and I understand it better now. Somehow even Mom being one hadn't shown me as much as this. Before, all I saw were women serving their men, and I never realized that they may really enjoy doing so. Because I do now. All I think about when you're away at work is what I can do to make life at home easier for you."

I smile. "Is this your way of telling me you don't want to get a job, baby?"

Her fingers move up my spine, looking for another knot to torture me with. "I think I'll probably end up picking up something small that I enjoy, like Mom does. But something full time and legit nine to five? No, I don't want that."

Her voice sounds far off, like she's in thought about the life she has envisioned. And I think she's using this opportunity of having my back to her to tell me something she's scared to talk about. Not because it's something she needs to keep private, but because she's scared of my reaction.

"I like that picture too, Emory. I can't tell you how much I've been dreading you getting a job and not being home to do the cooking and cleaning and laundry and all around run the house. I've gotten way too used to this new way these couple of weeks."

The first thing Emory did when she moved in was getting the food prepared when we got home from work, but it didn't stop there. After that, when Darius and I were at work, and Emory wasn't with Nana Isla and Papa Atti, she was cleaning the house and preparing meals. She organized everything and made a system for keeping the yards looking clean— something Tommy and I neglected most of the time though we tried to keep up with it. It was such a relief to come home to a hot home-cooked meal and a clean house. Such a relief not to have to spend our nights cooking when we were tired and our free time cleaning around the house.

Nana Isla has always tried to help with the hot meals, but these past couple of weeks have been different. Maybe it even felt different to me because it's Emory doing all of these things for me. I want to praise her to the stars and back because she does as much for us domestically as we do for her financially. More even.

She leans down and kisses the spot between my shoulder blades. "Good."

I flip us, so she's beneath me, and kiss her because she deserves that and so much more. I give her another kiss and sit up. "I should go. We need to get some sleep."

She pulls on my hand when I go to get out of bed and pulls me down. "Stay here. It's your bed, our bed. Sleep in it."

I smile. "Our bed?"

She shrugs, uncertain. "Isn't it?"

My hand cradles her face, and I lean in to kiss her. "Yeah. Yeah, it is."

CHAPTER 20
Emory

I HEAR Darius in the kitchen when I wake up, but Tommy is still asleep next to me. I love this—waking up with him beside me. It's not a matter of 'I could get used to this,' but a matter of 'I'm already used to this.'

I let him sleep as I get out of bed and head into the ensuite to get ready for the day. Then I move to the closet for some clothes. Funnily enough, I placed my clothes into his closet when I moved here, so we were sharing a closet before anything happened between us.

I know Tommy is really asleep because he doesn't make any lewd comments about my nakedness as I get dressed in the middle of the room. Poor baby, he must be so tired.

This is part of what I wanted to give him—the peace of mind that I'd take care of all home problems while he's at work. Or while he's resting because he deserves this. I never want him to worry about taking care of domestic matters ever again. I want to take care of him as much as he works to take care of me.

I move to him even though I don't want to disturb his sleep because I love our good morning kisses. He's on his stomach, facing my side of the bed. I lean over his form, feeling up his back as I move to hold myself up and kiss him once. "Good morning, Buttercup."

I don't realize he's awake until I go to move, and suddenly I'm flying through the air.

I hit the mattress and his entire body weight is on me. His head lies on my chest, and his arm and leg are thrown over my body so I can't move. His eyes are still closed when he says, "Where do you think you're going?"

"Darius is awake. I'd like to hang out with my brother too!" Part of me really doesn't want him to move because I love having him on top of me, but realistically, I do want to hang out with my brother. "C'mon, baby. Move."

He groans but moves off of me so I can get up again.

He pulls on my arm so I drop back down to him, and before I can reprimand him for it, he kisses me. "Good morning, baby girl."

I smile, give him a final kiss, then leave him sleeping in the room.

Darius is still in the kitchen when I walk out. "You know where Tommy went?"

"He's in his room."

Darius's brows furrow, but the look is gone so quickly, I'm not sure whether I made it up or not. Then he looks completely unconcerned with hearing Tommy's in his room. Maybe Darius doesn't think Tommy slept there all night. With me. Or maybe he doesn't care because we used to sleep together all the time. I don't know, but he's not asking so I'm not telling.

"Good," he says. "Then you're free for me to take out. Without the sister stealer."

I smile. "Yes, I'm free. That's why I came out here. Figured we could do something."

"Great. We can grab breakfast first!"

He drives us to a small diner about ten minutes away that the three of us came to every summer growing up. For some reason, only the summers.

We're sitting in the booth, looking at the menus as the waitress brings us waters and fills our cups with coffee.

She's walking away when the curiosity finally seems to catch up with Darius. He looks up at me with furrowed brows. "What was Tommy doing in his room? I didn't hear him walking around."

My heart stops. The more people that actually know, the more possibilities of disaster.

But Darius is my brother and Tommy's best friend. I shouldn't be worried. He may be slightly angry and definitely annoyed with hearing the two of us have the hots for each other, but Darius wouldn't wish anything but our happiness.

So I'm about to tell him that Tommy stayed because I wanted him to stay with me. Because I've got it bad for Darius's best friend. Because these dates we've been going on are real dates and not just us hanging out.

But when I open my mouth, all that comes out is, "He was sleeping."

He quirks a brow. "Where did you sleep?"

"In his bed." *Tell him it's because you're really in a relationship with his best friend.* "I figured it's his bed, there's no reason he shouldn't be able to sleep in it as well. It's our bed now."

His lips tip up.

Is Darius happy about it being our bed? Maybe I can tell him, and everything won't blow up in my face.

He rolls his eyes with a smirk. "Kinda like how my bed always became our bed when you couldn't sleep?"

I throw a sugar packet at him. "I was like five."

The waitress is back to take our orders, and I'm not surprised by the expansive one Darius gives. The boys sure do love to eat. And they need it too. With all the physicality that goes into their work, they need to load up on their calories.

I order a veggie omelette with dry toast.

When the waitress leaves, I stare at Darius and am about to tell him about Tommy when the memory of him kicking my throne comes to mind. How it was all going perfectly until it wasn't.

I know it was a long time ago, but my mind can't shut it off.

I also know Tommy is to blame as much as Darius in that scenario, but again, my mind doesn't seem to care.

So I don't mention Tommy. Won't mention anything until Darius asks me because I won't lie to my brother. That's the deal I made myself after everything—I wouldn't lie to those I cared about, but I also wouldn't voluntarily tell them anything I hold close to my heart.

It's worked perfectly with getting me through life. I'd had everything done—grades, extracurriculars, applications, scholarships, anything imaginable— before my family found out for certain that I wanted to go to school in London. I've always known they'd suspected, but I think they thought since I didn't mention it, I wasn't serious about it. I think that's when they really started learning that it was quite the opposite for me.

"So..." Darius takes a sip of his coffee. "Tommy mentioned you wanted to go back to your volleyball practices."

I smile. Tommy has been very excited about the booty perkiness volleyball is known for. "I missed playing. I'm thinking about joining a club. I figure at least once a week would be nice."

He smirks and wiggles his brows. "As long as you introduce me to the girls on your team."

I throw another sugar packet at him. "Never."

Monday and Tuesday end up being really long work days for the boys, so I don't add any pressure for Tommy and me to do anything. I actually really enjoy just spending time at home cuddled up on the couch with him and Darius. I think Darius still seems to think we're just cuddling like we did when we were younger and that it doesn't mean anything. Although, I do catch a couple of furrowed brows our way that are gone before I can really place them. I think he's fighting his own mind on the obvious.

But he's not asking about it.

On Wednesday after dinner, I expect us to be doing the same thing when Tommy smacks my ass as I'm putting leftovers into the fridge. I jump as I search the room for Darius and remember he's probably in the bathroom now.

"Go get dressed, baby girl."

"What? Why?"

"I'm taking you out." He's standing so close all I can smell is him.

"Baby, no. We don't have to go out. I like staying home with you guys." I don't want him going out if he's tired.

"I do too, but I want to take you out." Before I get the chance to fight, he throws in, "Plus, we're going to the movies. Nothing exhausting about that."

My smile is wicked as I stare up at him, and I know he's also remembering our last trip to the movies.

"Not that kind of movies." His breath brushes my lips, and I feel the tingling down in my core.

"Shame," I tease as I play with his shirt.

He chuckles, and it's so sexy. I'd much prefer to stay in for the night and let him take advantage of my body. "How're you gonna get Darius not to join us?"

"He's getting ready for his own date tonight. Found a new girl he likes." His brows dance because we both know Darius's end goal.

I laugh. "Okay. Give me ten minutes."

Darius is gone before I'm done getting dressed. He yelled out a "Don't wait up for me," and poof.

Tommy chooses the three-dollar movies that show oldies. My favorite.

Bonus, this theater is one of those that has reclining seats and every imaginable snack for reasonable prices. Tommy can afford to take me to a regular theater, but why would we ever do that when we have this one?

There's a showing of *Casablanca*, my mom's favorite.

There aren't many people here on a Wednesday night, so there's no one sitting around us. Extra bonus.

We move the armrest between us, and I snuggle into him. We have a slurpee, a large popcorn, and three bags of candy, and we're ready.

His fingers are skimming my arm as we wait when he says, "You know when we used to come here, and you would choose to snuggle with your brother instead of me, I'd get so jealous. I'd get antsy, like I couldn't focus knowing you were cuddled with him instead of me."

I look up at him and try to hold in my giggle. "Is that why sometimes when we would talk about the movie afterward, you would have no idea what was going on?"

He nods as a chuckle rumbles out of him. Poor kid was missing whole chunks of movies because of it.

"You could've said something," I say.

He scoffs. "And let your brother think I had a thing for his middle school aged sister? Absolutely not."

I hide my giggles in his neck, then look back up at him when something occurs to me. "You didn't like me back then either, right?"

"No." Both hands are wrapped around me now. "No, I just…I was so used to being the one you'd cuddle with that when you chose him, it got on my nerves."

"You're lucky it never got on his nerves that I basically always chose you."

He rolls his eyes and gives me a knowing smile. "Trust me, he was glad you chose me."

My mouth opens in an O. "Well, all right then, Mr. Cockypants."

He laughs. "He knew you started choosing me because you didn't like how much he talked about girls and liked that I kept it wholesome around you. Plus, it meant that whenever a girl *was* around, he wouldn't have to worry about you because you'd just snuggle up with me."

I've always cuddled with Tommy and Darius, but I started almost exclusively choosing Tommy around eleven. So when the boys were fifteen. Yup, right around the time Darius lost his virginity, and the whoring became a thing.

"Yeah, ruined your chances with the girls, though, didn't I?"

He considers it. "Yeah. Sometimes I was thankful, other times…" He shakes his head.

"You were thankful?" I quirk a brow because I definitely wasn't expecting that.

"When I didn't want to be on the double date. Those times it worked in my favor that several of Darius's previous girls had gotten it around school that 'we were together' so no one wanted to date me." He kisses me. "But then the times when I wanted the double date, or when I wanted a girl, and she'd also heard the rumors, not so good."

Mom had always insisted Tommy and I be there whenever Darius had a girl over. She didn't make me suffer through it whenever the double dates actually worked and Tommy also had a girl, but when it was just Darius, Tommy and I were always there too. Because Mom also insisted the first date—first few dates really—be watching movies at our house.

"The girls knew we weren't together, though, didn't they?"

"Yeah. I made it clear. Darius made it clear. And a lot believed us. But a lot were skeptical too. Some thought Darius believed it, but that I was hooking up with you on the side. Which, mind you, would've been disturbing. I mean I was sixteen and you were twelve. The four years mattered a lot more back then."

I kiss his throat. "I'm sorry for ruining your chances."

"I'm not." He tugs me so I'm basically on top of him. "It got us here. It means I didn't whore around as much before having you. It means you were mine before I even knew it."

"You're a little too romantic, Buttercup. It's making me feel like I need to step up my game."

He furrows his brows in a serious manner. "You do."

I push away, but he pulls me right back to his side. I look up at him and love the way his eyes shine down at me. My heart patters in my chest as I stare up, and I know I'd be content looking into his eyes for the rest of my life. "Well, Buttercup, who knew the skeptical ones would turn out right?"

He laughs as the speakers tell everyone the movie is about to begin. "Yeah. Gotta love those skeptics."

CHAPTER 21
Tommy

WE'RE at the hardwood store to pick up some materials for the kid's shed Lynette wants us to make for a woman she's become friends with at her pregnancy groups. She likes going to learn, but mostly to be around other pregnant women who have the same fears as her. Octavio says she's been calmer since going, and this girl, Ella, is the main reason why.

So I'm going to build her the best damn little shed ever.

Ella's pregnant with her third and runs the pregnancy group because she was in the same state as Lynette when she was having her first, so now, she helps first time expecting mothers.

Darius already has long slabs of wood in our panel truck, and Octavio is sifting through little windows while I look at colors. They have a girl and boy already, so I want something neutral, but fun.

I'm trying to stay away from the Lilac Camisole color that keeps calling my attention because it's feminine in its light lavender hues. But it's the perfect color for a little playhouse.

Next one's also a girl, so little man in the middle might have to deal. Teach him young to treat his sisters like queens and compromise for their benefit. Darius does it for Em all the time and has no complaints. He loves treating her like a princess and being the macho older brother when needed.

"I told Darius I want a homemade seesaw for my kids." Octavio's hand slams into my back.

A chuckle rumbles out of me as I turn to him. "Right after the treehouse. I'm looking forward to chasing after your little one. What do you think we'll pretend first? Pirates?"

Octavio laughs. "Or princesses."

"Princesses against pirates." I wink at him. "Aren't there romances about stuff like that?"

Octavio's grin is wide. "Teach 'em young to want a hard-working man instead of a pretty palace boy."

"Treehouse, seesaw, barbecue area." Darius's hand lands at my other side and the three of us are hip to hip in front of the paint colors. "You guys are gonna need a bigger place. We'll have to buy out the houses next to each other soon."

"Don't let Em hear that. She'll have five houses lined up in ten minutes. I let it slip the other day I was looking and she damn near flew out of herself in excitement."

"Don't worry. It won't be so easy. We need the houses together, Tomás," Octavio says in that accent of his.

I quirk my brow at him. "Give her a few extra hours. She'll find people willing to sell next door to each other."

Darius laughs. "He's not wrong."

Octavio squeezes my shoulder. "We can deal with that later. These first few months are already gonna be hell."

"Don't worry. Uncle Tommy will be there." I look at my best friend and imagine him with a baby. I've done it multiple times since finding out about Lynette, but now that the time is dwindling down, everything is feeling so much more real.

"Yeah." Darius clings to Octavio's back as if our presence would be a comfort to the baby. "And Emory will chastise us if we get anything wrong. She's already planning on kicking you guys out on a date night when you're allowed to have sex again."

Octavio shrugs with a wide grin. "Tommy y la princessa will get their practice in."

My gaze shoots to him in warning, but Darius merely laughs. "And I'm chopped liver?"

"Nah." Octavio's eyes are genuinely bright. "You'll make them a great uncle too."

I know he means for our kids, mine and Emory's together, but I also know how that could be misinterpreted to meaning mine and Emory's separately. I almost want to shove Darius because I've seen him come close to questioning us—me especially—multiple times before backing off. Even if he asks as a joke, I just want to shake him out of the clouds he's stuck behind.

But I can't do it, so I turn back to the paints and have a flash of Emory holding Octavio's baby as we babysit for the night, and I can't help but feel my heart skip a beat. "It *is* a nice picture, huh?"

Darius throws his arm around my neck and brings me in close. "The best, Brother."

The guilt makes its way back, but I ignore it.

I push him off me. "C'mon. We have a playhouse to build."

I scour the paints and settle on Skylight, a mix between baby blue and grey, but take my phone out to take a picture of the Lilac Camisole color for future reference.

Darius's habit of going away for the weekend—which coincidentally started when Emory got back—is really working in my favor.

My Saturday started with Emory straddling me, slowly riding my cock until I was wide awake. And when complete clarity filled my brain, she picked up her pace. It was the most glorious way to wake up. Ever.

Unlike the last weekend we had to ourselves when we went hiking, this time we choose to stay in.

Emory has one of my lousy button ups on—basically one of those that I wear to work—because she says she likes that I sweat in it all the time. It's clean now obviously, but she says just knowing I get dirty in it does it for her. Kinda gross, but she's into it.

Then we're in the kitchen making breakfast.

I ready the pancake mix and start a batch as she cuts the fruit and gets out the OJ and syrup. I have two pancakes done when she pops onto the counter beside the stove.

I'm only in sweatpants, and she doesn't try to hide her roaming eyes. To be fair, I don't try to hide mine either; she didn't button up the shirt all the way.

"You know," her finger trails my arm, "we could always skip breakfast and go back to the bedroom." I'm about to respond when her finger reaches me jaw. "Or better yet, we'll stay here. Just have another sort of breakfast."

I try to hide my chuckle. "I swear it must be in the genes. Your mind is always in the gutter."

"I've got a thing for dirty things." Her tongue lines her teeth as she finishes speaking, and it takes all of me to wrench my attention from staying fixed to that spot.

"I'm starting to believe it." I mean, she chose to be with me, and I get gross and dirty for a living.

"Good." She pulls me over. "So let's dirty the kitchen."

"Emory," I reprimand as I pull away and drop another two pancakes on the plate. "Your brother eats here too."

"I'll clean before he gets back." She brings me between her legs.

"Emory." I pull away and step out of reach, then pour the

final batch of pancake mix to cook. "Breakfast is the most important meal of the day."

Her eyes widen. "And I'm offering you breakfast."

I laugh. "Stop it, baby girl."

Her arms cross before her chest and my attention drops again to the opening. Her nipples are covered but her breasts are in full view, and they look delicious.

"Yes, sir," she says slowly, and by the look in her eyes, she knows what calling me sir is doing to me.

Luckily, Emory doesn't try anything with the syrup. She just eats her breakfast the same way she would if Darius was sitting with us. And I love knowing I get forever of this because one thing's for certain—I'm not letting go of her.

After eating, then cleaning the kitchen, we're back in our room, and I'm lying back in bed while Emory is in the bathroom. I'm scrolling through the photos and videos on my phone. There're a lot of Emory, of the two of us together. Most of them are innocent.

Her smiling at me in the canoe on our first date. Us cuddled together at the dance bar when the elderly couple insisted on taking a photo of us. Her selfies whenever she stole my phone in the car or at the house. Us lying on the couch on the nights we didn't go out. Her flipping me off on mile almost four of our hike. Us covered in mud. Her smiling at me on our first night sleeping together. Us at the grill, a photo Nana Isla or Lynn must've taken while Tommy insisted sex didn't exist in Emory's world.

There're a couple of short videos too, but not many.

I can remedy that.

I turn on the video on my phone when I hear her coming out of the bathroom.

She takes three steps and stops when she notices the camera on her. "What are you doing?"

"Capturing memories." My smile is wide.

"Oh." Her smile turns cunning. Then her fingers are moving to the buttons of the shirt she's wearing and slowly unbuttoning one of the four buttons actually fastened.

"Emory." My voice is stern. "What're *you* doing?"

"Giving you a memory to capture." Another button slowly pops open, but her arms are doing well in keeping the shirt in place, so nothing shows.

"Baby girl," I'm trying to reprimand her, but the need is clear in my voice.

Another button.

One final button holds the two pieces together before she's naked.

She bites her lip as she eyes me, and her fingers fall to that final button.

The shirt doesn't move from its original position even after all the buttons are loosened. She's doing a good job hiding any nakedness from the camera.

She loosely holds the folds together and gives me a spin. "You should flip the camera on yourself. Now that's a look you want captured."

"You're a tease, baby girl."

She tsks. "That would mean I don't intend to execute." Her tongue slowly licks her lips, and her eyes challenge me. "Or are you too tired? Unable?"

I growl and drop the phone to jump out of bed for her.

She screeches and turns to run, but my arms are already around her. I have her thrown on the bed in seconds, and I'm holding her arms above her head, so I have all the control now.

And because she's so graciously unbuttoned the shirt, it falls open, and she's completely at my will.

"Want to say that again?" One hand holds her arms down as the other begins to caress her body until it reaches my favorite best friend between her legs.

She struggles under me—poorly—but her gaze tells me she's not backing down. "Are you impotent, Buttercup?"

I growl again, and my sweatpant-clad hips thrust into her naked sex and she arches into me with a moan.

"Does it feel like I'm impotent, baby girl?" I'm doing better at controlling myself than I thought possible.

She shakes her head.

"Emory." My voice is demanding.

"No. Sir." She knows exactly what she's doing when she says that.

I thrust into her once more, then pull away so my fingers find the little nub at her center again. Her moan is so loud, I'm curious whether the neighbors can hear it.

She's slick between her legs, and I wonder how long it would take to get her to come by only touching her clit.

She reaches her head up to kiss me, but I pull away, holding her arms down tighter to get her to stay still.

"Tommy." Her hips thrust up at the same moment her back arches.

"Still feel like teasing me, baby girl?"

She can't answer through the incomprehensible things coming from her mouth.

Turns out, the answer is not long.

Not to that last question, but to my original one. How long would it take to make her come only rubbing on her clit? Not long at all.

She spasms beneath me, and it's one of the most erotic visuals of my life. "You are the best moments of my life, Emory Aabeck."

When she calms, and her lips try to smile up at me, my fingers dip and enter her, and her chest hits mine in pleasure.

I pump my fingers in a few times, then take them out and bring them up to her lips. "Have a taste of my favorite meal, baby girl."

Her gaze never leaves mine as her lips open, and she takes my fingers into her mouth, tasting herself.

I lied. *This* is the most erotic thing I've ever seen.

She moans as her gaze remains on mine, and I can't help it any longer. I thrust my hips into her. Now we're both moaning.

When there's nothing left on my fingers, I pull them away. "Now I'm ready to kiss that mouth, baby."

Her arms struggle against the hold I still have on them as she reaches up, and I meet her halfway.

I can taste *her* on her tongue. I want to fight that tongue, defeat it, and take the taste entirely for myself. I want all of it. All of her.

I'm growing harder by the millisecond as I continue thrusting into her, tongue and sweatpant-clad cock.

I can't take it any longer. I have to be inside her.

I already have condoms sitting on the nightstand in preparation for today, so grabbing one is too easy.

I'm running out, but I gotta write a thank you letter to Darius for giving me these condoms. And for giving us the day alone.

I'm sitting up in bed with Emory between my legs. Her legs are wrapped around my waist and hold me tightly as if she wants to cling to this moment. I know I do.

We're both naked, but there's nothing sensual about it at the moment. It's more an intimate meeting of souls than the sexual matter of us.

My fingers play with the hairs that insist on falling onto her face as my free hand traces up and down her back.

Her hands are coiled together at the back of my neck as she stares at me.

"What're you thinking about?" Her voice is soft, gentle.

Women have a thing for asking that question. Lucky for her, I suddenly always had an answer for her because she is always on my mind.

"I'm thinking about how incredible it is that we grew up together our entire lives, and I'm just now realizing that I'm in love with you."

She doesn't look scared by my admission. She just smiles like she knew how I felt about her already.

"I think about that a lot."

"That I'm just realizing I'm in love with you?"

She gives me an annoyed smirk and a small eye roll that has more love in it than any other expression ever could. "Yes."

I finally get that piece of hair to stay behind her ear and cradle her face. Her eyes are so full of trust, it's all I can do to calm my racing heart. "I'm so in love with you, Emory Aabeck."

Her fingers move to trace my face. "And I'm in love with you, Thomas Buttercup Rutherford."

I snort out a laugh and mutter, "Asshole."

"It's a family specialty. Get used to it." Her forehead leans into mine, and our lips are almost touching.

"I'm going to have to if my kids are also going to turn into assholes."

"We have strong genes." She kisses me. "There're no ifs about it."

I laugh and hold her close as our lips meet.

CHAPTER 22

Emory

THE OFFICE IS NOW clean but nowhere near where it should be for me to make it my room. I've now organized everything into cubbies with tags indicating what's in them and put them onto four large shelves that span the back wall.

The desk is clean, and I can finally see every bit of the surface. The papers within are organized, though I didn't move their position. If either Tommy or Darius put something in a specific drawer, it will still be there. I definitely don't want to be messing up and losing their things while they're off working.

After that bit of organization, it's instantly recognizable that there isn't much else in the room. Now it looks sort of bare.

Or maybe that's my excuse to take my brother shopping.

After that, it's time to vacuum the house. My favorite chore.

The boys have one of those robotic vacuums that travels around the house and does the work for you. Albeit it doesn't get every single bit, it's good for the boys when they come home tired.

But I don't like it.

I need a real one that you have to manually use. Though I am technologically advanced in that it's wireless.

I start in the office and will end up making my way through the hallway, into the guest bathroom, the bedrooms and their ensuites, to the living room, and finally. the kitchen.

It's a lot, but it gives me the perfect amount of time to think.

Like thinking about cleaning out the boys' closets. Or cleaning out the back hall closet. Or saying I love you.

I take a slow breath as the vacuum rumbles along the floors.

Like what I should make for dinner or the fact that I want to invite Nana and Papa over to host our own little dinner. Or saying I love you to Tommy.

I try to ignore my wavering thoughts and think of other matters.

Like the fact that Mom and Dad want to hang out later and Tommy said Dad knows about us. And if Dad knows, Mom knows. Like the fact that the most important thing in my life that was meant to be kept private is spiraling to the point where only Darius doesn't know.

I feel like a shitty sister for not mentioning it, but to be fair, we didn't mention it to anyone. They figured it out. And I've seen Darius come close to figuring it out multiple times before he pushed it out of his thoughts.

I know it's not fair to him because he's used to seeing me and Tommy flirty, but I can't help but panic a little any time I think about telling Darius. Before I came back from London, Darius had been my best friend. Now, it's Tommy, but that's only because of how quickly our feelings for each other developed.

But other than Tommy, it's Darius.

So it scares me the most what he'll think of us. Because

he's also Tommy's best friend and very protective of me, and though he always says he'll find a good guy for me, I don't think he thinks that guy exists.

And though it's sweet, I don't know what it means for me and Tommy.

Then the logical side of my brain kicks in and reminds me that he's going to have to find out at some point, and finding out at the beginning would be a whole lot better than later on in the relationship. That's when my heart races and my breath catches, and I have to pause vacuuming because I'm beginning to get a little shaky, and all I know is that I can't lose Tommy.

Why does it feel like telling Darius will cause me to lose Tommy?

Or you could think about Tommy saying he's in love with you, my mind reminds me, and I finally listen to it. Safe grounds for this little head of mine.

I close my eyes as the vacuum rumbles beside me and think about sitting between Tommy's legs as he so nonchalantly told me he was in love with me.

My breath calms back down.

I remember how sure I was that he meant it. How I knew it without his saying it. But also, how extraordinary it felt to hear the words from his lips.

I'm no longer shaky.

I remember telling him that I was in love with him and how not scary it felt. How I knew I could be as vulnerable as possible with him, and he'll always be around to pick up the pieces. How unafraid I was that he'd ever leave me.

My heart is beating steadily now, but it jumps a little because hello, I'm thinking of Thomas Buttercup Rutherford!

I open my eyes and smile. I love how calm he makes me feel even when he's not around. I love that I'll always have him.

So then why won't you tell Darius? My mind isn't on my side anymore, I see.

But I can't tell Darius. I know I won't lose Tommy in the sense that he'd leave me, but I could still lose this Tommy. The one who's best friends with my brother.

And that can't happen.

So you should tell your brother.

I know my logical side is right, but I just can't. Not yet.

I finish vacuuming, Lysoling, and folding the load in the laundry. Now it's time to get dinner ready. The boys will be home in a few hours, and I have yet to perfect my timing when cooking their meals. Especially when I'm making more than one thing and they finish cooking too far apart so half the meal is already cold.

And sometimes, dinner is ready far too early, and the entire thing is cold before they get home. Those times I try to leave pieces in the oven to keep warm.

Or the least terrible of the lot, when they get home and shower, and dinner is still cooking. They nibble while they wait and never complain, but I can always see how hungry they are. But it's the least terrible because they get a perfect hot meal.

I promise myself I'm going to tell Darius soon as I chop up vegetables for the crockpot roast. I need to tell Darius because I know I can't keep this up. Especially since everyone else knows now. I can trust in my relationship with my brother that he'll see how happy I am and be excited for his best friend and little sister.

After getting over the fact that said best friend has not only seen me naked, but also done certain things to my naked body.

• • •

Mom and Dad have me meet them at the mall because Mom wants to pick out baby clothes for little Rodriguez. We don't know if it's a boy or a girl, so Mom will do a whole lot of neutrals.

I leave the crockpot cooking with Nana Isla and take a Lyft because the mall is on the other side of town, and it would take me *hours* to walk to it. I know I should get a license, but a panic settles in me at the thought of driving. I've done it before, and that's how I know I get major panic attacks when it's my responsibility not to hit the cars beside me.

I love that Darius and Tommy never make fun of me for it. They've never even complained when I couldn't drive somewhere. Or insisted I get over it. They simply accepted it as part of who I am and moved on.

Mom has a little tub of cinnamon pretzel pieces in hand. Dad has a lemonade, but I'd bet my entire existence it's Mom's, and she's making him hold it while she eats.

When I say they are my role models, I mean it.

I open my mouth for my mom to drop a cinnamon rolled piece of dough into it as way of greeting. She does so with a wide smile and shining, proud eyes.

Then I turn to Dad and open my mouth for a sip of the lemonade.

He shakes his head as he brings it to my lips, but he can't hide the amusement on his features. "The baby will be here in a few weeks, Em. Then you won't be it anymore."

I stand taller with a smirk on my face. "I'll always be the baby."

He shoves me as he rolls his eyes so we can follow Mom to the baby shop she wants to check out. It's mostly a ton of small businesses that supply this store, so we're bound to find some cute, unique pieces. And help out smaller businesses.

Mom throws her empty bag away after making sure no

crumbs were left behind, then she claps her hands with excitement as she heads into the store with a cart. I can already imagine the amount of damage she's about to make.

"It's cute," I say as I follow her, pushing the cart because she's too busy already grabbing for different pieces. "You going crazy for their baby."

"That is my first grandchild," Mom defends, but doesn't turn to me. "Lynette is as much my daughter as you are. I mean, she's even named after me."

I roll my eyes. "If you're trying to get me jealous, it won't work. I'm cool with sharing you with her."

"Perfect." She turns with a wide smile and holds up the cutest set of tan corduroys. "What do you think?"

"Absolutely adorable." I'm not being sarcastic either. They are adorable. *I* want them.

Dad throws his arm over my shoulders because we both know I'm there for his moral support. Mom won't let me make decisions on these matters; she's a bit crazed about baby shopping.

"Tell me," he says, "how's Tommy?"

A blush erupts on my cheeks, and as much as I want to hide it, I can't. "He's good. Always is."

"I'm sure more so now, huh?" He wiggles his brows at me.

My cheeks heat up even more, and I push him off of me. "Of course. I was always his favorite person."

Dad chokes on a laugh. "*Way* more so now, huh?"

I push him. "Dad, stop it!"

Mom throws in three more sets and is pulling at two little shirts and debating over them as she throws over her shoulder, "Don't be shy, Em. He's an attractive young man. Be proud of what you have."

"I…" I stutter. "I don't know what you're talking about."

I know Dad's about to make a comment when Mom turns

to him with a little outfit. "Hold this in your arms as if you were holding the baby."

When he does so, I see them a quarter of a century younger, holding Darius for the first time. I see them as the parents they became when they had Darius, then me, and I kind of swoon at the lovey dovey way they look at each other. The way my dad still looks at my mom like she made all his dreams come true.

Mom claps, and her tone is so sweet when she speaks. I know she only sees Dad right now. "I cannot wait to see you holding the little one, Calvin."

Dad drops the set into the cart and takes her face in his hands to kiss her softly. "Then you can imagine how much I cannot wait to see you with the baby."

I fall over the handle of the cart. "You guys are so cute. I want this."

Dad comes back to my side as Mom faces me with all seriousness. "Who're you trying to kid, Emmie? You have this." She looks down to my stomach. "I'm extra excited for baby Rutherford."

She doesn't allow me time to say anything as she turns back to the baby clothes and pulls out a onesie, but my blush is back in full force, and my eyes widen at her insinuation.

I know they know. Or at least, they've guessed. They can tell something is happening with me and Tommy even if they don't know how far it is. How do I tell them that I'm in love with my brother's best friend, the man they've considered a second son our entire lives?

From the way they're acting, I'm sure they won't mind, but still, I divert as she throws another set into the cart. "Mom, that's a boys set." I pull out two others in the cart. "And those are girls'."

She takes them from me and drops them all into her cart.

"They won't be the only ones having babies. I'll save the unused for the next baby."

"And if the next baby is the same sex?" I question my ludicrous mother.

"Eventually, it won't be." She's looking at another set now.

I laugh. "That's not technically true, Maman."

She throws the new set—a boys one—into the cart and keeps walking. "Then I'll donate the unused half."

I lean into Dad. "Your wife's ridiculous, you know that?"

He laughs and throws his arm over me. "I've been told."

CHAPTER 23

Tommy

DARIUS TOOK Emory to the batting cages again, so I'm home alone when there's a knock at the door.

When I open it, Nana Isla is holding a covered tray in her hands, and Papa Atti has a pack of beers in his. I wonder how he won the argument to bring the beers along.

"You didn't have to bring me anything, Nana. I can manage a night."

"You mean the beauty left you a meal before leaving," Papa Atti interprets as they move for my kitchen.

"Exactly." I laugh.

"Have you eaten yet?" Nana asks.

"No," I answer as she takes out plates and pulls the aluminum off her tray. "And I'm guessing I'll be telling Em her meal can be had tomorrow?"

"That's a smart child." Her eyes sparkle at me, and I know even Emory won't be annoyed I didn't eat her food because of Nana. She'd probably chastise me if I refused Nana's meal right now.

"Do I have Em to thank for this thoughtful visit?" I gesture at them as I pull out cups and fill them with water.

Papa Atti shakes his head as he pops open a beer. "Wrong Aabeck."

I pause as I'm placing the waters before them. "Darius?"

Nana Isla fills my plate full of stew and adds a large chunk of bread on the side. "I'll presume he didn't know Emmie wouldn't have left you without food."

Like the guilt train wasn't eating me up enough, now I have this. Of course Darius would've asked Nana to feed me. We always asked Nana for food when we were too tired to do anything ourselves.

And I can't even tell him that I'm in love with his sister? I'm such a jackass.

I take my seat at the island and say nothing else because there is nothing I can say that would excuse my behavior toward my best friend. Other than the fact that said best friend's little sister is the reason I'm keeping this from him.

It's still a lousy excuse, but it's the only one I have.

"Thank you for the meal. We can take the leftovers to Octavio and Lynette. I'm sure they'll appreciate it."

"You really going to try to beat around this, boy?" Papa Atti asks.

"What?" I respond as if I don't know exactly what he's talking about.

"Darius is your *brother*. When are you going to tell him that you're in love with his little sister?"

I scoff and try to roll his comment off, but he doesn't let off.

"Look at me, boy. In all my time of knowing you boys, I've never seen you hide something from each other. What's got to be before you tell him?"

I pull out a beer from Papa's six pack and pop it open. "I know, Papa. I get it." I take a swig, and the guilt burns its way down my throat. "I get it."

Papa's voice softens, but he remains persistent. "Then

what is it, Thomas? That boy loves you more than life itself. Why hide this?"

I force myself to look up at them and see the pain in Nana's eyes. I know she's hurting for what her husband's putting me through, but she agrees with him, so she won't stop it. Hell, I agree with him.

"I love him too, Papa. I do. And if it was anyone but Emory, I would tell him. But she's deep rooted in her fears that things go bad once you tell people about them. I can't betray her trust in us." I make sure I have his full attention as I say, "I love him, Papa, but nowhere near as much as I love her."

He doesn't look shocked to hear the words. And I have to wonder if they would be a shock to anyone other than Darius at this point.

Nana's hand falls over mine. "You can't marry her without Darius knowing."

A humorless laugh leaves me. "Whenever she's ready, Nana."

Her hand squeezes ever so slightly then releases me. "Eat, boy."

I let a small smile lift my lips and meet Papa Atti's eyes. It takes him a few more minutes, but a softness that's not normally in Papa Atti's eyes makes an appearance. "Eat, boy."

Emory has her leg up on the chair in the corner of the room and is applying lotion over her smooth skin. My gaze follows her hands as they run up and down one leg before she seductively switches legs.

I don't think she's trying to be sexy. I don't even think she knows I'm there.

But fuck, she's so damn sexy.

Especially in that tiny white robe that's basically see-through with all the water dripping off her hair. That robe she's only allowed to wear when it's only us in the house, or when she's in our room. I don't need anyone else seeing her in it.

I don't say anything in hopes she'll drop that robe to moisturize the rest of her body while I watch. I already have the door locked behind me even though Darius is home, and there's no way we could do anything right now.

When she drops her leg back down and turns, she jumps at seeing me leaning against the wall, watching. "Hey, pervert."

"Hey, beautiful." She may not have taken the robe off, but it's so sheer, I can basically see everything, and it's all so tantalizing.

"What's that?" She nods to the bag in my hand.

My lips tip up on one side as I walk over and hand it to her. I stay on the other side of the bed though. If I get near her right now, her brother is definitely hearing us. "For you."

She eyes me suspiciously, but there's excitement in her gaze as she takes it and pulls out the big, white fluffy robe.

She quirks her brow. "A robe?"

"It's Thursday, and you're not wearing that around them again." I eye her delicious tiny robe.

She laughs. "I thought I could wear your shirts now?"

"Wear it under that. My shirts are still too short to be around those morons." I'm probably being a little too territorial, but I can't help it. That skin is mine to devour.

She rolls her eyes and drops the big robe. "Only because you're *asking* so nicely."

I chuckle. "Please, Emory, will you cover up with that giant robe tonight?"

She's at my dresser and pulling out one of my shirts when she looks over her shoulder at me. "Hm, I don't know.

I like the sound of you begging. Maybe I should draw this out."

I walk backward until my back hits the door, so I'm not tempted to shove her against the wall by the throat and take her roughly. "I'll beg for you later, baby girl. Preferably when you're on your knees."

She places my shirt on the bed and plays with the ties of her robe. "I like being on my knees for you, Tommy. I'm wet thinking about it right now."

I press harder against the door. "Stop it, Em."

She pulls at the ties, and the robe opens and slides slowly off her skin. "I still need to moisturize the rest of my body. Would you help me?"

"Emory, you're going to be the death of me." My tone is almost begging in and of itself.

She takes some lotion into her hands and rubs it onto her stomach, then she slowly moves to grab both her breasts, and I turn suddenly to face the door. I lean into it and close my eyes to catch my breath and delight in her giggles behind me.

I stand there for minutes until she's pressed into my back. "Can I join boys' night or will the others be annoyed?"

I can feel the fluff of the large robe, so I know she's done teasing me. For now.

I turn and cradle her face. "I actually think they'd be cool with it. As long as it's not an every week occurrence."

She smiles. "I don't think I could deal with a group of you morons *every* week, Buttercup."

I lean in and kiss her. "Why do I love you?"

"I'm fucking amazing." She gives a cheeky grin and pushes me aside to leave the room.

I smack her ass before we turn the corner to the room Darius and Octavio are already in. The fluff monstrosity I got her is perfect. I barely felt her ass which means it's plenty thick enough to hide her from the others. And it reaches her ankles, so those legs can't tantalize anyone else the way they do me.

"Isn't it a bit warm for that, princessa?" Octavio asks, and I throw him a glare.

"Surprisingly, it's cool in here." She snuggles into the robe and smiles. "But we'll see. I can always take it off and lay it over my lap later."

I know she's saying that last bit for me, and I feel a little guilty for making her wear it in the middle of summer. "Em's joining us tonight."

Darius smirks. "Does Em know how to play poker?"

She narrows her eyes at him. "You'll be nice."

"It's boys' night, princess. I'm not nice on boys' night."

I kiss the back of her head as I place the beers on the table. "I'll help you."

I take my seat, and she slumps down onto hers which is pressed so close to me, she's basically half on my lap as she says, "Thank you, Buttercup."

Darius eyes us suspiciously, and I know he recognizes how close Emory and I are. I know he sees she's snuggled into me and the way she leans into my ear to whisper how we're going to kick their asses. I know his protective brotherly instincts are screaming at him that we're being too touchy.

And I can see he's about two seconds from pulling us apart and spitting in my face that I'm being *too* friendly.

But then, the doorbell rings, and he does none of that. Rather, he's off to open it for the boys.

"You know he sees it," Octavio says as he brings in another chair for the table. "He just won't let himself believe it."

Emory leans into me. I know she feels bad about not telling him, but I don't know what to do to help.

I could just tell him, and once we're past his anger, this would be perfect.

But I won't break Em's trust like that.

The boys smile at Emory when they walk in, and Drew laughs. "Nice robe."

Em gives them a cheery smile in return. "Thanks. It's snuggly."

"Em is playing with Tommy tonight," Darius interrupts as he takes the deck and starts shuffling.

"Aw, Tommy boy, asking the girlfriend for help?" Mikey smirks between the two of us. Emory hasn't moved from being pressed into me, and I know the others see there's something now, even if they hadn't before.

My heart jumps at hearing her referred to as my girlfriend out loud for the first time, but all I do it smirk. "We'll see how smug you are when you lose, Mikey."

CHAPTER 24

Emory

NANA ISLA and Papa Atti invited us over for dinner at their house instead of a family BBQ this weekend. Darius, Tommy, and me. And Mom and Dad. And Octavio and Lynette. Our hodgepodge of the best family to exist.

Nana Isla and Papa Atti also insisted they do all the cooking.

All of it.

They actually made me take back a baked mac and cheese I'd brought. Said to leave it in the fridge and we could eat it tomorrow.

To be fair, they did a magnificent job.

Of course they did. They've been married for longer than my parents have been alive. They have the practice. And old age isn't a concept to them. Hasn't been since the moment I met them out on the curb.

They are how I aspire to be as an old couple.

I'm in the same dress I wore to surprise Mom and Dad when I first got back and a pair of beige summer wedges that give me a few inches. But I still only meet Tommy and Darius at their chins.

We're in the living room because Nana Isla refuses to even allow us to help, and I'm watching the boys as they try to touch the plants that are hanging a little too high for even their behemoth sizes.

I made them dress up too. Nice black button downs, dark jeans, and the boots they each have for nice occasions tucked beneath. They smell amazing too.

I have my phone out when I call to them and snap a picture of them turning to face me. Tommy's smile speaks volumes in the picture, and I'm suddenly so glad I took it.

"You guys look so handsome." I dote on them like a mother to her children because I know it'll make Darius roll his eyes and laugh.

"And you look beautiful, princess." Darius throws his arm around me and kisses the top of my head.

Tommy watches us like he wants to do the same thing.

And like he's happy to see us together. Because we're his two best friends.

Mom and Lynette walk into the house together with Dad and Octavio following behind, carrying fancy bottles of juice. Because Lynette can't drink alcohol, no one will be allowed to. It's more a problem for the men and their beer than anyone else.

But that means no bottles of wine either.

Nana Isla has the entire place smelling like heaven by the time we sit. She's prepared a traditional English Sunday roast. The beef, potatoes, vegetables, Yorkshire pudding, and assortment of condiments fill the table. It's so much food, if it weren't for how much the boys could eat, I'd think half of it would be left over.

And even though this is plenty of food, I know Nana Isla has an assortment of desserts down her sleeve too.

The first ten minutes of dinner are pretty silent as we devour our meals. The dishes are so good, they're going to be the next things I have Nana Isla teach me to make. Even after four years in England, I think this is the best English Sunday roast I've ever had.

On a Saturday.

The silence quickly ebbs away as we start on the debates regarding baby Rodriguez.

"I'm telling you guys," Darius argues, "it's a girl!"

"And I'm telling you, Son," Mom rebuts, "it's a boy."

"Mom," he insists, "it's not a boy."

"It is, Darius." Nana Isla looks smug like she's sure. "That belly is holding a little boy in it."

"Can someone else back me up, please?" Darius looks to Dad and Papa Atti.

They both shake their heads as Papa Atti says, "Isla's never been wrong about these things, Son. She's known from the beginning; it's a boy."

"It is a boy, Darius," Dad says.

"I'm never wrong either." Darius won't give it up. He's stubborn like that. "It's a girl!"

"I gotta agree with them, big brother. It's a boy." I'm not trying to instigate more of a fight. I actually think it's a boy. Always have.

"You guys are all insane!" Darius insists.

Dad turns to Tommy. "You've been quiet. What do you think?"

"Yeah, Buttercup, what do you think?" I turn smugly on my brother because I know Tommy's going to agree with me.

"I've gotta agree with your brother," Tommy leans back in his chair.

"Thank you!" Darius exclaims at the same time I gasp and snap around to look at him. "But you're always on my side."

He shrugs, and those sparkling eyes captivate me as he says, "Guess I just really want it to be a girl."

"Me too," Octavio says as he shoves more roast into his mouth. "But we have a feeling it's a boy."

Darius goes to fight when Lynette taps his arm. "You can argue with my husband about my baby after you get me a warm glass of water, please."

Darius leans in to kiss her temple with a smile. "Anything for you, Sister." He kisses the belly. "And you, my little *niece*."

He runs off to the kitchen as we yell after him "It's a boy."

"You want it to be a girl?" Dad turns back to Tommy.

He shrugs. "I didn't care at first. Thought both would be fun. I still do. But when we were preparing to build Ella's kids that playhouse, I saw this paint that I thought would be cute for a little girl. I imagined it for Octavio and Lynette's kid, and now I'm hoping for a girl."

I pinch his chin. "That's my sweet little Buttercup."

He bites my fingers as Mom asks to see the paint color.

Tommy's semi distracted by me, but he reaches for his phone anyway. His eyes barely leave mine as he taps his pockets before they furrow. "I must've left it in the kitchen when I was helping Nana bring the roast out. I'll go grab..."

"I'll come." Nana Isla stands. "I need to get dessert going."

"We can all go," Lynette says. "I need to move, and we can see what's taking Darius so long with my water."

We laugh because the rest of us had no intention to go to the kitchen, but now that Lynette's declared it, we're doing so. I have a feeling she's going to sit on a stool at the island, and the party will be transferred there.

Tommy somehow made it to the front and is leading us to the kitchen. The family lets me through so I can be beside him when we reach the kitchen, but he pauses.

Darius is on the other side of the island, and he has Tommy's phone in his hand. I know because Tommy's phone cover is a picture I took when I was in the Swiss Alps he and

Darius had sent me to. Has been even before I'd returned and things had gotten romantic between us.

Darius has Tommy's phone, and he's watching something.

It's my voice. *"That would mean I don't intend to execute. Or are you too tired? Unable?"*

CHAPTER 25

Tommy

I KNOW exactly what video he's watching. And exactly where that video leads. To a black screen with far too much audio.

There's the growl. Then the screech, then the laughs as I threw Emory onto the bed. *"Want to say that again?"*

"Darius," I break the silence that's filled the room. "Stop the video."

I'd forgotten all about that video and the fact that the phone hadn't stopped recording when I dropped it. Instead, it picked up every bit of mine and Emory's time together.

The video continues. *"Are you impotent, Buttercup?"*

"Does it feel like I'm impotent, baby girl? Emory..."

My heart is racing as I listen to the video in the silence of the room and watch Darius's face. He's showing nothing, and that makes my heart beat even faster. This is so far from how I wanted him to find out.

"Darius," I try to remain calm. "You really don't want to hear the rest of that."

"No. Sir."

The loud moan that I was sure would be heard by the

neighbors just begins when Darius drops the phone, and the video is finally off. On top of not wanting Darius to continue listening to it, Calvin is also standing right behind me, and he doesn't need to hear his little girl like that.

The rooms comes to a standstill as Darius stares into blank space. Then he slowly turns his eyes on me.

"Darius," Emory's voice is low as she steps up. I shoot my arm out to stop her. I don't want her in the middle if Darius loses it.

He steps out from behind the island, but his gaze never leaves me. "You're fucking my sister?"

That's a lewd way of putting it.

"Darius. I swear it's not what it looks like."

"Really? Because what it's *looks like* is that my best friend hasn't had any action in two years, and my baby sister came home right on time to take advantage of the opportunity! Like she doesn't matter at all."

I breathe slowly. "I swear, Darius, she matters. She matters more to me than anyone ever has. More than *you* matter to me."

His scoff is mixed with a snarl. "Bullshit."

I take a tiny step forward. "She is the most important par..."

"Bullshit," he yells at me. "Bullshit. If she were important to you, I would've heard about it from the beginning and *not* through a sex tape."

"I wanted to tell you." It's a weak thing to say, but it's true.

"Wanted." His fists clench at his side as he scoffs. "Wanted? You always tell me the most important things going on in your life. That's what we do. We tell each other those things. You not coming to me with this tells me exactly where you find my sister in your life choices." There's a bit of hurt in his eyes, but it's well masked by his anger.

"It's not like we haven't been showing everyone what's going on between us. Everyone else picked up on it!" It's the best argument I have.

He scoffs, and I'm beginning to understand that's how he's keeping his anger at bay. "Bullshit. You knew all I saw was the way you two acted when we were younger. Obviously, I wasn't gonna think anything of it. It's how you've always been together! Except I didn't realize that now you're also coming in her!"

"Would you stop talking about it like I'm using her for her body?" I say through clenched teeth.

He scoffs. "You're trying to tell me you didn't fuck her?"

My jaw ticks as I lose a bit of control on my anger. And though I know I should restrain myself because the entire family—Emory's father, especially—is behind me, I can't. "Oh, I absolutely fucked her. But she's not just the convenient hot chick in my house. I'm in love with her, Darius."

It's like I pulled a trigger with those words.

His fist hits me so fast, I don't have time to process it coming at me.

And so hard, it knocks me damn near ninety degrees.

Calvin and Octavio rush to Darius's side and hold him back so he doesn't try for another punch as Emory's soft touch reaches for me. She brings me to sit on one of the stools around the kitchen island.

She's gentle as she reaches for my jaw and lifts my gaze to meet hers. "Baby, are you all right?"

I shake my head, gaze already moving to meet Darius's. "Fine."

There's a look in his eyes I've never seen focused on me before, almost like hatred, and it rips at my heart to be it's target.

"So this entire time I've trusted you with my baby sister,

and you've just been treating her like your personal whore," he spits my way.

The pain in my heart is gone.

Everything is gone.

Everything turns to ice because all I'm processing is that he just called Emory a whore.

I have her pushed behind me and am out of my seat in a second, rushing toward him because I'm going to hit him harder than he just hit me. I'm going to kill him for speaking about Emory like that.

Octavio catches me before I make it, and now it's a power war of whether or not Octavio and Calvin can hold Darius and me back from killing one another. I know it kills them not to interrupt the fight, but I also know the family won't butt in. This is between us brothers.

Emory's before me again, and that's the only reason I force myself to calm down. I won't let her accidentally get hurt because of us.

"Sit down." Her voice is gentle, but authoritative as she pushes on my chest. "Baby, please go sit down."

I comply because that's what she wants from me, and I'm at mercy to giving her everything her heart desires.

She follows me and stands between my legs as she softly takes my face in her hands like it's just the two of us in the universe. "He didn't mean it, Tommy."

I know he didn't.

I know he loves his sister.

I know he would never look at or talk about Emory in that way.

But I still want to kill him for saying the words.

"He didn't mean it." Somehow her voice is still soft, gentle.

"I know," I finally whisper back because I realize she's waiting for me to say something.

She looks at me for another moment, kisses my forehead, then turns on her brother. "I'm the reason he didn't tell you, Darius. So if you're going to be mad at anyone, it's me."

"Baby, it's not your faul..." I'm immediately arguing, but she cuts me off.

"You know I need to keep the most important things in my life private. He wanted to tell you. Our first fight was actually because he wanted to tell you and I didn't. You know how I am. You never asked so we never said anything."

I know Emory truly believes this is her fault, but it's not. Darius is right, I've always gone to him with the important matters in my life.

There's hurt behind the hatred as Darius's gaze drops to Emory, and the silence is deafening as we wait. He finally turns to Calvin who still has a hand on his shoulder. "I'll see you at home."

Then he walks out of the kitchen, not deigning to look at Emory or me. And he's out of the house. Just like that.

He was serious. Darius didn't come home last night after finding out. A call to Calvin told me he was safe with them. That's all that mattered.

Sunday morning, we stay in bed late. I tried calling Darius three times and Emory tried twice.

He ignored every single call.

We eat a light breakfast in silence before we're back in bed. After last night, I don't really want to do much else.

What I really want to do is go talk to Darius, but I know he needs the time to cool off.

Emory shuts the blinds so it's dark in the room and cuddles in beside me as she pulls the blanket damn near over her face. She's snug against my chest, and even though Darius is pissed right now, I'm glad I have her with me.

I don't regret us. I don't regret any part of my relationship with her. And I don't regret not telling Darius.

Though I would like a bit of an explanation.

"Can I ask you something, baby?" I'm playing with strands of her hair as I stare at the tiny bits of sunlight beaming through the cracks of the curtains.

She snuggles into the crook of my neck and shoulder and kisses me lightly. "Always."

"I know you've always been the private, not secret kind. But is there a reason you needed to hide it from Darius the most?"

Because she hadn't seemed too bothered by everyone else finding out, but Darius had apparently been too much.

"I haven't always been the private, not secret kind," she says softly.

My brows furrow, and I try to look down at her, but with the way her head is placed under mine, I don't manage much. "You have, baby. I've known you damn near your whole life."

"And damn near my whole life I have been. But it really started when I was eight."

"Why?" This was *not* something I knew.

"And it's not just Darius. If I hadn't fallen for you, you would've been right beside Darius on keeping it private." She speaks so matter-of-factly about the fact that *I* have something to do with the reason she's like this.

I push her off me so she's lying on her side and scoot down so we're face-to-face. "Baby, what the fuck are you talking about?"

She smiles weakly at me. "The summer you guys destroyed La Aabehlooza. I know it's ridiculous to still be affected by it, but I can't help it."

La Aabehlooza?

"The little kingdom you made up?" I ask because I have a vague recollection of that name.

She nods. "You guys destroyed it because you were annoyed you had to babysit, and you knew it would hurt me."

My heart pangs, and I remember exactly what she's talking about. I want to correct her, tell her we didn't do it to hurt her. That we were just dumb pre-teens. But that's a lie. We *were* dumb pre-teens, but we did do it mostly to hurt her.

Fuck, we laughed and high-fived when she didn't tell on us to her parents.

I felt like such a little shit the next day when Emory didn't come down for breakfast or try to fix her little fantasy kingdom. It's how I knew we went too far. Because we bullied her before about her little make-believe worlds, and she always got up the next day and continued on with them.

"Emmie," I say breathlessly because I'm starting to realize how much that day must've affected her.

I thought she'd forgotten all about it. I had.

She shrugs and stares down at my chest. "I promised myself I would never give you guys the ammunition to hurt me like that again. That I would never lie, but I wouldn't freely give it up. Especially to you two."

"Emory." I take her face in my hands and try to force her to look at me. I can feel my eyes prickling, but I push the tears aside.

She's still staring at my chest as she says, "When you guys stopped being shits to me a few months later, I thought it wouldn't last. But it did. And as the years passed, I kept telling myself you guys wouldn't do anything like that to me again, but every time I came close to telling you guys something important, my heart would race, and I'd shut it down before I had a full-blown panic attack."

"Emory, please look at me."

She finally does. "I tried telling Darius. About us. But I couldn't do it. And if things had been different and I'd fallen for someone else, I wouldn't have been able to tell you either. Like, if Octavio had been single and I'd fallen for him. Like actually fallen, not the stupid crushes I had in London. There's no way I'd have been able to tell either one of you."

I press my forehead to hers. "Emory…"

"It's different with you now. Obviously. I feel like I can tell you literally everything and not a single part of me worries that you'll destroy it. But I know that's because I'm in love with you. And more importantly, you're in love with me."

"I am, Emory." I pull away so I can look her in the eyes. "So fucking in love with you."

Her lips tip up, but her eyes still look a little sad. "I know he's my brother, and he wants the literal best for me, but I don't know… My heart still beats too fast when I try telling him. Even knowing you'd never leave me, I was too scared."

I kiss her softly because I *need* to.

"Still in love with me?" She breaths against my lips. "Knowing I'm a coward?"

"Baby, look at me." When she does, I'm hypnotized by how beautiful she is. "You're not a coward. We were little shits, and we did this to you. I just wish I'd known how much it affected you."

"It's not your fault. You were twelve. Twelve-year-olds are all shits."

"I'm so sorry, Emory. Fuck, baby, I'm so fucking sorry." I lean into her again, and the words brush her lips.

She gives my lips a peck. "I should be the one apologizing."

I push away from her. "What?"

"It was a long time ago, and you and Darius have shown me a million and one times that you'd never hurt me. You have nothing to apologize for. I do. Because I'm the reason you two are fighting right now."

"Baby." I brush her hair back. "We would've been fighting whether I told him at the beginning or not."

"No. Not like this, and you know it."

I sigh. "Okay, not like this. But that doesn't change things. At the end of the day, it's our fault for putting that fear in you. *You* have nothing to apologize for."

She kisses the palm I have cradling her jaw. "We may have to agree to disagree, Buttercup."

"Fine." I kiss her forehead. "But I'm right."

She snuggles into me, and I can feel her smile against my neck. "If you want me to go down on you later, you're not right."

I laugh and hug her tighter to me. "Well, would you look at that? Turns out I am on the wrong side."

She giggles into my shoulder, and even though I'm fighting with Darius right now, all feels right in the world.

CHAPTER 26

Emory

ALL I CAN THINK about is how awful I feel. Because as much as Tommy likes to say it's not my fault, it is. If I'd just let him talk to Darius about this when he wanted to, things wouldn't have turned out so awful.

Even if I couldn't do it. I should've let him do it.

Yeah, they probably—definitely—still would've fought, but the shock factor of finding out through a sex tape wouldn't be there. I have a feeling that's a big part of the reason Darius thinks this is about sex and nothing more.

And maybe—definitely—the fact that his *best friend* hadn't told him about it when said best friend always tells him every important thing in the world.

Tommy is just coming out of the shower, dressed in his normal sweatpants and T-shirt, when the front door opens.

My heart stops. Could Darius be back?

We move to the living room immediately, and my heart sinks again. It's Mom.

She's got a weak smile as she looks between us. "How're my sweethearts doing?"

Tommy's answering smile is weak. I don't even attempt

one.

We all move to the couches, Mom sitting on the one opposite us as I take comfort in Tommy's proximity.

"How's Darius?" I ask because other than the guilt for the hurt Tommy's going through, it's all I can think about.

That small smile remains. "He's processing."

Tommy scoffs. "Yeah, how much of a mistake it was to trust me. Probably rethinking all our decisions, our business, our house. Probably trying to figure out if there's anything else I haven't told him, if anything I have told him was true. He hates me."

I turn to him, and my leg is thrown over his thigh in seconds. Then Mom is on his other side, hand resting on his arm.

"Baby," I say, "baby, he doesn't hate you."

He can't. He's one of the few men I love, and he has to get past this. Even if not for me, but for Tommy's sake, for their relationship. He's Tommy's platonic soulmate to my romantic.

Tommy's staring at nothing as his hand travels up and down my leg.

"Tommy." Mom's hand softly touches his jaw and turns him to face her. "You're as much my son as he is. You two are brothers. He will get past this."

"I've always known him better than I know myself. He's too upset. When it comes to Emory, he's always been of one mind." His tone cripples my heart.

"And if you ask him, he'll say the same thing. He knows you better than he knows himself." Mom's hand is rubbing circles on his hand now in that comforting way of hers. "And that's what's bothering him. That he's your best friend, your soulmate, and he didn't see it. *He* didn't see that his best friend was in love."

Tommy opens his mouth to say something, but nothing

comes out. He's looking at Mom so hopefully, I fall a little harder for him in that moment.

"That's why it bothers him so much when you say you're in love with Emory," Mom continues. "It's like you're rubbing it in his face that he couldn't tell. Because, let me tell you, he was suspicious of something. But he figured it was nothing because you would say something. He didn't allow himself to see how hard you'd fallen."

"What should I do?" he asks like a hopeful heartbroken child.

Mom brings his hand to her lips and kisses it. "Give him time, Son. He's going to come around. Just give him the time he needs to process this. He's already been thinking back to every interaction he's witnessed since Em came back. I swear that boxing bag has never seen so much frustration before. It's all coming together now in his head."

"Thank you," he says as his hand moves from my thigh to grab my hand, and I love the little attention he gives me even when he's not speaking with me. "Thank you for coming to tell me this, even though you're probably mad too."

Mom sputters. "I've known for some time. Dad basically confirmed it at that barbecue even though you refused to say the words. What do I have to be mad about?"

"That I basically made a sex tape with your daughter. Your little girl."

She smirks. "Oh, she may be younger than you boys, but trust me, she'll have the both of you by the balls. She's not the child I worry about. You and Darius on the other hand? Definitely worry about from time to time."

Tommy scoffs through a wide smile, and I'm trying to hold in my superior laugh.

"I don't know why that's so shocking." I turn on him. "I've always been independent. I lived across the world for four years!"

"Oh, and you never let anyone forget it," he interrupts in mock annoyance.

I smack him, and he quickly grabs for my arm and pulls me in for a kiss. We're about four seconds into the kiss when we remember we're not alone.

We pull away though the smiles are wide on our faces and turn back to our guest.

She shakes her head.

"What?" I ask because I'm kinda worried now. Did seeing us kiss make this a reality for her, and she doesn't like it?

"It's just amazing how right I could be. And over fifteen years ago too!" She looks like she's in a memory.

"Mom, what the hell are you talking about?"

Her gaze meets mine, and there's a spark in there that's jumping with excitement. "I said you two would be cute together. Also told your father you'd end up making some cute babies. I definitely see that one coming true as well."

I shake my head as a crippled laugh leaves me. "Mom! Do *not* jinx me like that!"

Tommy throws his arm over my shoulders and brings me in, his elbow keeping my neck locked in place as he moves in to kiss me. One big, sloppy kiss. Then he turns to my mom and winks. "Don't worry. I'll make sure it happens."

My mouth opens in the shape of an O past my smile. "Not yet! We're not married, and I'm too young!"

He turns toward my mom and stage whispers, "We'll remedy the first soon. The second…"

Mom helps him with the answer, "By the time she has it, she'll be a year older."

He snaps his fingers. "There we go!"

"Mom!" I exclaim.

She gives me a cheeky smile. "And you were asking what I'd do with all the extra baby clothes I bought."

"Mom, when did you turn into an asshole?" I cannot

believe she's joking with Tommy about getting me pregnant. She's totally jinxing it.

"What? Did you think the gene came from your father?"

We all laugh, and I'm so thankful to my mom for coming over and lightening the mood. And I know Tommy is too. I can just tell, but his next words solidify that knowledge.

"Thanks," Tommy takes her hand, "Mom."

While Tommy's in the bathroom, I play with the condoms he left on the nightstand. There is nothing particularly interesting about the condoms themselves; they're all basically the same.

It's their packaging that got my attention.

Apparently, this package had been of condoms with jokes on the packages. My favorite says, '*As I get older, I remember all the people I lost along the way. But hey, at least some of them got a nice place to stay. Others made homes in towels before getting washed out.*'

Perverted and hilarious.

"Something interesting about the condoms?"

I jump. I hadn't heard the door open.

"They have jokes on them. I like jokes." I smile up at him as he walks toward the side of the bed and picks up a condom.

"Should we rip this baby open and put it to use?"

He's already getting ready, and considering we haven't done it since before Darius found out, I know we're both ready.

"No."

He freezes, and his eyes shoot to meet mine, finding the seriousness there. "You...don't want to?"

"Want to what?"

"Have sex."

"Oh, I definitely want to have sex." My features don't give anything away.

"Then what are you saying no to?"

It's almost hilarious watching him get antsy with how badly he wants to rip the package open and get it on—all puns intended.

"Using the condom."

Now he's really frozen. "What?"

I know it's a dumb thing to say considering only a couple of hours ago I was adamant about not getting pregnant anytime soon. But I have a primal need to feel him in me without a barrier.

"I don't want to use the condom."

He quirks a brow at me. "Weren't you the one arguing against getting pregnant?"

I let a small smirk grace my lips. "If you pull out, the likelihood shouldn't be too much more than with a condom."

That's probably not true, but I'm telling myself it is.

His eyes grow darker with each passing moment. "And why would I pull out?"

I know my eyes are black as I say, "So you could cover me."

His eyes widen, and it makes me feel superior, dominant, on top of the world. I love this feeling.

"I want you to come all over me, Buttercup."

He groans. "This is not the moment to be using that name, Emory."

I give him a not so innocent smile as I sit back on my heels on the bed.

"I've never not used a condom before," he says softly.

"Really?"

I'm actually shocked as I sit up a little taller and look at his still standing form. He's still holding the condom between his hands like he's glued to the spot.

"I've never wanted to risk pregnancy. Darius neither. We've always made it a thing to never go bare." After a moment, his gaze turns sharp. "Have you...ever?"

I can't help the little smirk. "No. But to be fair, I've only ever been with two other people, and we've already done it more times than I did with either one of them."

His form relaxes a bit, and he goes back to staring off into space.

I grab his wrist. "We don't have to if you don't want to risk it."

His gaze meets mine when he finally comes out of his reverie. His thumb reaches for my mouth as his hand cradles my face, and he plays with my bottom lip. "You have no idea how much I want to risk it. If you hadn't specifically asked for me to come all over those luscious girls, I wouldn't even think about pulling out. I'd risk it all, baby girl."

My breath hitches, and my tongue pokes out to lick his thumb as it continues to play with my bottom lip. "Good."

He drops the condom and straddles me on the bed, grabbing my face in both hands and bringing our lips together. His tongue is a little too eager as it finds its way into my mouth.

I like him eager.

But then I pull away as something occurs to me. "I never asked you to come on my tits by the way. I said on me."

"Yeah, but the girls are basically begging for it. I wouldn't deny them this." His smile is almost cruel in its wickedness.

I crawl back on the bed, out from under him, and love the way his eyes drink me in as I move.

His hand reaches for the back of his shirt, and he flings it off with one swipe. Like the movies. Damn, did this ridiculous hotness occur in these past four years or was I just stupid blind before I left for Europe?

His hands drop to his sides, and he nods down. "I need help with the rest."

Sure he did.

I give him a wicked grin to match his own and move up to kiss him right where the happy trail goes into hiding. He flexes under my touch but doesn't move.

My nails graze their way up his sweatpants, and I know he can feel the teasing glide of nails through the fabric by the way he tenses.

I kiss him again as my hands reach for the edge of his pants and slowly pull them down, my mouth following them down from one hip to the next until I reach his cock.

He moans as my mouth and his dick meet.

My hands continue to travel the sweatpants down his legs until they get stuck at his knees while I lick his cock from base to tip, staring up at him through my lashes.

When I take the tip into my mouth, my nails make their way back up over his thighs, and his body flinches with sensitivity. "Fuck, baby."

I grin as I pull his cock from my mouth because I love seeing how I affect him.

My tongue swirls around the tip to collect any pre-cum, then I give it a final suck before licking him from base to tip again and continuing up his torso until I reach his neck. I bite down, hard enough to leave a mark. "In case anyone needs a reminder that you're mine."

His hand makes its way into my hair and tugs back sharply so my neck is exposed. "I believe the act should be reciprocated, baby, don't you?"

"Yes," I moan at the thought of him marking me.

He licks from my chest to my neck and sucks for a second before biting down. So hard I moan out in ecstasy. It'll leave a mark for sure.

His mouth finds mine. "I love the way you taste, Emory."

"Ditto." I push him off the bed so he can strip out of the sweatpants as I pull my tank off.

When he gets back on the bed, he takes my hips and flips me onto all four. He licks over my underwear and up my back until his teeth find my ear. "Spread your legs for me, baby," he whispers as his hands rip the underwear off my body.

I moan as my legs work on their own accord to please him.

His chuckle at my ear makes me so wet, I push back so I can rub against him, get any friction.

He runs his cock up my wet pussy and groans. "Fuck, baby girl, you're so fucking wet."

I turn to face him and lick his lips. "Stop playing, Tommy."

He kisses me as he shoves inside me, so hard my arms burn as they struggle to keep my body up. His tongue is harsh as he fucks me from behind, and it's making me wetter, the animalistic way he's taking me.

"Fuck, baby, you feel so good." He fists my hair and pulls like he needs to in order to keep his sanity. "This pussy was made for me, baby."

The bruising way his other hand holds my hip bites down even harder as he groans into my ear when I clench him inside of me. It'll be another mark to show that I'm his.

He releases my hair and holds both my hips as he pushes harder into me. When my arms can't hold me any longer and I fall onto my chest, he's deeper, and I moan out so loud, I don't even know what sounds are coming out of my mouth.

I'm reaching the edge fast. So fast.

Then he spits down at my ass, and his thumb moves to play at the edge of my asshole as the other hand slips beneath to play with my clit. He continues pounding into me, and it's too much.

I'm screaming. So loud, I might lose my voice, but I don't care.

When he pinches my clit as that other thumb plays at the edge of my other hole, I come so hard, my vision blacks out for long seconds, and I think I ripped the sheets with the force I'm pulling at them.

He flips me before I can fully come down, and I'm hazy as I look up at him.

He doesn't give me a break, just fists my hair again and pulls me to sit back on my heels. "Bring those tits together for me, baby."

Again, I comply without thought because I love pleasing him.

His cock comes between my tits, and he fucks my breasts. I moan because this is making me want him inside me again, but my sounds are lost on his groans.

As he fucks my tits, I catch his tip in my mouth and get just enough of a lick to taste myself on his cock before he pulls away harshly and groans through clenched teeth. "Hold the girls for me, Emory."

He comes all over my tits. Creams them in his cum so much that it drips down my chest, and I feel it sliding down my torso.

I take his cock into my mouth to get the last bits of his cum because I love the taste of him.

When I pop him out of my mouth and look up, he's staring down at me with awe. "I hope you know I'm never using a condom again."

My laugh is a mix of seduction and pure joy. "Good. Why should that crap get your cum when my body and mouth are so willing to take it?"

He groans and pulls me by my hair so we're face-to-face, and he kisses me hard enough to bruise.

CHAPTER 27

Tommy

WE CAN'T KEEP DOING this. Darius has been ignoring me all week at work, and it's starting to get fucking childish. He somehow has to get over it so we can get the job done.

We've gone through an entire day not talking on the job before. Not on purpose, but sometimes work was so busy that we didn't actually get to be around one another to speak, just sending our men with anything that needed to be said.

But this week hasn't been like that. Instead, Darius has been sending men to speak to me or straight up ignoring me when I went around. I get he's mad, but we have a business, and he needs to get over it and at least talk to me.

Even though he doesn't technically have to get over it just because we have work. In fact, with Octavio there, he can fully pretend I don't exist.

I breathe out a tired sigh as I watch him with his back to me as he patches up a wall. I step up so we're not yelling across the room. "Darius, please. We have to talk about this."

I've given him enough time to process this week.

"What? You fuck my sister again?" His tone is harsh, but

at least he's acknowledging my presence. He doesn't turn to face me, but he's talking.

But now the others are listening in.

They pretend like they're not, like they're just going about their jobs, but every single one of them has an ear out to our conversation. They've been curious about what had gotten between us all week so there's no doubt every single one of them is listening. This is juicy gossip to take back to their ladies.

I sigh again because this really is killing me. "Darius."

"You can stop lying now, Thomas."

I feel even more guilty now that the memory of coming all over that beautiful skin is forever ingrained in my mind.

"Darius, we go to bed together. I don't think you actually want to hear what we're doing, but this week hasn't exactly set the mood."

Because other than last night when we went dirtier than we'd ever gone before, it hasn't been the sexiest of weeks.

He stops patching and throws a dirty look over his shoulder. "Oh, I'm sorry. Did I mess up your chances of screwing my sister? Shame since I've given you two so many opportunities in the past."

He turns back to work.

And I should be back to work too. This is *our* business, and we're not going to be falling behind or running late hours because of this fight.

I get started on mixing the cement being used for the textured wall on the other side of the room since the men are beginning to run out. "You've got to stop talking about this like I'm just trying to get my dick wet."

"You're right. Sex tapes could mean so many things."

The men around us stiffen immediately, giving themselves away, but they recover quickly.

I make a frustrated exhale. "Darius, I'm in love with her. I'm going to marry her, and I'd like to do it with your blessing. You have to see it's not just sex. I'm *in love* with her. "

He throws me to the opposite wall—one that luckily hasn't needed any work, to it so we won't have any redos from this little attack.

He's glaring at me, nostrils flaring.

And that's when I realize the trigger hasn't been admitting to fucking his sister. Lynn was right—it was saying that I was in love with Emory. Somehow that is worse to him.

"Stop. Saying. That," he says through clenched teeth. "My best friend would've told me if he was in love!" He pulls and slams me harder into the wall. "He would've mentioned being in love with my *little sister*, Tommy!"

I recall the conversation with Emory about why she felt the need to keep this private and feel even worse.

"If Emory's anxiety permitted it, I would've. You know how she gets. How scared she is that once she tells others about the things she cares most about, they'll be destroyed."

"I'm her brother," he gets out, fists still clenched in my shirt.

"So imagine how scared she was of destroying us. She was too scared to tell you. You, who she trusts most in the world."

I'm hoping he's beginning to see it.

"Apparently not if she thought I'd destroy what she cared for most."

Nope, still angry.

But the fight isn't entirely there for me anymore. I'm tired, and I want my best friend back. My voice is softer when I speak. "I'm in love with her, Darius. I can't help it as much as she can't."

We stare at each other from only inches apart, and I can

see the hurt filling his eyes. His voice has lost its edge when he says, "So don't blame me if I can't help but see this as my best friend screwing my kid sister in the comfort of *our* home."

He walks away from me, away from the room, and all is silent.

The men are trying to act busy, act like they weren't all stopped and listening just seconds ago. But I feel their gazes on me, the one's they try to only make a second long.

And I don't care. All I can think about is my best friend walking away from me.

Octavio's at my side, clasping my shoulder as the others finally get themselves fully back to work. "He just needs time. After the shock wears off, he'll start to put together every time you two have been together and see the love there."

"Yeah," I mumble in a barely audible whisper.

Hopefully.

Surprisingly, this is our first time hanging out with Nana Isla and Papa Atti just the two of us. Kind of like a double date.

We're at the park that's only about a ten-minute walk from our houses and we've got blankets set out for a picnic. Even before Emory came back, Nana Isla loved coming on these picnics and would often invite me and Darius to join. Sometimes the four of us would come out. And other times the three of us, either Darius or me or Papa Atti not being able to make it. And sometimes—and secretly my favorite times—she'd ask just one of us on the picnic. I loved when I was the one.

Nana Isla had a few rules regarding these picnics.

One, no technology—this rule could only be broken on an emergency work or family matter. Which basically means it has yet to be broken.

Two, if you were on the picnic, you were there. No allowing your mind to wonder or any negativity to ruin everyone else's time.

Three, Nana Isla would be supplying all the food. She is very adamant about this rule.

She made with mini caprese sandwiches, cherry tomato couscous salad, and potato salad because we *always* have potato salad. She's also brought oatmeal raisin cookies—Papa Atti's and Emory's favorite—and strawberry rhubarb bars for dessert. For drinks, waters are the big deal. Water is usually the big deal during any of our meals.

"New rule," Emory starts. "Next time, I supply the food."

Papa Atti and I immediately bark out in laughter. Yeah right.

Nana Isla narrows her eyes on Em. "Is there something wrong with my food?"

"No. Of course not," Emory almost stutters. "I just want to do it, and you never let me."

That is one big thing Nana Isla and Emory have in common. They both love to cook. Especially for others.

"That's because I want to do it," Nana Isla says the last bit like it's the end of the discussion.

"But..." Emory starts but is cut off when Nana Isla turns to me.

"How were things at work with the flirt?" she asks like she's not changing the subject.

"Oh no, you're not going to get me in trouble." I back away and into Emory.

Papa Atti sticks a toothpick into his mouth as he laughs. "Smart man."

Nana Isla points a finger at me. "Answer my question, young man."

I look over to Emory to see if the coast is clear. I could get

233

in trouble with Nana Isla for not allowing her to change the subject, but better that than no-more-sex Emory.

Emory relents. "Yeah, yeah. I'll get her to give in later."

Nana Isla snorts—unhelpfully—but remains silently waiting for my response.

I sigh out. "Things are...how you would expect, I guess. He's angry with me, and the guys are loving hearing all the drama."

"Tell me something," Papa Atti interrupts. "When you two," he points the toothpick between Em and me, "have sex, what do you think about?"

I choke on my drink of water. "Excuse me?"

"What do you think about?" he insists.

"I think that's a little too inappropriate, *Papa* Atti."

He rolls his eyes. "Do you think about how pleasurable it is for you or..."

"Of course I do." I don't see where he's going with this.

"*Or* do you think about how pleasurable it is for her? How much more you could give her?"

"Well, the second obviously. I only think about the first after she's had her fill."

Emory is blushing, and she elbows me in the gut like that was too much information. Nana Isla's little laughs tell me she's used to Papa Atti's line of questioning.

"Then he'll come around," Papa Atti finishes.

"What?" Now I'm completely lost.

"Darius. He'll come around."

"What the hell did one have to do with the other?"

"When that boy saw that video, all he saw was sex. All he was thinking was of the way he's had sex, not the way he's heard of it. All he can imagine is personal pleasure. Though I'm sure he gives plenty of pleasure, otherwise he wouldn't be so popular with the ladies, his main goal is always personal pleasure. Your main goal is Emory. That much is obvious if Darius allows himself to see it. And he will."

I'm not sure if that makes complete sense, but I'll go with it.

"I know he'll accept it. It just hurts to have to wait for it," I respond.

I think Nana Isla is about to say something when my phone rings, and Lynn is calling. Nana Isla grumbles in a 'remember the rules' way, but I ignore her. I told Lynn we were on a picnic—we always made it a thing to tell her so she knew not to call unless it was an emergency. Which meant this was important.

"Hello," I pick up and ignore Nana Isla's death glare.

"Lynette's in the hospital. Apparently, her water broke last night and Octavio didn't want to say anything until it was push time."

My breath stops.

Lynette's in the hospital.

Lynette's going to have the baby.

"We're on our way," I say.

She knows we have Nana Isla and Papa Atti since we're on the picnic, so she doesn't bother to mention picking them up as well.

I hang up, and the smile is so shit-eating on my face, I can't help it.

"What's got you so giddy, boy?" Papa Atti asks.

"I'm going to be an uncle."

It's all I *can* say.

Darius is sitting with Calvin when we get there. Lynn is no doubt in the delivery room with Lynette and Octavio. She's not only been a surrogate mother to me, but to Octavio and Lynette as well.

Darius's gaze dips when it meets mine, but it doesn't entirely look like the I-can't-look-at-you-or-I'll-kill-you type. Watching Darius smile to Nana and Papa and give them hugs, I'm starting to believe what Lynn said. Maybe he is just upset that he couldn't see my feelings.

And though I want to knock him over the head and tell him it's okay, that I don't care that he couldn't see it, I don't. He needs to deal with this on his own time, and that's what I'll give him.

Calvin walks over to us with a smile. And after the hugs, he gives a knowing smile as he says, "You two next, huh."

Before Emory has time to smack him, he's off. Smart, run away before she kills you for jinxing her like that.

She smacks me instead.

I jump and look down at her. "What was that for?"

"You're smiling," she grumbles and moves to a seat where she can look out of the hospital's floor-to-ceiling windows, our backs to the others.

Time for the wait.

Lynette's already in the pushing stages, so it shouldn't be too long, but it's still a wait.

I take Emory's hand as we sit leaning on each other and play with her fingers. "Do you not imagine kids?"

She shrugs. "I always did before. Like *in the future*...but things have changed."

I close my eyes, so all my attention is on what she has to say.

"I think about them more and more now. And it scares me because I'm only twenty-two, and I still have some traveling I'd like to do, and I know we could just leave the kids with Mom and Dad, but it's like I know the worry will plague me the entire time I'm away from them, and I...we're young. I want some more carefree time."

"The most valid of arguments." Our fingers are still

tangled, but now she's also playing with my fingers as I play with hers. A mess. "And don't worry, we'll go on a safari for our honeymoon, and you'll get that one checked off the list."

She laughs and snuggles in closer to me. "What about you? Do you imagine kids? Did you ever?"

I take a breath because I know the answer, and it's kinda complicated.

"Yes and no," I say. "It's weird. I always imagined being a dad, but never imagined the kids. So yes because if I'm imagining being a dad, I'd have to imagine kids. But no because they were never the main focus of the thoughts."

It's weird, but I can hear her smile as she says, "So you're excited about being a dad. That's sweet."

"It wasn't necessarily being excited about being a dad. It was more the thought of Darius and me as dads together. Oh yeah, I figured all our kids would be the same age."

She gives a small laugh, and I chuckle in with her.

I shrug again. "So in a way, yeah, I've always thought of kids but only because I figured Darius and I would have them together, and we could be asshole fathers together and low-key torture our kids and laugh about it on the porch. Because in my fantasies, we bought houses right next door to each other."

Her giggling is back. "Technically, if we buy one of the houses next door, that could definitely come true."

"Why one of the houses and not a new neighborhood?"

She shrugs. "I wouldn't want to leave Nana Isla and Papa Atti. They'd be the children's great grandparents, and I want them to run havoc together."

My eyes are still closed, but I turn so my lips can find her hairline and give her a kiss. "I always figured they'd come and live in a guesthouse. Or with us. Or we'd buy three homes, and they'd be across the street again. Maybe four and your parents can have the other one. Five so Lynette and Octavio get the last."

She shakes her head through her laughter. "At least you considered them."

"Always."

We're quiet for a bit of time, and I can hear Papa Atti and Calvin's arguing over some sports game filling the room. They're not trying to keep their voices down, but thankfully, the staff doesn't care. We don't do voices down as a family.

I continue talking to Emory because I want her to know everything. "Anyway, the kid fantasies for me were always Darius fantasies, like this was another thing we could do together. But now…" She knows I love her, and still, this part is a bit nerve-racking. "Since that night you crashed the barbecue with your luggage and no announcement, it's all changed. Now all I think about is you wobbling around, swollen with my child, while more kids run around the house, probably causing havoc with Nana and Papa."

She laughs at the final bit and snuggles in closer to me, our fingers no longer playing but just holding each other.

"I think about walking into the house or coming out of the bathroom or waking up, all of it. I think about every possible opportunity you could sit me down and tell me you're pregnant, and my heart breaks at how much I want it. I think about making you swear you won't tell anyone when I cry—because I will cry—and making love to you afterward. Because that time would definitely not be fucking or shagging or sex. I'd be giving you all of my love for making my dreams come true."

Her fingers are on my chin, and I open my eyes as she turns me to face her. Her eyes are watering. "I love you, Buttercup."

"Not as much as I love you, baby girl."

I lean in to kiss her, and every part of my soul is alight

with fireworks. Darius is upset and that part sucks, but every other part of my life is exactly how I've always wanted it. Emory chose me. She didn't push away at hearing every one of my thoughts of our future. We've just gotten together, and yet, she didn't run in fear at hearing how badly I wanted to marry her and get her pregnant.

CHAPTER 28

Emory

OUR KISS IS BROKEN when Octavio runs through the double doors leading to the labor rooms, and we all jump out of our seats. I'm shocked to see Darius sitting right behind us when we get up. I thought he was beside Dad on the other side. And I don't know if it's Octavio's booming presence or something else, but when our eyes meet, he doesn't look angry any longer.

"It's a girl!" Octavio announces.

And there's a breath that fills the room at finding out the gender. This makes it real. And wow, is it real because she's here!

My eyes are still watery from what Tommy has been saying to me, but now they're watery for a whole other reason. I turn to him. "It's a girl!"

His smile is wide as he brings me in for a hug, and it's like that first BBQ all over again. He squeezes me so hard for a moment, I think we're meshed as one.

We all turn to Octavio as Dad says, "Well, can we see her?"

Octavio nods his head back and we're all pushing our

way through to be the first. Nana Isla and I win. Well, technically she wins, but I'm a close second.

Lynette is holding the baby girl, and oh, I'm so in love already.

Mom is at her side. Nana Isla takes the other, and I come up right behind her.

"My precious girl." Nana Isla softly caresses Lynette's hand, and it's the first time she truly gives off an elderly aura. "Do we have a name?"

Lynette looks to her and smiles. "Navy Isla Rodriguez."

Nana Isla's eyes shoot to hers, widening, and there's a question in there, but she asks it too. "Really?"

"She deserves to be named after such an incredible person."

Nana Isla's eyes are watering as she smiles at the new mother. I'm feeling so incredibly joyous, I genuinely cannot imagine not being here for this moment. Cannot imagine not meeting Octavio and Lynette. Cannot imagine not having Nana Isla and Papa Atti in my life.

I look up to find Tommy's eyes and feel overwhelmed. I cannot imagine not coming home to Tommy. Cannot imagine a life without his eyes on me and that smile following me around. Cannot imagine a child of mine without the name Rutherford.

I cannot imagine a life had I not chosen to come home after finishing school in London. Because that had been an option. I'd been offered a position at a pretty well-known company in the heart of the English city, and I had really considered taking it.

But missing Mom and Dad and Darius and Tommy brought me back. Wanting our kids to grow up together and my kids to grow up with their grandparents brought me back.

I look back to baby Navy and know it was the best decision I could've ever made.

"I told you it'd be a girl," Darius comments as he looks at the little girl over Mom's shoulder, and we all laugh because Darius does *always* know.

The nurse kicks us out after about twenty minutes—just enough time for each of us to get to hold the newborn—and it's off home for us all. There's the option for everyone to go to Mom and Dad's, but I think we all want a bit of time apart before coming back together tomorrow. They said Lynette is doing so well; she could be released after a day rather than two.

When we get home, Darius is there.

I definitely wasn't expecting that. And by the way Tommy freezes as we see him sitting on the couch, he wasn't either.

"You're home," I say because we need to get past this awkwardness.

"I'm home." His gaze jumps between Tommy and me, but he doesn't say anything else.

I move to sit beside him, Tommy taking the armchair beside our couch, and we wait. I don't know whether I should say something more. If so, I don't know what.

Darius looks down at his hands as he leans over his knees. "I heard you."

I turn to Tommy, and his confusion equals mine.

Darius finally continues, "I heard you talk about it, about becoming a father with me. About seeing it now, kids and a pregnant wife. About seeing Emmie as that pregnant wife."

Ah, so he'd been sitting behind us the entire time at the hospital. I wondered earlier but figured he had just moved when Octavio walked out.

"Mom keeps telling me I'm angrier with myself than anyone else," he changes topics. "She says it's not only that I'm mad that I couldn't see that you were in love, but also the fact that I'm not in love. She said part of me always thought we'd do everything together, like you thought about becoming fathers."

Darius won't look up to meet Tommy's eyes, but he's definitely talking to Tommy. And Tommy's watching him closely.

"And you know how I hate when Mom is right." He scoffs and runs his hands through his hair, lightly pulling like he has to get himself to do something.

I know Darius is still angry with the fact that he wasn't told about us, but damn, Mom *was* right. He really was angrier with himself. I almost can't believe it.

Finally, he looks up and meets Tommy's gaze. "The same way you figured we'd be fathers together, I did. I thought we'd fall in love together. I thought we'd buy our family homes together. I thought we'd both go through every stage of life together. And now...now, you're there and I'm not and up until the moment I found out about you two, I didn't care. When I finally got past the fact that you're fucking my sister—which let me tell you, took a *fucking* while—all I could think was you were going to do it all without me, and I was still whoring around. I don't want to whore around if it means I won't be getting married and having kids with you."

My heart is breaking for my big brother, my superhero, my best friend. This is his love letter to his soulmate, and it's so perfect. I love that the both of us get to share a best friend.

"And I know it's too late now. You two will have that wedding soon..."

"Excuse me, he hasn't even proposed," I can't help but interrupt. But hey, it broke a lot of the tension because we're all laughing. Of course that would be the part I would be focused on.

Darius rolls his eyes at me, then moves them back to Tommy. "You're going to get married soon, have her walking barefoot and pregnant, and living that entire life without me, and I'm jealous."

"I get it," Tommy says. "And honestly, I can't say anything to help with it. It fucking sucks."

Darius's smile is humorless and knowing. "It does. And I don't want anything to help with it. I needed this. That's what Mom says at least. She says now I can get my ass into gear and find a proper woman rather than whoring around, then we could be fathers together, at least with your second or third child."

I wriggle my arm around Darius's bicep and snuggle in close. "I'd love that, Douchebag."

He shoves me. "How is it that he got Buttercup and I got Douchebag?"

"I've always had a predisposition for him, obviously."

He really shoves me away this time, so my hold on him breaks, and that makes me really laugh.

"So what does this mean? Are you okay with your sister and me?" Tommy brings the conversation back to its serious note.

Darius's smile drops, and he meets Tommy's stare again. "All of that anger wasn't toward myself, Tom. At the beginning, it really was because of...your relationship."

"I know," Tommy's voice is so sincere.

"I...I couldn't process it. All I could think was there was this video, physical proof, that you and my baby sister have been...together. And all I could think was, you haven't been with anyone in two years, and now Emory iss back, and she's looking as beautiful as ever, and of course you would notice. All I could think was you took advantage of the situation and the fact that I wouldn't think anything of it. I honestly just felt betrayed."

My eyes are watering again, but not enough to cry. Just enough for me to finally understand what keeping us private did to Darius. I'd selfishly only been thinking of me when I insisted on the privacy, then only about Tommy when it came out. I never truly considered what it would do to Darius to think his sister kept it from him.

"It was after our fight at work that I finally started to see it as love and not just screwing around. I was punching a bag in Mom's basement, getting that anger out and replaying all of it, every conversation and scenario since Emory came back. Every time I'd been suspicious and pushed it aside. That's when I realized how much it really was about more than just sex." He chuckles a little. "Then I was mad because I hadn't seen it, and I blamed you for that too. Because I could."

We all laugh.

"But I get it now. I'm okay with it. I'm not mad. Really, how could I be? My best friend is going to become my brother for real? This is literally a dream come true. If it didn't involve the part where you see my sister naked, it would've been a dream come true."

Tommy smirks as his eyes shoot to me. "I do more than see her naked. I..."

"Hey!" Darius jumps out of his seat. "I said I'm okay with it, not that I want to hear anything more!"

"But I tell you everything," Tommy teases. "Especially the *most* important parts of my life."

Darius's gaze is almost murderous in a humor-filled way. "That's come to an immediate end, *Brother*."

We all laugh because this, this is the old us, and it's honestly all we could have wanted. All I wanted.

It's late. Like late late. But I can't sleep, so I'm heating up water for some hot lemon water. I don't think it'll help, but I'm craving it, so I don't care.

I stare at the kettle as I wait for it to whistle so I can snap it up before it makes too much noise and wakes the boys up.

And...snap.

The stove is turned off, and I'm pouring my water into a cup. Then half a lemon goes into the lemon squeezer to get the most out of the juices and voilà. I love steaming lemon waters.

I sit on the counter, facing the entrance to the kitchen, and let my head fall back to rest on the cabinet as I take a sip from my cup then set it down beside me.

I miss London. I miss the atmosphere and the life I had there. I miss being so close to all those European cities and traveling to the little English towns. I miss taking the tube to get everywhere and never really having to worry about driving. I miss all of it.

But I can't seem to miss it half as much as I thought I would.

I now have Octavio and Lynette and baby Navy in my life. I have Nana Isla and Papa Atti. I have Mom and Dad. I have Darius. And most importantly, I have Tommy. And as much as I may miss London, I can't imagine leaving him for the city. I miss him when he's off to work, a mere few miles away. The thought that I could be any farther is unfathomable. He's become my entire life.

"Imagine my surprise when I turned over in bed and tried to stick my dick into thin air," Tommy says.

I jump from my thoughts and look back to the entrance. My gaze had wavered to the ceiling, and I definitely hadn't noticed him walk in.

"What're you doing, baby girl?" He walks up and stops between my legs.

I wrap my arms around his neck. "Thinking about London."

A bit of worry edges the corners of his eyes. "Do you want to go back?"

"Yes." My hands are playing with his hair, and I feel completely at peace under his frozen stance. "At some point. With you."

He relaxes as his forehead knocks into mine. "After our African honeymoon. Next stop."

I laugh. "Yes, sir."

His hands reach for my hips, and he pulls me in closer. My center touches his, and a light, almost inaudible moan leaves me as he says, "Behave, baby girl."

My hand slips around and slides down his chest, the little hairs prickling my fingers and inviting me to trace the happy trail. I comply because I'm a good girl.

My hand slips beneath the waist band to his sweatpants, and of course he's commando so I hit the treasure-chest immediately. My fingers wrap around his cock, and he wasn't kidding. He's so hard, I have no doubt he would've tried to turn and stick it in me. Especially because I was basically always wet around him. My panties are kind of annoyed with the fact.

I stroke him a couple of times and watch as his eyes close and his breathing becomes controlled. He'll have to be very careful to not make any noise and wake Darius up.

I reach up and pull on his waistband, just enough so his cock springs out. Then I'm stroking again.

He leans in close and whispers, "Can you tease me later? I need to be inside you."

I'm only slightly shocked. He was the one adamant about not doing anything in the kitchen the other day. He was the one hesitant about not using condoms. He was the one who had asked me not to touch him earlier because my brother was in the house.

And now?

Now he's ready to take me in the kitchen, raw, and with my brother still in his room.

My hand releases him, and I wrap it back around his neck. "I'm all yours, Buttercup."

I'm in one of his crazy bit T-shirts and nothing more. Easy access. Perfect for right now.

His fingers reach for me, moving up my folds, and one finger slides in. Now I'm the one trying to keep quiet.

He puts in another finger, pumping and letting his palm hit my clit every time. I have to bite down on his shoulder to keep entirely quiet.

When he pulls out, I almost let out a whimper, but somehow hold myself together.

He licks at his fingers, the glint in his eyes telling me he could tease me just as much as I could tease him.

Then he's angling his cock to my entrance and pushing in hard. I have to bite down again to keep quiet. His breathing is labored at my ear, but he's not making any noise. If the simple act of sex didn't make noise by itself, it would've been indiscernible.

Then our foreheads are pressed together, and we're breathing each other's air as we both look down and watch him enter me then pull out. Again and again and again.

Then he's kissing me, and I get the heavenly sensation of both his tongue and cock pumping into me.

He bites my lip as he finally pulls away. "You taste like lemons, baby."

I don't respond. I can't. If I try to say anything right now, I know I'll moan so loud, Nana Isla and Papa Atti will hear me from across the street.

So instead, I kiss him again and rejoice in the feeling of having him fill me over and over and...

"What the fuck!" Darius's voice invades my cloudy mind like a bucket of ice.

We freeze, Tommy deep inside me. And I know exactly what Darius is seeing: Tommy's half bare ass—my foot pressed there tells me the sweatpants are still covering some of it—and that much gives up enough information.

I can see Darius from over Tommy's shoulder as he feigns vomiting. "Are you fucking kidding me? I'm going to be sick. Oh, my…" A shoe comes flying at us. Well, at Tommy. "That's my baby sister, asshole."

Then he's gone, because of course he is; he wouldn't stay.

I'm mortified as I look at Tommy and I see a bit of shame there, but not half as much as there should be.

I'm so lucky this shirt is ginormous, and his body is covering anything else, so Darius didn't technically see anything.

He pulls out of me and pulls the sweatpants up. Then he wraps my legs around his waist and my full weight is in his arms.

He picks up my cup of lemon water because he's a gentleman like that and turns for our room. "Well, now that he knows, no real reason to be quiet."

I smack him as we enter the room, and he puts the lemon water on the nightstand. "Yes, there is, asshole."

He drops us on the bed so he's hovering over me, but my legs never drop from around his waist. "I thought I was Buttercup."

"Apparently today you're Asshole."

He kisses me. "I can live with that."

He pulls his sweatpants down, then he's entering me again.

CHAPTER 29

Tommy

I'M warm when I wake up. And somehow, still not sweaty. Darius turned on the A.C. last night no doubt.

Emory's body is perfectly fitted to my front, my arm thrown around her keeping her in place. Her hair, thrown haphazardly around, is blocking my view, but I have no doubt that she looks absolutely stunning in such a relaxed state.

I pull my hand away softly so I can slowly push her hair out of her face, but the light disturbance has her moving entirely. She falls onto her back, and her face falls away from me.

It gives me a perfect opening of her neck.

I kiss her lightly. When nothing happens, I do it again and nibble on the skin there.

She moans so soft, if I hadn't been right beside her, I wouldn't have heard it.

I do it again because I love hearing her.

This time she calls my name, so softly, I barely hear it.

I move to her ear. "I love you, Emory."

Her face turns to me, and she snuggles into my neck. I

chuckle and whisper into her other ear this time. "Marry me, Emory."

Her breathing doesn't change, and that's how I know she's still deep in sleep.

"Marry me, baby girl." I kiss her ear. "Make me yours. Officially."

She fidgets a bit, then turns to her side so we're flush, chest-to-chest. My arm around her waist pulls her in closer.

I peck her a few times until I know she's coming out of sleep, but not entirely there yet. "I can get used to this..." I say as she snuggles into me, and her lips tip up so slightly, I would've missed it if I weren't obsessed with staring at her. "Your morning breath hitting my face every day."

She laughs. Completely breaks from acting like she's still asleep and laughs. "I hate you, Buttercup."

"Open your eyes for me, baby girl."

She complies, and her chocolate browns are shining up at me. "I love waking up in your arms, Buttercup."

"I love waking up with you in my arms, baby girl."

"I love suffocating you with my morning breath." Her eyes narrow on me, and all it does is turn me on.

I know she can feel it with our bottom halves flush the way they are. "I love your morning breath on me. I love all your breaths on me."

"I love..." her index plays with my lips, "how you make me feel. All lovey-dovey, gooey and gross inside."

I laugh. "I love that I make you feel all lovey-dovey, gooey and gross."

She smacks me. "You mean you love how I make you feel!"

"Nope." I don't think I've ever grinned so much so early in the morning. "I meant what I said."

"Say I make you feel gooey and gross, Asshole!" she

admonishes, and it makes me harder how wide her eyes get when she's passionate.

"Will that make you happy, baby girl?"

"Only if you mean it," she grumbles, but I know she wants to hear it.

I laugh again and kiss her, my arm bringing her in closer to me because I have an obsession with having her close to me. "I love how you make me feel too, baby girl. Not all lovey-dovey, gooey and gross, but perfect. Whole. I don't feel like a kid in love for the first time when I'm with you. I feel like I've loved you my whole life, and yet, everyday it gets stronger. I feel genuinely ready to walk through Hell to make sure you live every day in Heaven. I feel the need to protect you and possess you, but also to push you to accomplish everything you want because that's what you do for me. You make me want to be better than I was yesterday, better than I am now. You make me want to keep working to deserve you, and I love how it feels in my chest. *Perfect.*"

"Buttercup." She smacks me. "Why are you always so romantic and make me look like the asshole?"

I take her bottom lip between my teeth, then kiss her hard. "You are the asshole, baby."

She just holds my face in her hand and runs her thumb along my light stubble. "I love you, Buttercup. And I can't wait to have you every day until the end."

Her kiss is soft, but there's so much passion in it that I feel like she's putting into it everything I just said to her. She's telling me in her own way that I make her whole too.

When we pull away, we just stare at each other.

Eventually, I break the silence. "Did you hear what I was telling you?" I don't know if I hope she did or didn't.

Her brows furrow, and I know the answer is no. "Of course."

My lips tip up in a smirk. "You're not gonna get me to say it again by acting like you already know, baby."

She pouts. "Please, Buttercup."

I kiss those lips. "Okay." I kiss her bright smile. "But not today."

She grumbles and tries to push away, but I'm much stronger. I drop her onto her back and get on top. "Are you mad at me, baby girl?"

"Yes," she grumbles, and it's damn near the cutest thing I've ever seen.

"Oh no. We can't have that."

Her eyes widen when she sees the mischief in mine. "Tommy, whatever you're thinking, no!"

I kiss her neck. "You sure about that?" I'm moving slowly down her body, and her legs are spreading more and more to accommodate me.

"Mmhm," she breaths hard as I kiss her breast.

I kiss her nipple through the top she has on. "I need words, baby." I kiss her stomach through that shirt and love how affected she is even though I haven't touched skin yet.

"Tommy," she moans as her hands falls into my hair and softly tug and play with it.

I laugh and kiss the bare skin between her bunched top and pussy. "Yes?"

Her legs are spread as far as they can go, but she visibly tries to spread them wider. "I hate you."

I tsk three times and her back arches in anticipation. "Can't have that, baby girl."

I kiss her pussy once, and I know she's mine forever.

I'm on my way to the kitchen when I see Darius walk in the front door with a tray in hand. On the tray is a plate of food, a cup of OJ, and a cup of coffee.

"Why do you have all that on a tray? And what the hell were you doing outside?" I ask.

"Nana Isla kicked me out. Said breakfast is a moment for only her and Papa Atti," he grumbles and takes a seat on one of the couches, placing the tray on the coffee table and leaning over it.

"What were you doing over there anyway? And what the hell are you doing? We have a kitchen."

I'm watching him as he shovels a loaded forkful of an omelette into his mouth.

He looks up at me, and there's a threat there almost as hateful as when he'd found out about me and Emory. "If you think I'm using that kitchen after what you two were doing in there last night, you're dumber than a death wish."

My lips twitch because he has every right to be angry, but it's still funny.

"I'm gonna fucking kill you," he grumbles again as he eats his breakfast.

"What's he mad about now?" Emory wraps an arm around me and looks at her brother like he's the crazy one.

I can't help the grin. "Guess."

Her cheeks burn as she remembers, and suddenly, she's not standing so straight anymore. "Last night."

"That a girl," I laugh as Darius snickers.

"Ugh." She hides that beautiful face behind her hands. "Please don't remind me."

"Don't remind you!" Darius's eyes go wide as they find her. "I can never use my kitchen again!"

"I'll clean it while you guys are at work today. Deep clean." She looks miserable, and I know I should be comforting her, but I still find it kind of hilarious.

"Yeah. Like that'll get the memory out of my mind." He shovels the last bit of his breakfast into his mouth and downs his OJ. He moves to the front door and turns to me. "I'm waiting in the truck. Get ready, let's go."

We haven't driven to work together all week. I know it's a small thing, but it's something Darius and I have always done together. It's how we've always started our workdays. And it had killed me not doing it all week. I can't imagine having to go longer with him so pissed off.

I turn to Emory. "Whip me up something fast while I get changed?" Guess I don't have time for eating with her this morning.

She's still pink, but she kisses me and nods.

When I come out dressed in my usual work attire, Emory's got a cup of coffee in a to-go mug, a bottle of water, and a breakfast burrito ready for me. Damn, the girl works fast.

Darius is still giving me a death glare when I get in the car and open my breakfast. "You know the only reason I'm not killing you right now is because it would upset her."

I smirk his way. "I know."

The rest of the ride is silent, like our usuals, as I finish my breakfast. I'll have to have Em make Darius one of these next time so he can stop being so angry. Because, damn, it's good. A kick of hot sauce in there is surprisingly perfect for breakfast.

When we get to the site, most of the men are already there. Some of them look up and seem almost shocked to see us together. Wonder where their pool was at for how long we would fight for. And who won.

Octavio isn't here, obviously. It's our second to last day on the job, so we'll be fine without him anyway. And for the next few jobs, we planned knowing he wouldn't be around, so really, it's no loss to the job. It's more important for him to stay home with his girls anyway.

I'm about to get out of the car when Darius says, "Hey."

I turn to him.

There's a little smile there that I haven't seen aimed at me since he was trying to set me up with random girls a couple weeks ago. "I actually *am* happy it's you she's found."

My heart kinda shatters. I knew I'd wanted to hear those words from him, but I hadn't known how much I'd wanted it. Now I know the answer was a lot. A lot, a lot.

"I love you, Brother," I respond because it's the most honest answer I have.

He winks and gets out of the car.

CHAPTER 30

Emory

IT'S another Sunday family BBQ.

These family days have fast become my favorite thing. And while summer is shining, we're taking advantage.

To be fair, spring and fall are pretty warm around here anyway, so we could probably carry this on until November. Then indoors we'll go.

Everyone is here and very distracted with baby Navy. She's only about ten days old, but she's become the most popular person in the family.

We grilled vegetables today and I peeled them and cut them up into a salad while the boys finished with the beef. It all smells so good.

Too good.

I'm thinking about eating far past my fill.

Then we're finally seated, and I'm watching Mom feed Navy a bottle Lynette pumped because she knew how much we all wanted our turns with the newest addition. Tommy's hand reaches for the one I have casually resting in my lap and holds it.

That's it.

He just holds it.

And it feels so good. So normal. So…us.

And the guilt of basically making Tommy hide us is hitting me again. I know technically we never hid our relationship; it was more of a 'just don't talk about it' situation, but we also never did things like this. I could hug him, and we may have held hands before, but they were all surrounded by jokes that sort of pushed past our relationship. Now, we can casually hold hands, and everyone knows why. Not just because they *know*, but because touching without the need to bring attention to it like before is like being fully myself.

Tommy is in a debate with Dad and Darius about the best way to make the beef. They've gone with Dad's way this time, but he was adamant his way was better. The smiles on their faces as they all fight about which of the three ways was superior lightened my soul in a way I hadn't realized I needed.

I lean into him as Darius's voice raises above every other conversation at the table and whisper, "I'm sorry, Tommy."

His full attention is immediately on me—I love that I'm always at the top of his priorities—and the smile is now gone. "For what?"

I squeeze his hand that's in my lap. "Darius is right. The way we were before could've easily been misconstrued as us just being the old us. There's no way we would've gotten away with it if we did this. Just touched the entire time we're at the table. The questions definitely would've come, and I think the way we did it was probably more of a secret than I let myself believe. Because if not, we would've done this weeks ago, and Darius would've asked about it, and it would've been out."

His free hand reaches for my face. "I don't regret any of it. Think about it, if it hadn't come out the way it did, Darius wouldn't be thinking about settling down and finding someone so we could be dads together."

I chuckle and shove his shoulder with mine. "I'm serious."

His thumb is drawing light circles on my cheek, and he brings our faces close. "I am too, baby. I don't regret any of it, and you have nothing to apologize for. You never said anything was off limits. I didn't touch you at the table either so it's as much my fault."

"What the fuck are you two talking about?" Darius breaks our little bubble before I can respond.

Tommy looks over and winks at him. Since Darius okayed our relationship, Tommy's had a lot of fun—maybe a bit too much—teasing Darius about what we do or say.

"Tommy, I swear to the lords, I will skewer your dick off. Keep it up, you piece of..."

"Hey," I interrupt. "Stop talking to him like that."

Tommy's chuckling at my side, and Darius's mouth opens in an O. Darius's eyes narrow on his best friend. "You've turned her against me now? Dead man, Rutherford. The second I get you away from her. Dead man."

Everyone's laughing because obviously it's an empty threat, and Tommy is enjoying it as he leans in and kisses my neck.

A bread roll flies at Tommy's head.

And Darius used to be a pitcher, so it's hard and fast.

Tommy turns back to me, so we're in our little bubble again and his lips brush mine as he says, "I'm glad things worked out the way they did. I'm actually glad I got my time with you before your brother knew. I mean, I love that he knows, and we're actually gonna be brothers, but those few weeks when we got to sneak around a bit were fun, Em."

"Yeah? Maybe next time we could make a legit sex tape. Spice things up." I wiggle my eyebrows, and he laughs.

"I love you, Emory. And I don't regret a second of us."

"Why are you such a romantic, Buttercup?" I pout, and his tongue plays with my bottom lip. I'm so glad my hair covers our faces so my parents can't see us right now. Even though I'm pretty sure they wouldn't care. Mom wouldn't. "You make me sound like a dog."

"It's not your fault. It's in the genes, baby girl." He kisses my cheek, and the act sends more butterflies to my stomach than the one on my lips.

He sits back.

Without him in my little bubble, I look out to the table and see Darius's death glare. Tommy plays with him as he smirks and winks.

Yeah, he's definitely having too much fun with this. Darius is definitely gonna beat him at some point if he keeps it up.

I lean into Tommy because I like being held by him.

And because as much as he likes messing with Darius, I like teasing him.

I tilt my head so my lips are at his ear and whisper, "I was serious about the sex tape, Buttercup."

Tommy

3 months later

SUMMER'S COMING TO AN END, so it's one of the last chances to come out here before it's a little too chilly to be by the water.

I have the canoe out and have my leg settled in it to keep it steady as Emory drops our waters into the end and takes my hand.

"You're such a gentleman, Buttercup."

It's ironic, that compliment. Because she looks so beautiful in that white sundress, I want to do so many ungentlemanly things to her.

"Your parents knew what they were doing when they raised me," I say as I get in across from her.

She smiles as I begin rowing, and the beauty of her makes me forget the burn of rowing the canoe around the lake. It's honestly some of the best exercise out there, and I love watching her gaze latch onto my biceps.

"Tommy," she chastises after watching me for long minutes, "why would you insist on leaving the phones in the shed? I wanna get a picture of how great you look."

I smirk. "You can hang on to the memory."

She rolls her eyes. "I *can*, but it's so much better to touch myself if I have a picture."

I laugh. "We'll make a video later."

Her eyes widen with delight. "Promise?"

"Promise."

She bites her lip, and I shift a little in my seat as I row us around.

"I'm still annoyed I can't get the picture, Buttercup."

I quirk a brow. "With how clumsy you are in this thing, I think it's the smartest thing to leave the technology away from the water."

I roll my eyes again. "One time! And we didn't even fall in!"

I laugh as I stop in the middle of the lake, leaving the paddles hanging off to the side as I lean forward. "Barely, baby. We barely didn't fall in."

She's been a little excited a few weeks ago and jumped at me for a hug and we'd almost gone over with the way the canoe had rocked. The attack was less due to her clumsiness and more just the suddenness of the hug, but still, I don't want to risk losing the photos and videos in my phone. I have most of it backed up, but I need to do so again for the rest. It's the only part of my phone I care about.

She gives me a knowing grin. "Well, that only happened because I was excited. It hasn't happened again since."

"That's because I haven't had something I wanted to tell you before," I hint.

Her eyes narrow. "What, Buttercup?"

"What?" I act aloof.

"Buttercup," she warns as her smile grows. "Is it something that's going to get me as excited as last time?"

Last time, I told her about the trip to the forests of New England I have planned for this fall. Something just for us to be out in a cabin and enjoying one another for three uninterrupted days.

She was so excited, the first thing I did when we got home was look at where to next because I wanted to continue seeing that smile.

"I hope more so, baby."

She jumps excitedly in her seat, and we already begin rocking.

"See! I haven't even said anything, and we're already unsteady."

"Shut up and tell me, Tommy!"

"How am I meant to shut up *and* tell you?" I ask to be annoying and because I love seeing the anticipation grow in her.

"Tommy!"

I lean forward so I'm touching her knees and look at her with all the love I feel. "I think you know what I wanna ask you back at our first date spot, baby girl."

Her eyes widen, and the excitement radiates off her as she giddily moves forward. "Tommy, please!"

I know she knows, and she just wants to hear me say it. It's the same with her answer. I know it already, but I still want to hear it.

"Will you marry me, Emory?"

A shriek fills the air as she throws herself at me, and we're both flying off the canoe and into the water. I'm laughing so much, I get a bit of water in my mouth but don't care as I kiss her beneath the water.

We come out, and she's clinging around my hips as I

stand in the lake that's barely shallow enough to allow me to stand in.

And I kiss her again and again. "That's not an answer, baby."

Her laugh is exhilarating. "Yes, Buttercup, yes! Forever ever ever yes!"

Her lips are on mine before I can say much more, and our tongues are fighting for dominance. I have to wonder if hearing the question felt half as good as hearing that answer did.

So our next trip after New England will be Africa. That honeymoon is something I've been looking forward to since she first spoke of the safaris.

I pull away and barely force her to keep her lips off mine.

"Baby," she complains.

I laugh as I reach into my shirt and pull out the chain I've been wearing. "I just wanna show you this, baby."

Her gaze latches onto the ring her mother and Lynette helped me custom make with an old diamond from one of Nana Isla's favorite necklaces.

Her eyes water, and she bites her lip to keep from crying as her eyes jump up to meet mine. "Buttercup..."

My arm holds her tighter against my body as my free hand cradles her face into mine. "You'll get it when we get back on land, but I've been dying to show it to you. It's Nana's diamond. I figured you'd prefer something vintage to a brand new one."

"How are you so fucking perfect, Buttercup?"

I smirk. "With a nickname like that, I had no choice."

She laughs, and we're kissing again.

As much as I'm enjoying this moment in the lake with her, I need to see the ring on her finger even more. I pull away to her protests and swim us back to the canoe where we flop in so ungracefully, we're both dying of laughter.

I row us to land quickly and help her out, then pull the canoe out as well.

I turn to her and start taking the chain off as she stares at me with the widest grin across her face.

I let the ring slip into my palm and pocket the chain, then I drop to one knee. "Maybe I should do this traditionally too, baby."

She laughs, and the tears are back in her eyes.

"Will you marry me, Emory Aabeck?"

She takes my face between her hands. "A million times yes, Thomas Buttercup Rutherford."

I kiss her around the laugh at that nickname, then finally pull away enough to look at her hand. We both stare at her finger as I slip the ring on, and my heart explodes at the sight of it on her finger.

I look back up to her and catch her staring at me. The tears are falling down her face as she says, "I'm finally gonna be a Rutherford."

I stand and take her face in my hands. "I'm finally gonna officially be an Aabeck."

She laughs and kisses me, and tears are falling down our faces, but I don't care. I'm going to cherish this moment for the rest of my life.

The rest of our lives.

Join My Author Newsletter

Sign up for Nelly Alikyan's newsletter to be the first to know about new releases and cover reveals, receive exclusive content—like a special scene or two—and be up to date about any other exciting news, i.e. events, signed copies, etc.

www.nellyalikyan.com

About the Author

—————

Nelly Alikyan is a girl from the Los Angeles Valley who moved to Boston for school and found she prefers the East Coast. But really, London is where she'd like to be since it's her favorite city ever. She's the only reader in her family—not her only cause as the black sheep—and has dreamt of being a writer for as long as she can remember.

When she's not working on her books or in the real world, she's on Youtube at Nelly Alikyan!

For more books and updates:
www.nellyalikyan.com

- tiktok.com/@authornellyalikyan
- instagram.com/authornellyalikyan
- youtube.com/NellyAlikyan
- amazon.com/author/n.alikyan
- goodreads.com/authornalikyan
- facebook.com/authornellyalikyan
- pinterest.com/insinpublishing

Acknowledgments

Guilty as charged.

I definitely wrote this because I love a man who works with his hands. Most of my characters tend to have aspects that are completely me and aspects that are nothing like me. Emory's love for men who get dirty and sweaty? Me!

I also wrote this because I had this story stuck in my head for days on end—I remember writing the *full* outline for it in the last two days of June 2021. *Two days!* I have never written a full outline so quickly, and don't see myself doing so again. At least not anytime soon!

This was completely created by stories I make up in order to put myself to sleep at nights. I've always loved the brother's best friend trope and have made an infinite amount of these stories to help myself fall asleep, but this one stuck out. I don't know why, but I do know that I love Tommy and Emory and the entire gang. Darius especially seems to be a favorite by all those who have read this book in its earlier stages. I love Darius too. A lot.

I'd like to thank my beta readers. Nishka, especially, your comments made me so happy!

I'd like to thank my copyeditor, Michelle, for helping me find my fixes and even suggesting a couple of words that seemed to have left my brain during the many drafts of this story.

I'd like to thank my cover designer, Murphy Rae, for the

cover that came out basically how I had it in my head. It's such a sweet, summery cover for this sweet, summery read.

And finally, a thank you to my family for continuing to support me. For being excited for the books even though they don't read; for helping me when I need something done with marketing—i.e. text messages videos lol; for continuing to find it crazy that I can do this.

Printed in Great Britain
by Amazon